MAVERICKS

SHIPMENT 1

Paging Dr. Right by Stella Bagwell
Her Best Man by Crystal Green
I Do! I Do! by Pamela Toth
A Family for the Holidays by Victoria Pade
A Cowboy Under Her Tree by Allison Leigh
Stranded with the Groom by Christine Rimmer

SHIPMENT 2

All He Ever Wanted by Allison Leigh
Prescription: Love by Pamela Toth
Their Unexpected Family by Judy Duarte
Cabin Fever by Karen Rose Smith
Million-Dollar Makeover by Cheryl St.John
McFarlane's Perfect Bride by Christine Rimmer

SHIPMENT 3

Taming the Montana Millionaire by Teresa Southwick
From Doctor...to Daddy by Karen Rose Smith
When the Cowboy Said "I Do" by Crystal Green
Thunder Canyon Homecoming by Brenda Harlen
A Thunder Canyon Christmas by RaeAnne Thayne
Resisting Mr. Tall, Dark & Texan by Christine Rimmer
The Baby Wore a Badge by Marie Ferrarella

SHIPMENT 4

His Country Cinderella by Karen Rose Smith
The Hard-to-Get Cowboy by Crystal Green
A Maverick for Christmas by Leanne Banks
Her Montana Christmas Groom by Teresa Southwick
The Bounty Hunter by Cheryl St.John
The Guardian by Elizabeth Lane

SHIPMENT 5

Big Sky Rancher by Carolyn Davidson
The Tracker by Mary Burton
A Convenient Wife by Carolyn Davidson
Whitefeather's Woman by Deborah Hale
Moon Over Montana by Jackie Merritt
Marry Me...Again by Cheryl St.John

SHIPMENT 6

Big Sky Baby by Judy Duarte
The Rancher's Daughter by Jodi O'Donnell
Her Montana Millionaire by Crystal Green
Sweet Talk by Jackie Merritt
Big Sky Cowboy by Jennifer Mikels
Montana Lawman by Allison Leigh
Montana Mavericks Weddings
by Diana Palmer, Susan Mallery

SHIPMENT 7

You Belong to Me by Jennifer Greene
The Marriage Bargain by Victoria Pade
It Happened One Wedding Night by Karen Rose Smith
The Birth Mother by Pamela Toth
A Montana Mavericks Christmas
by Susan Mallery, Karen Rose Smith
Christmas in Whitehorn by Susan Mallery

SHIPMENT 8

In Love with Her Boss by Christie Ridgway
Marked for Marriage by Jackie Merritt
Rich, Rugged...Ruthless by Jennifer Mikels
The Magnificent Seven by Cheryl St.John
Outlaw Marriage by Laurie Paige
Nighthawk's Child by Linda Turner

THE
GUARDIAN

ELIZABETH LANE

HARLEQUIN® MONTANA MAVERICKS

Special thanks and acknowledgment are given
to Elizabeth Lane for her contribution
to the Montana Mavericks series.

ISBN-13: 978-0-373-41826-8

The Guardian

Recycling programs
for this product may
not exist in your area.

Printed in U.S.A.

www.Harlequin.com

Elizabeth Lane has lived and traveled in many parts of the world, including Europe, Latin America and the Far East, but her heart remains in the American West, where she was born and raised. Her idea of heaven is hiking a mountain trail on a clear autumn day. She also enjoys music, animals and dancing. You can learn more about Elizabeth by visiting her website, elizabethlaneauthor.com.

Chapter One

April 1837

Charity Bennett braced her feet against the rattling tailgate of the covered wagon. Her buttocks, already bruised raw, thumped painfully against the crate where she sat. Her arms clasped her bulging belly as if to protect the unborn child that stirred beneath her ribs.

"It's all right," she murmured to the kicking baby. "It's all right, my little love. We'll get through this day and a good many more before life is finished with us."

The wagon lurched sideways as one wheel struck a jutting rock. The grease bucket that dangled from the rear axle clanged like a bell. Pots and tools clattered as they swung from iron nails that served as hooks.

Breaking through its frayed jute lashings, a flour barrel slid across the wagon bed and crashed against a massive trunk that was packed with bibles and hymnals. The impact split the barrel open, releasing a cloud of flour that filled the confined space like ash from an explosion. Charity coughed and sputtered, wiping her eyes to clear away the dust. Silas would be furious about the spilled flour. He despised waste of any kind and had charged her with keeping their precious supplies in order. Once he saw the mess, she would not hear the end of it for the rest of the week.

Glancing forward through the sunlit opening in the wagon cover, Charity could see the outline of her husband's back. He was hunched over the reins, his hair hanging in sparse gray strings below the brim of his shapeless felt hat. She would have chosen to sit beside him on the wagon bench where she could breathe cool April air and enjoy the view of the sweeping short-grass prairie, but he had ordered her to stay hidden. The sight of a young, blond, white woman in this wild country, he'd insisted, could bring a horde of heathen savages sweeping down upon them to carry her off to unspeakable sin and degradation. Until they reached the Flathead Indian encampment on the Swan River, it was imperative that she stay beneath the cover of the wagon—a wagon she had come to hate with every bone in her tortured body.

Charity's grandparents, who'd raised her after her parents died, had been elated when the widowed preacher had asked for her hand. With their granddaughter on the brink of spinsterhood at two and twenty, they had fretted over what would become of her when they were gone. And what an honor for Charity to have been chosen! In their closely knit congregation, there was no higher calling for a woman than to be a minister's wife.

Charity had felt no stirrings of romantic love for the grim, graying Reverend Silas Bennett. But her long-denied adventurous spirit had been caught up in Silas's plan to convert the heathen tribes beyond the upper Missouri. As for her own feelings, she had accepted him with blind faith in her grandmother's assurance that, in time, they would come to care for each other.

In time. For Charity, those words had long since lost their meaning.

Charity's arms tightened around her belly. She had long since given up any hope of a happy union with Silas. But in performing his so-called husbandly duty, he had given her a priceless gift. She might have lost the reverend to his God and to his grandiose dreams. But no matter. The baby would be all hers to cherish and care for, hers to shower with a lifetime of love.

"You all right in there, Miz Bennett?" Rueben Potter, the bewhiskered trapper who'd hired on as their guide, reined his spotted Indian pony up behind the wagon. When he'd met the little party at a trading post out of Fort Leavenworth, wearing a coonskin cap and grease-stained buckskins that looked as if they hadn't been off his body in years, Charity had thought him the filthiest person she had ever seen. But the old man had proven to have a kind heart. In truth, these days he treated her with more consideration than Silas did.

Along the way, as they'd traveled and camped, Rueben had taught Charity about the wilderness. He had shown her how to read a game trail, make a fire and find her way by the stars. He had pointed out which plants were safe to eat and which were poisonous, and instructed her in dozens of little skills that would help her survive. For this, she would always be grateful.

Now Charity nodded, forced a smile as she clung to the bouncing wagon. "I'm quite well, thank you, Mr. Potter. But why are we…going so…fast? Can't we slow…down?"

A green horsefly rose from Rueben's beard as the trapper shook his head. "'Tain't safe." He grunted. "This here be Blackfoot Injun country, and we seen signs of the murderin' varmints less'n two miles back. Looked to be a huntin' party by my guess, but with those bastards you can never tell. Things could turn nasty in the flick of a mule's tail. Sooner we git our tail feathers through this valley and across the river, the better!"

Charity's stomach, already queasy, contracted at Rueben's mention of the Blackfoot. All the way west, she had heard tales of these bloodthirsty raiders and the terror they had wreaked on white travelers. She had felt safe enough as long as their little party of missionaries and traders kept to the well-marked Oregon trail. But in the nine days since they had turned off and cut due north, through the trackless valleys that fronted the Rocky Mountains, she'd been unable to shake the feeling that they were being watched by unseen eyes.

"God will protect us," Silas had declared when she'd voiced her concerns to him. Charity knew better than to argue. But God had not protected her parents when their loaded wagon broke through the ice on the frozen Ohio River. Nor had God kept her little brother from dying of diphtheria that same terrible winter. Given the past, she had no reason to believe an angel with a flaming sword would swoop down and defend a little band of zealots who had forged their way into hostile territory.

"Sure as spittin' the bastards be out there, and they know we're here." Rueben spoke as if he had read her mind. "But we ain't made no dangerous moves, and we ain't got much to steal. With luck, if'n we keep our noses clean, they'll look us over and let us move on." The old man spat a stream of tobacco beneath the wheels. "Had a talk with your husband this mornin'. Told 'im we might oughta leave some vittles behind for 'em, so's they'll know we's peaceful. But he wouldn't have no part o' that idee. Give me a right smart dressin' down, he did, beggin' your pardon, ma'am. Said we got no grub to spare for heathen savages."

Touching the edge of his filthy coonskin cap, he turned his horse as if to leave, then pulled close to the back of the wagon once more and caught the tailgate with one horny hand. His bloodshot blue eyes burned into Charity's as he spoke.

"If'n I had a daughter, I reckon she'd be about your age," he said in a hoarse whisper. "Listen, girl, if them Injuns ride at us, you stay in the wagon, and stay hid, no matter what, y' hear now?"

Cold fear twisted Charity's stomach as she nodded.

He turned to go, then hesitated yet again. Still keeping pace with the wagon, he reached into the depths of his greasy buckskin tunic and pulled out a small, dark object, which he thrust toward her.

"Take it, girl," he rasped. "It be loaded and ready to fire, but it only shoots one ball, so save it till the last. If'n them red devils take you alive, you'll curse God and the mother what borned you!"

A leaden chill passed through Charity's body as her fist closed around the weight of a tiny pistol, the sort of gun that might be carried by gamblers and fancy men. She could only imagine how Rueben might have come by the weapon.

Momentarily puzzled, she stared down at it as Rueben wheeled his pony and galloped away. A gun that fired only a single bullet would be of little use against a charging band of Indians. Even if she was lucky enough to shoot one brave, others would swiftly take his place.

If'n them red devils take you alive, you'll curse God and the mother what borned you!

A moan escaped Charity's lips as the truth struck home. Rueben Potter had given her the gift of mercy. The single shot was not meant to be used against the Blackfoot. It was meant for her.

Shuddering with horror, she raised the gun, wanting nothing more than to be rid of the awful weapon, to fling it out of the wagon as if it were a venomous snake. Her arm went back, poised for the throw. But at the last possible instant her fingers convulsed around the tiny grip, holding on to it so tightly that her knuckles whitened with strain.

Suddenly, uncontrollably, her whole body began to shake.

Black Sun crouched at the edge of the bluff, his dark eyes narrowed to slits against the afternoon glare. His long brown fingers curled into angry fists as he gazed down into the valley at the *Nih'oo'oo,* the spider people. Even here they came, with their lumbering wagons, their iron-jawed traps, their picks and shovels, their thundering guns and their monstrous greed. Even here, where the land was unspoiled by their wagon tracks and the deer, elk and buffalo were still plentiful, they came to plunder the earth, the trees and the animals. They came to take everything they could and to destroy what was left.

Black Sun had seen wagons like these on the long trail to the south. The wagons always appeared from the direction of the rising sun, crawling westward in slow single file, toward a distant place the whites called Oregon. With their bulging canvas tops, they reminded him of swollen caterpillars.

The travelers tended to move in small groups, and so far there had not been many of them. But where there were few now, there would be more later. Many more, like the ones he was seeing now. This party troubled him deeply because they had left the common trail and cut north into unmarked territory. Their wagons, as many as the fingers on one hand, were rumbling swiftly now, along the flatland that skirted this range of high bluffs. Their iron-rimmed wheels cut into the tender skin of the earth, leaving a wake of flattened grass and blood-red soil.

Black Sun leaned forward, straining to catch a glimpse of the men in the wagons without showing himself. But their path was angled away from him now and he could not see the drivers on the benches where they sat. A single rider, clad in the ragged buckskins and fur hat of a trapper, darted among the wagons on his spotted pony, pausing now and again as if to speak to the drivers. The man would be their guide, Black Sun surmised, and the others were most likely hunters and skinners, here to kill buffalo now that their kind had scoured the land of beaver.

Black Sun's fingers gripped the hasp of the long steel knife—the knife he had taken from his white stepfather on that long-ago night when he had fled, beaten and bleeding, into the wilderness. He knew the ways of white men all too well—their laziness, their brutality, their blind greed. Anger rose like a sickness in his throat as he stared down at the moving wagons. With a handful of seasoned warriors, he could wipe them from the face of the earth, take their horses and their guns, and leave their wagons in flames.

A bitter smile tightened Black Sun's lips as

he erased the thought from his mind. It had been nothing more than an idle wish. He had no warriors with him. He was alone, far from home in this remote, mountain-rimmed valley. And his people, the Arapaho, had never raised a lance against the white man.

Black Sun's body tensed as a movement in the trees below the bluff caught his eye. An aspen branch, laden with spring catkins, moved against the wind. Sunlight glinted on a bare, bronze shoulder, then another. Under Black Sun's careful gaze, heads and limbs materialized beneath the branches. The low nicker of a horse rose to his ears. Flattening himself against the ledge, he slid forward until he could see them all. Ten—no, eleven—mounted braves were moving stealthily through the trees, on a parallel course with the wagons.

Black Sun studied the riders, taking in their long, plainly braided hair, their fringed buckskin shirts and the moccasins that showed blackened soles when they leaned forward on their mounts. They were *Siksika,* members of the tribe the white men called Blackfoot, and all of them had the look of youth and inexperience. Little more than boys, they were outfitted for hunting, not for war. But now they were following far more dangerous game than deer or even buffalo. For their own sakes, Black Sun could only wish them the wisdom to stay out of sight and leave these white travelers alone. He had no great love for the *Siksika,* but these youths were as vulnerable as a gang of half-grown coyote pups toying with a rattlesnake. They were too young to understand the danger.

It would be the horses that drew them like moths to flame. Four powerful brown animals pulled each wagon. Compared to the wiry ponies the young braves rode, the white men's horses looked as massive as full-grown elk. The possession of such horses would make any man rich in the eyes of his people. Black Sun could not blame the young *Siksika* for wanting to get close to them, to touch them, to take them.

An experienced warrior would not risk a confrontation with the whites. He would follow at a distance and wait for darkness, when the travelers would be asleep and the horses tethered for the night. Then he would use stealth and cunning to slash their hobbles and lead them away. But not these young fools. They were only asking for trouble.

Black Sun eased his way down the rear of the bluff to the stand of lodgepole pines where his own two ponies were tied. This was dangerous country for a lone Arapaho, with his tribe more than twenty sleeps to the east. He had come here to his mother's burial place seeking a vision that would bring him the medicine he needed to serve his people. But even after four days of fasting, the vision had not come. Long years of bitterness had walled it out, and now the sight of the hated wagons had destroyed all sense of purpose. It was time to abandon the quest and to go back to his tribe on the open plains; back to his aging grandfather and to the small son he had left in the care of his dead wife's sister. He had been away from the boy too long.

The dun-colored buffalo pony pricked its ears at his approach. Swinging easily onto its bare back, Black Sun took up the lead of the packhorse and chose a narrow deer trail that zigzagged downward through the pines. Below him, the trail forked. One branch wound over a rock slide and down to a rushing creek. The other, easier on the horses but more exposed to danger, circled the back of the bluff to emerge into the valley below.

He hesitated, glancing up at the sky. The sun was well past its high point and he had a long way to go before dark. The easier route would be faster, but he would need to go quietly and keep to the trees. It would not do to have the young *Siksika* abandon the wagon train and turn their mischief on him.

For a moment longer he paused, scanning the steep hillside for any sign of danger. Finding none, he nudged the horse and swung left onto the path that would take him down the bluff and into the valley.

Charity struggled to her knees and peered over the back of the wagon. Through the choking dust, she could make out the swaying cover of the next wagon behind. She could hear the driver shouting at the straining team as he slapped the reins down on their pumping haunches. The lead horses were so close that she could see the red linings of their flared nostrils and the whites of their eyes. She could see Rueben flashing among the wagons on his spotted Indian pony.

The one thing she could not see was Indians.

Boiling with anxiety, she righted herself and began crawling forward amid the jouncing boxes and barrels. Silas would scold her if she violated his orders to stay put. But never mind. She had to find out what was happening.

As leader of the little party, Silas drove the first wagon. The other wagons carried missionaries, a mason, a carpenter and a pale, consumptive young man with enough medical training to call himself a doctor. The two missionaries were married to sisters—plain, humorless women in their forties with little use for Silas Bennett's pretty young bride. Other women might have fussed over Charity and her condition, but these two, who'd evidently been friends with Silas's first wife, treated her with undisguised spite.

There were no children along. Charity's baby, as far as she knew, would be the only white child in hundreds of miles.

As she moved ahead, steadying herself against the big trunk, the cold weight of Rueben Potter's pistol pressed against her leg. What if she were forced to use the tiny weapon with its single shot? If she fired the lead ball into her own brain, how long would the baby live? Long enough to be torn from her body and ripped apart? Would she have the courage to shoot into her bulging belly, killing the child before it could know terror or pain? Even the thought was too awful to bear.

Gasping with effort, she reached the front of the wagon. Silas was driving the team hard, his long musket balanced across his knees. Reaching forward, Charity laid her hand on Silas's bony shoulder.

"Get back, Charity," he snapped without turning around. "Stay out of sight."

"I'm not a child, Silas," she said. "I need to know what's happening. Where are the Indians?"

His head jerked slightly to the left. "Trees," he muttered, too busy driving the team to rebuke her impertinence. "They're staying even with us. We can see them moving, but as long as they stay back, we can't get a clear shot at them."

Charity stretched, trying to see the Indians, but her eyes were dazzled by the afternoon sunlight. She could make out nothing. "You'd think, if they were going to attack us, they would have done it by now," she said. "Maybe they're only curious."

"D'you want to wager your life on that, woman?" Silas's metallic voice quivered with a nervous undertone. "According to Rueben, the Blackfoot are the devil's own spawn. I'm willing to take his word for that."

"Look!" Charity pointed. Her vision had cleared and she could now see the Blackfoot warriors riding out of the trees. Their sharp young faces were unpainted, their bows and quivers slung over their backs. They sat their horses proudly, their bare chests gleaming like copper. The thought flashed through Charity's mind that these youthful warriors were the most beautiful people she had ever seen.

The leader raised his right hand in an unmistakable sign of peace, but Silas appeared not to notice. "Spawn of the devil!" he muttered, raising his musket.

"No!" Charity's scream was lost in the shattering explosion of powder and lead. She saw the young Blackfoot's body jerk backward with the impact of the shot. Then the plunge of the startled horses threw her back into the wagon, into the shifting chaos of boxes, bins and barrels. She heard the blood-chilling screams of the Indians and the whistle of objects flying through the air. Only when Silas moaned and fell to one side, with a feathered shaft protruding from his chest, did she realize they were arrows.

"Silas!" She fought her way toward him, but his glazing eyes and the trickle of blood from a corner of his mouth told her he was already dead.

Lunging past his body, Charity grabbed the reins. She was fighting to slow the racing team when Rueben galloped past her, his coonskin cap gone and his sparse hair blowing in the wind. "Git down!" he screamed at her. "Git down an' hide!"

He dashed to the far side of the wagon in an effort to turn her horses into the circle the other wagons were forming. An instant later, Charity heard a whistle and an abrupt thud. When Rueben's pony reappeared, its saddle was empty except for a single battered boot dangling from the stirrup.

Choking on her own terror now, she dived for the wagon bed and covered herself with the heavy patchwork quilt she and Silas had used for sleeping. From outside she could hear scattered gunfire. A woman screamed as an arrow struck its target. Charity pulled the quilt over her head to shut out the horror. People all around her were dying on this sunlit spring day, and she could do nothing except try to save herself and her baby.

The wagon had stopped moving. Dimly, through the quilt, she could hear young male voices speaking in a rapid-fire tongue that made no more sense to her than the gabble of wild mallards. She could hear the jingle of harnesses falling to the ground and the sound of the horses being led away. They would want the horses, of course. Rueben had told her that

Indians prized horses the way white men valued gold. Kindly, gruff old Rueben would be lying dead now, with an arrow through his body. Charity gulped back her tears.

The sounds of gunfire had ceased. In the silence, Charity's heartbeat filled her senses like a throbbing drum. Was the massacre over? Would the young braves take the horses and go now, leaving her here alone?

Fear jolted through her as she heard the creak of a footstep and felt, through the floorboards, the pressure of quiet movement. She lay as still as death, feeling the weight of Rueben's pistol in her pocket. Beneath her body, her hand eased downward until she could touch the grip. As her fingers found the cold metal trigger, she knew that she could never be desperate enough to shoot herself or her baby. She would only use the tiny weapon in defense of their lives.

The intruder was opening boxes and barrels, muttering in disgust and dumping their useless contents into the wagon bed. Charity bit back a groan of pain as the corner of a hardbound hymnal struck her back. Her hand tightened around the pistol grip. If he was going to find her, it would probably be in the next few seconds.

The angry brave shouted something at his companions outside, telling them, most likely, that nothing in this wagon was worth taking.

An instant later, he strode to the front of the wagon. The boards creaked again as he jumped to the ground. Charity exhaled, her body limp and dripping with perspiration. The young Blackfoot had freed the horses and probably gathered up the guns. Surely they would leave now. She would only have to keep still a little longer.

She heard their voices again, muffled by distance this time. Yes, they were going away, leaving her to face whatever lay ahead. Charity's heart leaped with a strange, desperate elation. She was alive, her baby was alive. Somehow she would survive the grim days ahead and find a way to reach safety.

The baby, too long confined to one position, kicked. "It's all right, Little One," Charity whispered, shifting against the hard boards. "We're going to make it. We're going to be fine."

The last reassuring word had no sooner left Charity's lips than an arrow thunked into one of the wooden hoops that supported the wagon cover. Scarcely daring to breathe, she shrank beneath the quilt once more. Her lips moved in silent prayer as she waited, hoping against hope that the Blackfoot would not return.

Seconds crawled past, then minutes. Huddled beneath the quilt, Charity strained her ears for the sound of footsteps or voices. When she could no longer stand the silence, she raised the edge of the heavy quilt.

Choking gray smoke stung her eyes and flooded her lungs.

The wagon was on fire.

Chapter Two

Charity's first impulse was to clamber out of the wagon and dash for safety. But there was no safety to be found. Above the hissing and crackling of the flames, she could hear the triumphant whoops of the Blackfoot braves. She could almost picture them dancing around the wagon, celebrating as they watched it burn. If she tried to escape, they would be on her like a pack of coyotes on a wounded sheep.

Forced to choose, she weighed the prospect of a brief but agonizing death against the horrors she'd heard described in whispers around nighttime campfires. The baby was her biggest concern. Surely it would be more merciful for the small life to be snuffed out now, inside her body, than to suffer the terror that waited outside the wagon.

Charity pressed her face against a knothole in the floor and gulped the precious air. No, she resolved, she wasn't ready to die. Somehow she would survive. She would live to have this baby, to see her child grow up and to cradle her grandchildren on her lap. She would live, heaven help her, or die fighting.

The crackle of burning canvas, soaked in linseed oil for waterproofing, had become a roar. Sparks were dropping like fiery hail on the surface of the quilt. Charity heard the popping sound as they struck the thick fabric and began to smolder. She thought of the water barrel, which sat just a few feet away, now hopelessly out of reach. Why hadn't she had the foresight to soak the quilt with water? She should have known that if the Indians attacked, they would set fire to the wagons.

Little cat tongues of flame were licking their way through the quilt. A red sheet of agony spread through Charity's body as they reached the back of her dress and began to consume the worn cotton fabric.

She could no longer hear the shouts of the young braves, but by now it would have made no difference if they'd been screaming in her ears. The fire had reached her. Seconds from now, if she could not get out of the wagon, she and her baby would be dead.

Choking and blinded by smoke, she groped her way to the rear of the wagon. She could feel the skin blistering on her back as she found the tailgate and the iron hook that held it in place. Only the pain kept her moving. She could feel her reason ebbing, feel her mind sinking into a smoky black void.

With the last of her conscious strength, she worked the hook free. As the darkness closed in, her frantic lunge shoved the tailgate open and her momentum carried her forward over its edge. With her gown smoking, Charity dropped to the ground, rolled onto her back and lay still.

Black Sun had followed the deer trail, which zigzagged down through the pines and into the ghost-pale aspens. By the time he emerged from the trees, he was east of the bluff, a safe distance from where he had seen the *Siksika* youths. He had heard the gunfire echoing in the distance but had willed himself to ignore it and to keep moving. Let his enemies destroy each other. He had no more use for the *Siksika* than he did for the *Nih'oo'oo*.

He had dismounted and was watering his horses at a spring when the cry of a golden eagle called his gaze upward. High above, he could see the outline of the great bird against the blue sky. On wings that stretched as wide as his own arms, it was soaring lazily westward, toward the place where a rising column of gray smoke gave testament to what had taken place.

Black Sun studied the smoke with narrowed eyes. Burning wagons could mean only one thing—the *Siksika* youths had won their fight. Even now they would be galloping home with their trophies—horses, guns, ammunition, whiskey and anything else they could lay their hands on. The prizes might even include a few white captives, whose slow deaths would provide amusement for the entire band.

And what had they left behind, among the burning wagons? Black Sun swung back onto his horse, struggling to wipe the thought from his mind. Let the *Siksika* have their victory. He had never relished the sight of death, and he was no scavenger, to hunt among the bodies for plunder that the braves might have left behind. Ride away and try to forget what had happened in this valley of blood, that would be the easiest and safest course.

But even as Black Sun turned his mount eastward, duty tugged at him. Word of the battle would surely trickle back across the plains, from band to band, from tribe to tribe. With each retelling, the story would change. His people would need a true report, so that they could discuss what had happened and how it might influence their own dealings with the *Nih'oo'oo*. He owed it to them to go back and learn all he could.

His lips hardened into a thin line as he turned toward the rising smoke. In the sky, the vultures and ravens had already begun to circle. By the time he reached the burned wagons, the birds would already be flocking onto the bodies. Black Sun braced himself for what he was about to see. He could only hope that everyone he found in that evil place would be dead.

Charity drifted in and out of nightmares. Now she was in the wagon with her mother and father. They were trying to cross the ice, which had cracked beneath them, causing them to tumble into the freezing water. As she sank into its black depths, the water became a whirlpool of fire that seared her skin, her hair and her lungs. She fought her way upward, gasping for breath.

As she rose through a red fog, Charity felt something prick her cheek. She flinched, moaned and opened her eyes.

A huge raven was perched on her chest, its bright, beady eyes a handbreadth from her face. As she stared, still dazed, its massive black beak jabbed straight toward her.

"No!" Her head jerked to one side. Her arms thrashed upward, knocking the bird off its feet. Startled, the hellish creature squawked, fluttered upright and flapped away.

Only then did Charity become aware of the searing pain that shot through her body with every shift in the position of her arms. And only then did she remember what had happened.

The baby—her pulse jumped in sudden dread. Her hands darted reflexively to the bulge below her ribs. The movement triggered another jolt of agony, like the red-hot points of a hundred needles jabbing into her back. But even the pain was forgotten in the rush of relief that swept over her as she felt the familiar kick of a tiny foot against her palm. Her baby was all right. For that one joyful instant, nothing else mattered.

Cautiously she shifted her head and inspected her surroundings. The sun was low in the sky, its amber light slanting through the blackened skeleton of the wagon. By some miracle, she had tumbled clear of the fire. The iron-rimmed wheels and axle that supported the frame had prevented the blazing wood from collapsing on top of her. Otherwise, Charity realized, she and the baby would not have survived.

Silas might have claimed that God had been watching over her. But God hadn't been watching over Silas. She had seen her husband die with an arrow in his chest. And she had every reason to believe that Rueben Potter had died the same way.

But what about the others?

For the space of a long breath she lay perfectly still, trying to catch any human sound— a word, even a moan of pain. Nothing reached her ears but the squabbling cries of birds and the rustle of wind through blades of grass still damp from snowmelt.

Again she raised her head, bracing against the skin-splitting pain as she twisted to look beyond her ruined wagon. Nausea seized her stomach as she saw the sprawl of death around her. Rueben Potter lay a stone's throw away, his body impaled on a feathered lance. Charity recognized the two sisters from their fluttering skirts and narrow black boots. They had perished in a hail of arrows, clutching each other to the end. Their missionary husbands, the young medic and the two bachelor tradesmen were likewise dead, and all of the wagons were in smoking ruin. Charity could see no sign of Silas. But then she remembered that he had died on the wagon seat. The flames would have consumed his body like the hellfire and brimstone that peppered his sermons.

Charity lay back in the grass, shaking uncontrollably as the reality of what had happened swept over her. She was alone and injured in hostile Indian territory, the only survivor of a horrible massacre. She had no food or water, no shelter, no resources of any kind except her own two hands.

For a brief time she closed her eyes and rested, willing herself not to hear the raucous cries of the death birds that flocked around her companions. The thought struck her that she should get up, find a shovel and bury them. But she did not have the strength to dig one grave, let alone nine. With her seared back lancing agony through her body, it would be all she could do to stand up and walk.

The day was cool. Even so, the slanting sunlight felt hot on her face. When she tried to swallow, she discovered that her mouth was cotton-dry, her throat parched and burning. If she lay here much longer, she would die of thirst.

A low, breathy sound reached her ears, gentle and familiar, almost lost amid the squawks of the scavengers. For a long moment Charity let it seep into her senses, her pain-fogged mind recalling the warmth of her grandfather's barn and the stalls where the massive draft horses had stood munching hay and oats.

She heard the sound again, closer now. As its meaning slammed home, Charity froze in terror.

It was the uneasy snort of an approaching horse.

Scarcely daring to breathe, she lay rigid on the ground, her eyes closed in what she hoped would be taken for death. Where there was a horse, there would likely be a rider. And no rider would come to this killing ground for any good reason.

By now, the horse was close enough that Charity could feel the vibrations of the animal's skittish gait. She could sense the agitation in its low, rough nickering. But it was what she could *not* hear that frightened her most. The metal parts of a white man's bridle would jingle when the horse shook its head. Indian bridles, those she had seen, consisted of little more than a leather thong looped over the animal's lower jaw. The horse coming toward her was clearly nervous. But there was no metallic sound to reassure her that its rider was white.

Hidden by her fluttering skirt, her hand eased downward to the pocket that held Rueben's pistol. The small weapon was still there, cold and solid to the touch. Her fingers closed around the grip and found the trigger. One shot. She would have to make it count.

The horse halted beside her and lowered its head. Charity willed herself not to breathe. The animal was so close now that she could feel the hot, damp air emerging from its nostrils. Its velvety muzzle nudged her cheek, long whiskers pricking her skin.

She clenched her teeth, willing herself not to react, but when the creature sneezed, spraying her face with drops of moisture, her reflexes betrayed her. She jerked sharply. Her eyes flew open.

A towering figure blocked the light of the sun, casting a long shadow across her face.

Charity gasped as her gaze traveled upward. The horse, a rangy, dun-colored Indian pony, was unremarkable. But the man on its back took her breath away.

He was tall for an Indian, with fierce aquiline features and skin the color of polished mahogany. His glossy black hair was parted in the center and hung over his chest in two long braids. His moccasins and fringed buckskin leggings were not so different from the ones Rueben Potter had worn, but the long buckskin shirt, belted at the waist and edged with fringe that brushed his lower thighs, was decorated with exquisite quillwork around the open neck.

He was a wild, magnificent, utterly terrifying creature. But it was his eyes that impaled Charity where she lay, making her feel as helpless as a wounded bird in a snare. Dark, hooded eyes with glints of fire in their depths, they gazed down at her with undisguised hatred. Fierce and dignified, he bore little resemblance to the young Blackfoot who had attacked the wagons, but she had no doubt that he was every bit as dangerous.

Charity's fingers tightened around the grip of Rueben's pistol. She had no way of knowing what this Indian planned to do with her, but there was a single bullet in the little gun. If he made one wrong move, it would go straight through his heart.

Black Sun studied the woman, concealing his emotions behind the stony mask of his face. He had never seen a white female before. This one was young, and might even be judged pretty in the eyes of the *Nih'oo'oo*. But to him she looked as pale and strange as a ghost. Dirty, tangled hair, its color like dried cattail stems, lay in dank strings around her soot-smeared face. The cloud-gray eyes that stared up at him were bloodshot and wide with terror. One hand splayed protectively over her bulging belly. The other lay concealed beneath her skirt as if hiding something, a knife, perhaps. He would be wise to watch that treacherous little hand.

The Arapaho life path was built upon giving to others. As a follower of that path, he was duty-bound to take pity on all those in need, even nonhuman beings like this *Nih'oo'oo* woman. To turn away and leave her to die, along with her unborn child, would bring disgrace upon himself and his people.

Still, as he shifted in the saddle and made ready to dismount, Black Sun found himself paralyzed by warring emotions. The nine years he had spent in a filthy cabin, with the white trapper who had bought his widowed mother for a few strings of beads, had separated him from the true way of the Arapaho. Those same nine years had spawned a hatred of whites that ran as deep as the marrow of his bones.

Following the counsel of his grandfather, Four Winds, he had returned to his mother's burial place seeking reconciliation and asking for a vision that would bind him to his people once more and enable him to serve them. Weak from fasting, he had pleaded with Heisonoonin, the great creator and father of all, to cleanse his spirit and bring him peace. But because his heart was hardened by old angers, the vision would not come. Heisonoonin had sent him away empty.

Now, as if to mock him, fate had flung this helpless white woman across his path, giving him no choice except to take compassion and help her.

As he eased his leg over the pony's withers, the vile curses his drunken stepfather had screamed at his cringing mother echoed in his memory. Part of him wanted to shout them into the woman's ears, to let her know exactly what he thought of her kind. But when he finally cleared his throat and spoke, the words that emerged were simple.

"Don't be afraid. I won't hurt you."

Charity could not have been more startled if the man's horse had opened its mouth and begun quoting from the Book of Revelations. She stared up into the stern bronze face, scarcely able to believe her ears.

"You speak... English." She forced each word from her smoke-parched throat.

"Some." He squatted beside her, his smooth-muscled shoulders blotting out most of the landscape. His hands worked a wooden stopper from the narrow neck of a seamless rawhide pouch—the bladder of some large animal, she realized.

"You are... Blackfoot?" Charity's dry lips cracked as she spoke.

"Arapaho." His hand moved none too gently beneath her head, supporting her neck as he tipped the open pouch to her mouth. "Drink," he said gruffly.

The water trickled into her mouth. She gulped it eagerly, not caring that it was neither cool nor particularly fresh but only that it quenched her burning throat. Her hand loosed its grip on the pistol in her pocket. Rueben had told her that the Arapaho were known as the Blue Sky people because of their kindly behavior toward outsiders. Unless this man was lying, he was not likely to harm her.

"Don't drink too much. It will make you sick," he cautioned, pulling the bag away. When she moaned, he lowered her head and poured a little of the water into his palm. With an odd, rough gentleness, he smoothed the water onto her forehead, her cheeks, her throat and her cracked lips. She whimpered, wanting to lick the moisture from his hand, to take his long fingers in her mouth and suck them dry.

When he took his hand away and stoppered the bag, she tried to plead for more with her eyes, but he ignored her distress. "You can't stay here," he said, glancing toward the trees.

Charity nodded, knowing what his words implied. She would have to get up, no matter how much it hurt. Bracing against the pain, she worked one arm beneath her and rolled onto her side. The strain of that simple movement on the skin of her blistered back sent arrows of hot agony shooting through her body. A scream rose in her throat. She gulped it back. Their lives could depend on her keeping quiet.

For a moment she stilled, feeling the baby shift and resettle inside her. She heard the sharp intake of his breath as he bent to examine her back.

"How bad is it?" she asked.

"Bad, but I've seen worse." He exhaled sharply. "I can do something to help, but not here." He rose to his feet and moved around her so that he could look into her face. "Give me your hands," he said. "It will hurt, but you must let me pull you up."

"I know." Charity extended her hands and felt his grip close around them. His fingers were long and sinewy, and his palms possessed the timeworn toughness of pliant leather. She held on, knowing she had no choice except to do as she was told. If she remained here, she and the baby would die.

Twisting, she bent her legs so that they would catch her weight and push her upward. "Ready," she murmured. "Make it quick."

"Now!" He jerked her upward. She sucked her scream inward as the pain swept through her. On her feet now, she sagged dizzily against him. His body went rigid at her touch, as if a serpent had crawled across his chest. This man had not been happy to find her, Charity realized. To him, she was nothing but a danger and a burden, as much to be hated as to be pitied. Only some strange quirk of conscience

had kept him from riding away and leaving her to die.

Seized by a flash of pride, she pushed herself away from him. "As you see, I'm quite all right!" she declared, swaying like a drunkard. "Get me to a safe place where I can rest. After that, you can wash your hands of me and be on your way!"

His anthracite eyes flashed her a look of cold contempt. "Don't be a silly child," he snapped. "Come on. We have to get out of here."

Glancing beyond the wagons, she noticed that he had brought a second horse. But that horse, a short-legged brown pinto, was wearing a loaded packsaddle with no room for a rider. Unless her rescuer planned to abandon his supplies, they would have no choice except to ride double.

He seized her wrist and pulled her toward his mount, then hesitated. Charity could guess what he was thinking. If she rode in front of him, the contact with her burned back would cause her excruciating pain. But her bulging belly would not allow her to fit easily behind him.

He deliberated for the space of a breath. Then, wasting no more time, he sprang onto the horse's bare back, shifted forward almost to its shoulders, and used his grip on her elbow to swing her up behind him. The sudden pull on her arm caused Charity to gasp, but the strain was brief. Without being told, she reached past the expanse of her belly and clasped his ribs. She felt his body flinch at her touch, but he said nothing as he caught the lead of the pack-horse and urged his mount to a gallop.

He raced the horses full-out until they reached the shelter of the trees. Then he slowed their pace to a walk, so smooth and stealthy that they glided like shadows among the bone-white aspens. Charity murmured a silent prayer for the dead she was leaving behind—kindly old Rueben, the young carpenter and mason and medic, the two grim women and their even grimmer husbands. And Silas, for whom she had not shed one tear.

Had she loved him? Perhaps she would never know. Her girlish notions of love had been crushed under the weight of guilt, duty and obedience, crushed by his self-righteous harangues and his cold indifference to her needs. After this ordeal was over, she might find the time to mourn him. Now, however, the only feeling left in her was the hunger to survive.

"What kind of man would bring a white woman to a place like this?"

The tall Arapaho's question, coming after such a long silence, startled her. His English, she noted, was very good, but spoken with a slight singsong quality, as if he had learned much of it from books.

"My late husband was a missionary," she said, refusing to be put off by his icy tone. "And I do believe that's the longest string of words you've spoken to me. Is that where you learned English, from missionaries? Are you a Christian?"

His only response was a derisive snort of laughter.

"I don't think we've been properly introduced," she persisted, taking refuge in formality. "My name is Charity Bennett. You may call me Charity. And kindly tell me what I should call you."

His eyes followed the flutter of a chickadee from branch to branch. "My Arapaho name means Black Sun," he said. "And you ask too many questions, Charity Bennett."

"Indeed?" She feigned mild outrage, using their verbal duel to distract her thoughts from the agony of her seared skin. "May I remind you that the first question was yours?"

"I did not know that moving one rock would set off a rock slide." He guided the horses around a deadfall, his sharp eyes scanning the trees around them for any sign of danger.

"Why are you named Black Sun?" She grimaced as the horse jumped over a log, its motion shooting daggers up her back. "It must be an interesting story."

He exhaled wearily, as if he had explained the name too many times before. "Not so interesting. I was born at a time when the moon shadow was passing across the face of the sun."

"You were born during an eclipse."

"Yes."

"My mother always said that children born during an eclipse had the gift of second sight. Do you have any special gifts, Black Sun?"

He did not reply, and for a moment Charity took his silence for dismissal. She was groping for a retort that would put him in his place when she realized that he had halted the horses and was leaning forward, his body taut and wary.

"What is it?" she whispered into the stillness.

"Shh!" he hissed. "Listen."

Charity held her breath and strained to hear the sound that had alerted him. She could hear the wind that whistled through the aspens, making their long catkins dance and shimmer. She could hear the distant squawks from the awful ring of dead bodies and burned wagons they had left behind. But she could hear nothing more. Her ears were not attuned to the pitch of danger as his were.

"What is it?" she whispered again. "I can't hear—"

"Listen!"

She heard it then, the faint, galloping cadence of unshod hoofbeats, muffled by the soft prairie earth. Her pulse surged, pumping terror through her veins as she realized what it meant.

The Blackfoot were coming back and her life was in the hands of a man she scarcely knew.

Chapter Three

Black Sun listened long enough to estimate the number of riders and judge their speed and direction. The party was small, very likely the same *Siksika* who'd burned the wagons. After hiding the stolen horses, they could have decided to return to the killing ground for more prizes, such as jewelry, clothing, knives and scalps. Drunk on victory, they would be in a wildly dangerous mood.

The white woman's fingers dug into his ribs as he swung his horses to the left, moving deeper into the trees. Had the young braves seen her lying beneath the wagon and mistaken her for dead? Would they notice that she was gone and try to trail her?

His spirits darkened as their peril sank home. The *Siksika* were known to be superb trackers, and Charity Bennett's pale, tawny hair would be a trophy worth pursuing. If the braves picked up her trail, they would be relentless.

Charity gasped as the horse swerved around a massive boulder. The woman was in terrible pain, he reminded himself. She was bearing up stoically, but in her injured condition she could not travel fast or far. They needed a safe place to hide, where she could rest for a day or two while he treated her blistered skin.

And then what? Black Sun suppressed a groan as he thought of Charity's swollen belly. Judging from the size of her, she was less than a moon from giving birth. If he didn't get her back to her people soon, she would go into labor with no women or doctors to help her. If her labor went badly, she and the child could die. And even if things went well, he would be stranded in hostile territory with a helpless woman and a newborn baby on his hands.

What a joke Heisonoonin had played on him! He had asked for a vision to cleanse his spirit and make him one with his people. Instead this white woman had been flung across his path, bringing him nothing but danger and difficulty.

The *Siksika* were coming closer, making no effort to keep their presence a secret. Young and careless, they were laughing and singing about their victory. Had he wanted to risk it, Black Sun might have found a vantage point and tried to pick them off one by one with his arrows. But he did not make war on children—not even cruel, dangerous children like these. Right now, the only prudent course was to get himself and this woman out of their reach.

As they slipped through the trees, Charity clung to his back as if using his body to shield her unborn child. So far she had displayed remarkable courage. But her strength wouldn't last much longer. They needed to find a safe place where the *Siksika* might not look for them.

Black Sun knew of one such place, a deep box canyon fed by springs and riddled with small caves. It was close enough to be reached before nightfall. But the canyon held its own dangers. It was sacred ground—sacred to the *Siksika,* to the Shoshone, to the Crow and to many other tribes, including his own people. To enter the canyon, especially in this season of renewal, would be to invite disaster and death.

Almost any place of refuge would be better than that forbidden canyon, Black Sun thought. But unless they could find another way to elude the *Siksika,* it might be their only choice.

So far, he had not taken time to cover their trail. But now that would have to change. Moving deeper into the trees, he began to wind back and forth, avoiding soft earth and patches of melting snow that would show the prints of the horses hooves. When they crossed a shallow brook, he traveled upstream before emerging onto the bank again; and where the trail forked, he chose a treacherous path across a rock slide instead of keeping to the easy game trail below.

Even so, Black Sun felt uneasy. The tricks he'd used to cover the way they'd gone were simple ones, known to any good tracker. Worse, he could no longer hear the braves. Either they'd gone off in the opposite direction, or they had picked up his trail and were moving stealthily along it. Only by going back to scout could he be sure. And that would mean leaving Charity alone.

The sun lay like a burning coal above the trees. Daylight was fading, but the moon would be full tonight. A hunter's moon—and they would be the hunted, fleeing from shadow to shadow.

Their path had taken them into a small, rock-sheltered clearing. Black Sun halted the horses while he took stock of their situation. Would it be best to keep moving or to stop for some badly needed rest?

Charity moaned, her weight sagging against his back. Black Sun felt her start to slip sideways, down the flank of the horse. His hand flashed out, catching her arm before she could topple headfirst to the ground. She gasped with pain. Her closed eyes flew open.

"Where…are we?" she whispered. "What's happening?"

Black Sun made his decision. "We're stopping for now," he said. "The horses need rest. So do you."

"And what about you?" She blinked, still dazed and confused.

He eased her to the ground, then dismounted. "I need to know if we're being followed. You stay here with the horses. I'll take a shortcut back the way we came and see if those braves are on our trail."

"And if they are?" She stared up at him, fully awake now.

"Then I'll come back and we'll keep moving. Otherwise, we'll make camp here and try to get some sleep."

"You're leaving me here alone, then. For how long?" He caught the flicker of fear in her storm-colored eyes.

"Not long." He strode to the packhorse, unrolled the buffalo robe he used for sleeping and arranged it in the lee of an overhanging rock. Opening a parfleche, he took out a strip of smoked venison and thrust it toward her. "Chew on this. I'll leave you the water bag, too."

He had expected her to whine and argue, but she accepted the dried meat and took an experimental nibble. "What if you don't come back?"

"I'll come back. Just stay where you are and keep still." He turned away from her and tied both horses to a nearby aspen. "Anybody who comes after you will have to deal with me first."

The look she flashed him in the dying light did not reflect much confidence, but she said no more as he slipped off into the trees. When he glanced back, she was still standing where he'd left her, looking small and afraid as she clutched her swollen stomach. She was a spirited little thing, Black Sun reflected with grudging admiration. But nothing could change the fact that she was terrified and in pain. It would be foolhardy to leave her for long, but he needed to know whether they were being trailed. Both their lives could depend on that knowledge.

Forcing his eyes away from her, he set off through the trees at a silent run.

Charity watched her rescuer until he vanished into the deepening twilight. Then, turning away, she eased under the overhanging rock, sank onto one end of the buffalo robe and pulled the other over her belly to ward off the chilly wind.

There was no part of her that did not hurt. Her spine and pelvis ached from the jarring ride, and her thighs were raw where they'd gripped the horse's flanks. Her head throbbed, her eyes and throat burned, and the slightest movement of her arms pulled at the blistered skin on her back, making her want to scream.

There were no words for what she'd been through today. Her husband and companions had all been murdered, her wagon had been burned, along with all her meager possessions and the things she'd made for the baby, and now her savage rescuer had gone off and left her alone in this awful place. Right now, all she wanted to do was to cover her head, close her eyes and wait for death.

The firm jab of a tiny foot against her bladder startled Charity out of her despondency. She was not alone, after all, and this was no time to give up on life.

In the balance, she had much to be thankful for. She was alive. Her baby was alive. And although the burns on her back were miserable, the fire had spared her face, her hair, her hands and the rest of her body. Her burns would heal in time, as would her grief. Somehow her life would go on.

But only if she fought for it now, she reminded herself. Only if she refused to give in to the forces of pain, fear and despair would she be strong enough to walk out of this wilderness alive.

The light had faded from the sky, leaving only the glimmer of emerging stars. From the hollow beneath the boulder, Charity could barely make out the chalk-white aspen trunks and the pale rumps of the horses beneath them. She could hear their big teeth munching the spring grass that had sprouted from under the fallen leaves. The sounds of their quiet breathing and the familiar aroma of their manure soothed her in the darkness.

She bit off a strip of the tough, smoky meat Black Sun had given her. Its salty taste stung her throat, but she chewed it hungrily, knowing how much her body needed the nourishment.

How long had Black Sun been gone? An hour? More? Charity stirred beneath the buffalo robe. The baby moved with her, shifting its small limbs in the confining space of her womb. What would she do if the tall Arapaho failed to return? He had promised to come back, and he struck her as too proud to break his word. He had even left the horses behind—surely he would have taken them if he'd meant to go off and leave her stranded. But sometimes the best of intentions could not be carried out. Any number of things could have gone wrong. By now he could be lying at the bottom of a cliff or serving as target practice for the young Blackfoot braves. By now, Black Sun could easily be dead.

Seconds crawled by at the pace of hours, and still he did not return. She would wait until first light, Charity resolved. Then she would take the horses, set her course toward the rising sun and hope for the best.

The baby fluttered and shifted inside her

once more. How much longer would it be, she wondered, before she held her little one in her arms? A month? A week? Her grandmother had told her nothing about having babies, and the two grim, hostile missionary wives had been no help at all. She could only pray that the baby would be born in a safe place, with someone who knew how to help her.

She tried closing her eyes, but she was too miserable to sleep. Black Sun's lean, dark face seemed to float in front of her, his eyes blazing like an angry eagle's. Why did he hate her so much? He *did* hate her—she was certain of it. Even when he treated her kindly, she could feel the tension in him, the reluctance even to touch her. When he spoke to her, the contempt in his voice cut like a blade. Why, when she'd done nothing to harm him?

Was it because she was a white woman? That was the most likely guess. Black Sun's fluent English could only have been learned from living among whites. What could they have done to ignite the smoldering disgust she saw in his eyes every time he looked at her?

Charity tugged the buffalo robe up to her chin, shivering at the touch of the cool night breeze. Black Sun was a man of the most puzzling contradictions. If he loathed whites so much, why had he taken on the burden of saving her life? It couldn't give him any pleasure, caring for a helpless, injured white woman, let alone one who was great with child. Clearly he hadn't wanted to take her along with him. Yet, he had.

A low peal of thunder rumbled over the western mountains. The wind freshened, carrying the smell of rain to her nostrils. Charity's heart sank. Most of the time she enjoyed rain, but she was miserable enough already without being soaked to the skin. Where in heaven's name was Black Sun? Why hadn't he returned?

As the rim of a full moon rose above the treetops, an anxious snort from one of the horses riveted her attention. Both animals seemed nervous. They were tossing their heads, rearing and stamping, becoming almost frantic as they tugged at their tethers.

Charity crept out from under the overhang and peered through the trees. She could see nothing, but the sudden sound that ripped the darkness turned her blood to cold jelly. It was a high-pitched scream, almost like the scream of a woman. But it wasn't a woman. Charity knew, because she'd heard the same scream one night on the wagon trail. Once heard, it could never be forgotten.

It was the cry of a great, golden cat. A mountain lion. A cougar.

Panic welled in her throat. She gulped it back. The cat would likely be after the horses, not her. Rueben had said that cougars were usually afraid of people. But she was alone, and if the beast picked her out as the easier prey, she would have no way to defend herself.

Only then did Charity remember the little single-shot pistol in her pocket.

As her fingers reached down and closed around the cold iron grip, the cougar screamed again. The big cat was close, very close. Panic-stricken, the horses snorted and reared. She could see the whites of their wild eyes by the light of the rising moon. There was no time to check the firing mechanism. She could only hold the tiny weapon at the ready and pray that it would work.

In a flash of sheet lightning, Charity spotted the cat. It was crouched on top of the boulder where she'd been resting, its sleek tawny head thrust forward, its fangs bared in a snarl. It was a huge animal, and there was just one shot in her little gun. What if she only wounded it, leaving it in pain and more dangerous than ever? How could she take such a chance?

The cat's steely muscles tensed like springs

as it inched forward. Then, like an arrow shot from a bow, it leaped into the air.

Thunder echoed across the sky as Charity pointed the pistol and squeezed the trigger.

Black Sun had found the *Siksika* braves camped in a meadow at the edge of the forest. They'd been feasting and laughing around their campfire, so careless that they hadn't even posted a lookout. To teach the young fools a lesson, he had removed the hobbles on their ponies, allowing the animals to wander off. The youths would be a long time rounding up their mounts in the morning.

Satisfied that the braves were not trailing anyone, Black Sun slipped back the way he'd come and broke into a ground-burning lope. He had covered about half the distance to the spot where he'd left Charity when he heard the sharp explosion of a gunshot.

He froze for an instant, scarcely daring to trust his ears. Maybe it had only been the thunder he'd heard. But his instincts told him otherwise. Heart slamming, he stretched his legs to a sprint. Somewhere out there in the forest, there was trouble. And if the sound of a gun had reached his ears, the *Siksika* would have heard it, too.

He thought of Charity, alone and helpless in the night. Had someone come across her by chance? Someone with a gun?

No story he could piece together made any sense. Black Sun only knew that he had to reach her side before it was too late.

He was out of breath by the time he burst into the clearing where he'd tied the horses. His knees weakened with relief as he saw Charity. She was sitting in a patch of moonlight, her eyes wide with terror, her hands clutching the base of a long, dead tree limb.

As he came closer, his eyes caught the gleam of moonlight on a miniature pistol, no bigger than a child's toy, lying next to her knee.

"You shot that gun." The words came out as a harsh rasp.

She clutched the limb tighter, as if she meant to strike him with it. "I shot at a cougar," she said defensively. "My shot missed, but I think I scared it away. I don't have any more bullets, just this...limb." Her voice trailed off and broke. He realized she was on the verge of tears.

Black Sun exhaled sharply. He might have dismissed her story as a woman's imagination, but the huge, fresh pug marks in the earth gave testimony to the truth. He should never have left her here alone.

"You shot at the cat and missed, and now you're sitting there expecting to beat it off with a stick." He was angry at himself, not at her, but when Charity straightened her spine and thrust out her chin, it was clear that she hadn't understood things that way.

"Yes," she declared. "It was all I could find. I didn't want the cougar to attack the horses."

"You're sure you missed? We can't leave a wounded cat out there."

"I'm sure. The bullet knocked this limb off a tree. Stop treating me like a child." She shot him a scathing look. "Did you find the Blackfoot?"

"Yes." He strode toward the horses, glancing back at her as he untied their tethers. "They were camped for the night. We'd have been fine. But your gunshot changed all that. They'll be after us as soon as they can round up their horses. We've got to get moving."

"If you hadn't gone off and left me for cougar bait, there'd have been no gunshot." She scooped the little weapon into her pocket and staggered to her feet, swaying with exhaustion. She'd been remarkably brave, Black Sun thought, but this was no time to tell her so.

Pain rippled across her moon-pale face as he helped her mount, but she did not cry out. "Where are you taking me?" she asked.

"That depends on how far we can ride before the horses give out." Black Sun caught the lead of the packhorse and swung the animal into line. Best not to mention the forbidden canyon. As a white woman, she would not understand the importance of respecting sacred ground, and she might argue for stopping there.

Nudging the dun pony, he started out of the clearing at a brisk trot. There would be other hiding places beyond the canyon. The trick would be to reach them without being discovered. The *Siksika* would lose a little time catching their mounts, but they had the advantage of speed and endurance. Riding double and with an injured woman, Black Sun calculated, he would not be able to stay ahead of them for long. Even if he were to unload the packhorse, progress would be slow, and the two of them would have to do without much-needed food, clothing and blankets.

Charity held on to him tightly as they picked their way down a creek bed to hide their trail. The hands that gripped his ribs were small and cold. What was she thinking? he wondered. Was she mourning her husband, the father of her child? Had the man been good to her? Had she loved him? But such questions were none of his concern, Black Sun reminded himself. Charity Bennett was not, and never would be, his woman.

Her belly pressed the small of his back, so close that Black Sun could feel the thrust of a small foot against his spine. The movement sent a strange, warm quiver through his body, but he quickly steeled himself against it. He could not let himself feel anything for this white woman and her unborn child. His only aim was to get her back to her own people before the time came for her to give birth.

And how soon would that be? It was not a seemly question to ask a woman, but her time had to be close at hand. And if her pains started here in the wilderness, with only his unskilled hands to help her, she could die.

Like his mother.

Like his wife.

"Tell me how you learned English." Her voice startled him in the darkness. Earlier he had found her personal questions irritating, but Black Sun had since come to realize that she made such careless talk to take her mind off her fear and the pain of her blistered back, so he resolved to be patient.

"I learned English from the white trapper who bought my mother," he said.

"He *bought* her? Like he'd buy a horse?"

"Such things happen where there are white men and no white women. Because my mother was a widow with a child, her price was lower than the price for a maiden, but she was pretty and a hard worker. A bargain, as your people would say. We stayed with him for nine years." Black Sun spoke carefully, hiding the bitterness that gnawed at his spirit whenever he thought about those nine years.

"Was he good to you?"

"Not so bad at first. He'd gone to school, and he taught both of us to speak English. I even learned to read from some books he had. But then the drinking started. It made him...vile." He had to grope for the last word, which he had read, but never heard spoken.

Charity was silent for a time. Black Sun could feel her shifting behind him. "What happened at the end of those nine years?" she finally asked. "How did you get away from him?"

Black Sun sighed. "You ask too many questions, Charity Bennett. And your questions knock on doors that I choose not to open."

"I'm...sorry," she said in a low voice. "I meant no offense."

"You are a *Nih'oo'oo,* a white person, and not expected to know better," he said. "Among my people it's disrespectful to ask such private questions. Let's be still for a while. Stillness is good."

She did not reply and, after a few moments, he knew she would not. Had he hurt her? Thinking back on his words, he realized they had sounded pompous and silly in English— not the way they would sound in Arapaho, as spoken by an elder to rebuke an unruly child. Not the way they had once been spoken to him.

In truth, he mused, he had never mastered correct Arapaho behavior. The Arapaho life way was something that had to be learned day by day, year by year, moving through the lodges, the lessons, games and rituals and ceremonies with one's own age mates. Living apart for nine years, as the stepson of a drunken white man, had taught him to speak and read English. But it had robbed him of an Arapaho boy's education.

His accident of birth, during the time of the black sun, had marked him for a life as a healer and medicine man. But on returning to his people after his mother's death, he had discovered that the gift was gone. In his life as an adult, he had performed the sun dance four times. His chest was laced with scars where his flesh had hung from the sharp bone hooks while he'd danced in a slow circle around the sacred pole. He had fasted countless days while he pleaded for a vision. But the *beetee,* the spiritual power he needed to serve his people, hadn't come to him. Maybe it never would.

The darkness lay like a quiet lake around him, its silence broken only by the movement of the horses and the low, edgy sound of Charity's breathing. Had his words made her weep? No, that would not be like her, he thought. She was too strong for that. But she would be weary and in pain. Soon, regardless of the danger, he would need to stop, make camp and tend her burns.

To the west, the mouth of the forbidden canyon cut like a deep black gash into the foothills. He turned his eyes away, struggling to ignore its call. There were other canyons, other shelters, he reminded himself. But none of them were so temptingly near.

Lightning flashed across the dark sky, followed by a shattering boom of thunder. Rain began to fall around them, first in stinging drops, then in sheets of water that streamed off their hair, their shoulders, their backs and down the flanks of the horses.

"C-can't we stop somewhere?" Charity's teeth were chattering with cold.

"Soon." Black Sun willed his gaze away from the canyon, despite the fact that the weather seemed to be driving them toward its shadowy entrance.

"Please, I'm so— Oh!" She gave a muffled gasp. Her fingertips dug hard into his ribs.

"What is it?" he asked, alarmed.

She gripped him harder, writhing. "The baby!" she gasped. "I—think it's coming!"

Chapter Four

Charity clenched her jaws, biting back the cry that pushed upward into her throat. She could feel the resistance in Black Sun's body as he halted the horses. She could hear the unspoken dread in the low rasp of his breathing. Oh, why couldn't the baby have waited? Why did her pains have to start tonight, in this miserable storm, with no one but an Indian brave to help her?

"Are you sure it's the baby?" He spoke above the hissing sound of the rain.

"Yes. I'm sure. I'm…wet." She hoped he would understand and not point out that they were both soaked from the rain. The surge of warm fluid between her thighs had come just before the first pain stabbed through her body. Charity knew far too little about having babies, but what was happening to her could hardly be mistaken for anything else.

"How soon, do you think?" He glanced ahead, then to his left, as if torn between one danger and another. Where her fingertips rested on his ribs, Charity could feel the rapid pulsing of his heart.

"I don't *know!*" She found herself wanting to pummel his body with her fists. "It's my first baby! How could you expect me to know something like that?"

The words Black Sun muttered under his breath could have been a curse or a prayer. "Hold on tight," he snapped, swinging his mount to the left. As he kicked the horse to a gallop, Charity saw that they were headed toward an inky shadow that spilled across the foothills. Seen through the thick curtain of rain, it slowly took on the form of a deep cleft, then a canyon with a wide mouth and steep, rocky sides.

Charity was trying to pick out more details when another pain knifed through her. She gasped, her body doubling against his back.

"Hold on!" Black Sun spoke quietly but his

voice was hoarse with strain. How much did this man know about delivering babies? Not a great deal, she suspected. Right now, Charity would have given anything for the presence of her grandmother, or even one of the hatchet-faced sisters who'd perished beside their wagons in a hail of arrows. She could only hope the birth would be easy and natural. If there were complications, she and the baby might not live to see morning.

Her fingers pressed into the hard knots of Black Sun's shoulder muscles as she wondered what dying might be like. Pain, she imagined, perhaps terrible pain, and after that a feeling of blessed release, or maybe sadness at all one was leaving behind. Then darkness, to be followed by whatever came next. Dying might not be so bad after all.

But no, she wasn't ready to die—she who had tasted so little of life. Whatever this man must do to save her and her baby, she would see that he did it. If she had to scream at him, curse at him, threaten him…

Slowly the gripping agony slid away from her. They were in the canyon now, with tall stone buttresses rising on both sides of them. How quiet it was here. Even the rain had become a fine, silent mist. High above them, the night sky flowed like a river of thinning clouds. Stars emerged as the storm moved eastward, and now the pale rim of the moon peeped over the rim of the canyon, flooding their path with a ghostly silver light.

The packhorse snorted, the sound exploding in the stillness. Charity could hear the splash and gurgle of a stream and the whispering chirp of crickets. Black Sun had not spoken but he seemed unusually anxious, leaning forward on the horse, his eyes peering into the darkness. Was there some danger in this oddly peaceful place? Something she didn't understand?

Charity had no more time to wonder. Another contraction seized her like a brutal fist closing tight around her, squeezing, pushing and twisting. Her hands seized Black Sun's shoulders from behind, gripping them to hold back a scream. "Please," she muttered through clenched teeth. "Please, can't we stop now? I need to get down! I can't have this baby on horseback!"

"As soon as we come to a good, safe place." He maneuvered the horses around a cabin-size boulder that blocked their path. "If they find us in here—"

"No!" Pushing against his back, Charity slid

across the horse's rump and dropped to the ground. As she landed on the damp moss, her knees buckled beneath her. Burned, soaked and hurting, she huddled on the earth in a ball of misery, her arms clutching her swollen belly. Her eyes glared up at him.

"*This* is a good, safe place," she hissed. "And if it's not, it will just have to do! I'm not going another step!"

Black Sun stared down at her, amazed that such a small, punished body could endure with such determination. She reminded him of a cornered bobcat, wounded and chased down by hunters, spitting defiance with the last of its strength. But he had no mind to argue with what she'd said. Charity Bennett was not going another step.

Dismounting, he glanced around at the rocky glade where she'd forced him to stop. They could do worse than this, he decided. The giant boulder they'd just made their way around formed a barrier against anyone approaching from the mouth of the canyon. The stream was nearby, and the overhanging willows and alder trees, heavy with catkins, offered shelter from the wind and rain.

With a sigh of resignation, Black Sun tethered the horses and removed the bundled supplies and the rawhide-covered packsaddle from the little brown pinto. He had hoped to get the woman back to her people, but that was no longer possible. Her life and her child's life were in his hands now. If things went badly, their deaths would be on his conscience to the end of his days.

By the time he turned back toward Charity, the contraction appeared to have passed. In the light of the cloud-veiled moon, she looked like a spirit child, so small, pale and vulnerable that her helplessness tore at his heart. But he could not allow himself to feel any softness toward this woman, Black Sun reminded himself. She was one of the *Nih'oo'oo,* the spider people, and bringing her to this canyon was a violation of all respect for sacred places. There would be a price to pay for what he'd done, but for now he had no choice. He had taken pity on Charity Bennett and it was his duty to help her.

"Let me look at your burns," he said, taking a step toward her. "Maybe I can do something for the pain."

Charity did not answer but turned away, offering him a view of her back. Black Sun lowered himself to a crouch beside her, turning her shoulders to expose her burns to the brightest angle of the moonlight. He had glanced at her injuries earlier; but now he suppressed a gasp as he saw, in detail, the fragments of charred fabric clinging to an expanse of seared and blistered flesh as large as the span of his two hands. How had this small person endured the agony of the bouncing horse, the lashing tree branches and the roughness of his own hands? Her strength astounded him. But Charity's ordeal, he realized, had only just begun.

"How bad is it?" She spoke in a whisper.

"The burns will heal. But you will have scars." Black Sun had once been told by a *Nih'oo'oo* trader that white women were very vain about their bodies, wanting them to be perfectly shaped and flawlessly smooth to please their men. He had expected her to be dismayed. Her edgy little laugh startled him.

"Scars? Good heavens, do you think that matters at a time like—"

Her words ended in a gasp as another birth pain seized her. Her body arched and her fingers dug into the wet grass, but she did not cry out. The *Nih'oo'oo* trader had said that white women in labor squealed like pigs. Either the man was lying, or he had never known a woman like Charity Bennett.

Moving swiftly now, he tugged the buffalo robe out of the pack and spread it at the base of a sturdy pine tree. The dry needles beneath would cushion the ground, and the spreading branches would keep out the worst of the weather. As the pain receded, she uncurled her legs, crawled onto the buffalo robe and stretched out on her side, resting with her eyes closed. Her spent, swollen body quivered with each breath.

Would she survive the night? Black Sun wondered. Would she deliver her child safely, or would he find himself digging a grave by the light of dawn? His own people laid their honored dead beneath the sky, but whites, he knew, required burial in the earth. If Charity died, he would prepare such a grave to honor her courage.

But this was no time to think of death. Such thoughts only invited the gloomy spirits to come and lurk in the darkness, waiting to snatch fragile spirits in their greedy claws and carry them away. Charity Bennett was a fighter, and he was here to help her live, not to watch her die.

Images of his battered, bleeding mother and his beautiful wife rose in his mind. Both of them had died in agony and he had been helpless to save them. Now Black Sun forced those images back into the shadows of his memory. The past was the past and he could not change it. He could only pray for the skill and luck to pull this brave white woman and her child from the claws of death.

Charity was still resting, so he put himself to the task of gathering herbs to soothe her burned back. Yarrow would be best if he could find some. It was early in the season for the feathery green leaves to be sprouting, but maybe in this sheltered canyon, close to water…

The spring was only a few paces away. At the base of a decaying stump, where the midday sun had warmed the soil, he found a clump of the precious yarrow sprouts, enough for a generous fistful of soft green leaves. Where there were these, there would be more, Black Sun told himself. At first light he would look for them—if Charity Bennett was still alive.

He returned to the pine tree to find her on her knees, doubled over in pain. Black Sun dropped to a crouch beside her. He was hesitant to touch her, for fear that he might startle her, but one small hand flashed out and caught his wrist in a frenzy of need. The fingers squeezed and kneaded his flesh, blunt nails digging into his skin.

Tentatively he stroked the soggy mat of her hair. "It's all right," he found himself murmuring. "I won't let anything happen to you, Charity Bennett. I'll take care of you and the baby for as long as you need me…"

The sound of his own words frightened and astonished him. What sort of craziness was this? He owed nothing to this woman. In the eyes of his people, she was not even a human being. In his own eyes, she was a member of the same race as the drunken monster who'd destroyed his mother. But as he squatted beside her, stroking her hair, the desire to protect her was like a blazing fire inside him.

Her grip on his wrist eased as her pain receded. The silvery eyes that looked up at him were calm, almost cold. "Why would you say such a thing, Black Sun? I can tell you have no love for my people—and as for me, I'm nothing but a burden and a danger to you. You could have ridden away and left me to die. Why didn't you?"

"Because you needed my help." The words came without hesitation. "Taking pity on those in need is the way of my people."

A little smile tugged at her childlike mouth. "Then you are like the good Samaritan," she said. "Do you know the story?"

He frowned as the memory emerged from the past—the thick, leather-bound book in his stepfather's cabin; the pages filled with columns of tiny print. He remembered chapters and verses. And he remembered the stories. So many stories.

"I have read your Christian Bible," he said. "But I am not a Christian."

Again he saw the smile, as brief and enchanting as the flicker of a butterfly's wing. "As I recall, neither was the... Samaritan."

By the time the last word was spoken, Charity was in the grip of another pain. While her frenzied fingers clutched his upper arm, Black Sun began to prepare the yarrow for her burns. Since he had no grinding stone, he chewed the leaves lightly between his teeth, then mixed them with water to make a lumpy paste in the palm of his hand.

"Have you...ever...helped with a baby before?" she asked, her teeth clenched.

Black Sun hesitated, wondering how much he should tell her. "Once," he said at last. "My mother—I tried my best to help her. But I was only a boy. There was nothing I could do."

"She died?" Charity whispered the question. Her fingers had begun to relax their grip on his arm.

"Turn around," Black Sun said. "I'm going to put this poultice on your burns."

With a shudder of release, she turned away from him, exposing the length of her back. There was no need to cut away her dress or the undergarment beneath, since the cloth had burned through. She winced at the first touch of the mashed yarrow. Then, as the herb's cooling effects began to work, her breath eased out in a broken little sigh. "The pains are getting worse," she murmured. "I'm hoping it won't be much longer."

"People say that first babies can take a long time." Black Sun tried to sound calm and confident, hiding his fear as he dabbed the yarrow paste across the backs of her shoulders. "Your baby may be getting ready to give you a lesson in patience."

"Will I have to lie on my back when the baby comes?" Her question sounded as if she'd been thinking about it for a long time. "With the burns, I don't know if I can…" She glanced away from him, as if suddenly aware that she'd crossed a line, discussing such an intimate subject with a man who was not her husband.

But this was no time to be proper, Black Sun told himself. Charity was close to giving birth, with no woman or doctor to help her. It was important that they learn to speak frankly with one another.

"Among my people, women squat to give birth," he said. "The earth pulls the baby down, which makes it come easier."

"I understand, but what an odd idea. I don't know if I can—" She gasped as another pain took her. This time her groping fingers found his hand, squeezing it so hard that Black Sun could feel his knucklebones cracking together. Her hands were surprisingly strong, the palms and fingers lightly callused. Her skin was cold, and he found himself wishing he could build a fire to warm her. But that would be too risky. The *Siksika* could be near enough to see the smoke.

"Tell me about your mother, Black Sun."

Her question caught him off guard, like the sudden jab of a thorny branch. Her fingers still furrowed his flesh, a sure sign that the pain had not passed. But the eyes that met his were clear and calm. "You told me you couldn't help her," she said. "What happened?"

"Nothing that you would want to hear at a time like this."

"She died then, in childbirth." Charity's voice was a pain-laced whisper. "Tell me about it."

"For your entertainment? To pass the time

and take your mind off the pain?" He shot her a contemptuous glare. "For that I have better stories, Charity Bennett. Wouldn't you rather hear the tale about the wolf and the spider?"

"No." Her grip on his arm had relaxed, but her hand remained. "I need to know why you're putting your own life at risk to help me. I think it has something to do with your mother. And yes, it will take my mind off the pain. That, too."

Black Sun felt the tightness like a clenched fist in the pit of his stomach. He had never told anyone the full story of his mother's death— not even his wife, whom he had loved. That he should bare the past to this small, irritating white woman was unthinkable. And yet, because she had asked, he found himself struggling for a way to begin. He stared up at the sky, groping for words.

"How old were you?" she asked gently.

"Fourteen winters," he said, feeling the raw unwinding of the story begin inside him. "My mother had lost many of the white man's babies—he was very big and she was small, and they always seemed to come too soon. But this one she did not lose. Her time was close on that night...when it happened."

He felt the light pressure of her fingers on

his wrist, as if she sensed the awfulness of what he was about to tell her. It was only when he glanced down at her face that he realized she was having another contraction.

"Go on," she whispered, her voice taut and husky with the effort of holding back the pain.

"The white man—he had a name, but I always thought of him as the monster—had traded some furs for a jug of whiskey that day. He got drunk, and when he got drunk, he got mean. My mother had made a stew for him, and he threw it, pot and all, against the wall. Then he started screaming at her and kicking her with his boots. I was only a boy, and not very big for my age. When I tried to stop him, he grabbed me, threw me out into the snow and barred the door."

Black Sun felt the tightening of her fingers. This pain seemed to be lasting longer than the others.

"Go...on, please." She was breathing in gasps now. "Please..."

"I pounded on the door," Black Sun continued, though his mind was no longer on the story. "From inside the cabin, I could hear him screaming, hear her screaming, and then—"

"Oh!" She pressed her lips together to muf-

fle the moan. "I think it's...coming," she whispered. "Sweet heaven, the baby, it's coming!"

"Try not to push!" Black Sun scrambled to his feet, wishing he'd thought to make preparations sooner. Attending a birth was women's business and he had only the barest knowledge of what needed to be done. Now he improvised as best he could.

Yanking a rope from the pack, he tossed the end over a stout limb of the pine tree. Finding a short, strong stick, he made a knot around it so that the stick hung crosswise, a forearm's length above Charity's head. "Hold on to this," he said, guiding her hands around the stick until she could clasp it easily. "Pull as hard as you need to."

Her body went limp as the pain abated, but her hands kept their grip on the stick, so that, for a moment, she simply dangled, with her knees resting lightly on the ground.

Tugging the buffalo robe aside, Black Sun used his hands to scoop out the ground beneath her and line the hollow with swiftly gathered handfuls of fresh leaves and grass. By the time he finished, Charity was writhing in agony. Her eyes locked with his for an instant, then closed in a grimace of pain and effort.

Seared into memory, the images of his

mother and his wife rose again in Black Sun's mind. Once more he willed them away. Charity was young and strong and full of fight, he told himself. Even with her small size and the trials she had suffered, there was no reason to doubt that her child would come swiftly and safely, unless…

But no, he would not even voice that thought. He had done all he could. Now he could only wait, hope and try to ignore the fear that lay like a coiled thing inside him—the fear that this woman, too, would die and that somehow it would be his fault.

Black Sun raised his eyes and murmured a plea for forgiveness to the sacred canyon— to the rocks, the trees, the water, the animals that had lived here undisturbed for generations. Then, turning his attention to Charity Bennett, he made ready to do what he could for her.

Charity clung to the stick that Black Sun had rigged for her. Her sweat-slimed palms gripped the papery bark as the pain twisted her body—*good* pain, she told herself repeatedly. Good, good pain that was bringing her baby into the world.

"Hold on…hold on…" Black Sun's deep voice droned in her ear. His presence calmed her, reassured her that everything would be all right. He was her rescuer, her guardian angel who had covered her with his wings in this time of danger. He would not let anything happen to her or the baby. She had to make herself believe that or she would lose her will to fight.

Why was the baby taking so long? She had thought, when the pains worsened, that it would be a matter of a few pushes and then she would feel the lightening of her body and hear the mewling cry that would bind her heart forever. But time had crawled on and on, agony-filled minutes flowing into what seemed like agony-filled hours. The moon had drifted along the high rim of the canyon, then vanished from sight like a curious lady visitor grown bored with waiting for something to happen.

All this time, all this torment, and there seemed to be no end to it.

The knifing contraction slid away, giving her a few moments of blessed relief. Charity let go of the stick and slumped to the ground, the folds of her filthy, ragged skirt falling around her like the petals of a mud-trampled flower. Her arms felt as if they'd been wrenched from their sockets. She massaged her aching shoulder joints, fighting tears of frustration.

"Here." Black Sun offered her a sip of water from the skin bag, which he'd refilled at the spring. His face was etched with weary shadows, as if he'd shared every pain with her.

"It won't be much longer," she said. "Surely it won't."

He reached out and brushed the matted hair back from her face with his rough brown fingers. She closed her eyes, savoring his gentle touch. Where had he been going when he found her? she wondered. Who would be waiting for him, worrying because he hadn't arrived?

"Do you have a family, Black Sun?" she asked, suddenly needing to know.

"A boy of six winters." His voice rasped with fatigue.

"And his mother?"

He glanced away without answering her. For the space of a breath, Charity was puzzled. Then, with the certainty of instinct, she understood why. Black Sun's wife was dead. Like his mother, she had died in childbirth.

Other things began to fall into place, as well: why he had taken it upon himself to save her, and why he took such pains to hide the depth of his anxiety. If she and the baby lived, it would be a token of his salvation. If they died, it would plunge him that much deeper into purgatory or whatever the Arapahos might call that self-made prison of the soul.

Black Sun had never finished telling her the story of his mother's death. But Charity had no wish to hear it now. To know that it had happened was already as much as she could bear.

She reached for the stick as the tightening began once more. Black Sun watched her, his eyes hooded in shadow.

"I need…a story," she gasped as the pain surged through her body. "A good story—you said you knew one about a wolf and a spider."

A bitter smile twitched at a corner of his mouth. "That is a story for children," he said.

"Then tell me a story for…grown-ups!" Her hands clawed at the stick as she fought to keep from crying out. If the pains grew any worse, they would rip her in two, she thought. But she would endure anything to get this baby into the world, and the contractions were good because they meant the baby was coming. Surely it was. She could not—would not—be dying.

The tears she'd been holding back all night overflowed and spilled down her cheeks. She began to cry, quietly at first, then in big, gulping sobs that shook her whole body. All she wanted was to have this baby, and she was trying so hard, so hard…

Through her tears, she saw that Black Sun had risen to his feet and was looming above her. Gently but firmly, he uncurled her fingers from around the stick and enfolded them in his big hands. She gripped his warm, solid flesh as her tears continued. "I'm sorry," she whispered, ashamed of her own weakness. "Making such a fuss. I've read that when it comes to having babies, the women of your people are strong and brave, not like…like *this*."

"Your tears are tears of courage, Charity Bennett." His voice was rough with weariness. "Hold my hands when the pains come, and I will tell you the story of this canyon where we have come for refuge. It is, as you say, a story for grown-ups."

"Thank you." Charity rested her forehead against the back of his hand, feeling the pressure of cords and tendons against her skin. How good it would feel to stop and rest for a while, to lie on the buffalo robe, protected by the circle of his arms, and to drift off to a place where there was no fear. But she knew better than to wish such a thing. No part of that wish could possibly come true.

Steeling herself against the pain, she waited for the story to begin.

Chapter Five

"It happened a long time ago." Black Sun's voice drifted over and through her like smoke from a glowing campfire, and Charity realized she was listening to a gifted storyteller. "The great Thunderbird who rules the sky decided he would take the form of a man and walk on the earth for the space of a moon. This canyon is where he made his camp."

"Here?" She looked up at him, astonished and delighted in spite of her tortured body.

"You're kneeling on sacred ground right now," Black Sun said. "The whole canyon is sacred ground."

"Then…we really shouldn't be here, should we?"

His gaze flickered away for an instant. "We had no choice," he said. "I have asked forgiveness, but what is done can't be undone."

"I see." A contraction twisted through her body. If she and the baby lived, she would know that forgiveness had been granted, she told herself. If not… But what would forgiveness matter then? What would anything matter?

"Tell me what happened here," she gasped, clutching his hands as if they were her only anchor to life. "I want to hear the rest of the… story."

"The Thunderbird had planned to walk out over the land to see how men and women lived and how they treated each other. But on his very first day in the canyon, those plans changed."

"Changed how?" Charity kept her gaze locked with his.

"A beautiful woman came up the canyon, looking for roots to dig. Thunderbird saw her, and because the desires of a man had become part of him when he changed his body, he wanted her."

"And the woman?"

"She saw that he was kind and handsome, and she wanted him, too. He took her to a cave, high in the canyon. She became his wife, and in her arms Thunderbird learned everything he had ever wanted to know about men and women. The two of them were so happy together they didn't come out of the cave until it was time for Thunderbird to change his form and go back to the sky."

"So, did he leave her there and become a bird again?" Charity's pain had eased. She felt wrung out and exhausted, but the story had pulled her in. She knelt on the ground, her hands lying limp across her knees, her eyes gazing up at him.

"Yes," Black Sun said. "He left her and went back to his place in the sky."

"What a sad story."

"Sad? Why?"

"Because he didn't take her with him or stay here with her. They loved each other, and they couldn't be together."

Black Sun shook his head. "It had to be that way. He belonged to the sky. She belonged to the earth. They could only be together here in the canyon."

"Then, that's all?"

"No, there's much more to the story. When

they came out of the cave, they discovered that their lovemaking had caused the rain to fall and the sun to shine. The grass, which had been dry and brown, was fresh and green. There were leaves and flowers, and this was the very first springtime. They made a vow that every year they would come back to the canyon and stay together for a moon, so that spring would come to the earth."

"Spring is coming now. Does that mean they're here with us, in this canyon?" Charity asked, only half in fun.

"If you choose to believe their spirits are here, then they are." His voice was solemn.

"Is that the end of the…story?" She sucked in a breath as the twisting sensation began low in her body.

"Not quite." He gazed down at her in the moonlight. "After the woman left the canyon, she gave birth to twin sons. One of the sons gave her people the gift of fire. The other gave them the gifts of language and music. So you see, it's not a sad story, after all."

"No…it's quite a lovely story, in fact." Her voice caught in a muffled sob as the pain ripped through her. How much longer could she stand this before her strength gave out? She was so tired, so utterly spent. All she wanted was to lie down and close her eyes and slip into merciful darkness.

And this contraction seemed worse than all the others combined. Charity bit her lip to keep from screaming. The salty taste of blood seeped into her mouth.

"Push…" Black Sun had caught her wrists and was pulling her upward. "You have to push…now!"

"I…can't." She sagged toward the ground, held upright only by the grip of his hands. "I'm tired…so tired…"

He jerked her upward, the sudden strain on her arms jarring her to full awareness. His hands slid up to enfold hers in a fierce clasp.

"Listen to me, Charity Bennett." His eyes blazed like hot coals. "This child of yours also has gifts to give the world. Gifts of beauty and courage and love—but only if you're strong enough to do your part now! If you give up, you and the baby will die—and I won't let that happen. I won't watch you die the way I watched my mother die!"

His voice was fierce, almost angry, but his hands were gentle. She could almost feel their warmth flowing into her, nourishing her, filling her. She felt the magic of the story he had told her, felt the peace of the canyon enfolding her as she struggled.

"Don't fight the pain," Black Sun's voice urged her. "Use it. Help it to do its work. *Push!*"

Charity braced her feet against the sacred earth and flung all her reserves of strength and spirit into one excruciating push. She moaned like an animal as she felt her stubborn flesh begin to yield, felt the downward pressure as the baby moved into the birth canal. Sensing what was about to happen, Black Sun shifted her hands to the stick above her head. She hung from it, gripping with all her strength as he crouched beside her and moved his hands beneath her skirt. He seemed to be chanting something in a low voice. The words that drifted up to Charity made no sense; then it penetrated her fogged mind that he was chanting in Arapaho. She could only hope it was some kind of blessing.

Spent, she hung limply from the stick. Was it over? Was her baby really here? Then why couldn't she hear it crying?

Why couldn't she hear her baby crying?

Panic exploded through her like flame through black powder. Then, before she could react, she heard it—the sharpness of a slap, followed by a tiny gasp and a loud, indignant squall.

It was the most beautiful sound Charity had ever heard.

Black Sun was fumbling with something in the darkness. Charity's eyes caught the glint of moonlight on a knife blade, and the motion of his fingers tying some kind of knot. With effort, she found her voice.

"Is my baby all right?"

"Yes." Black Sun's voice floated up to her. He sounded light-headed, almost giddy with relief. "She's fine. She's just upset with me for spanking her."

"She?" Charity's heart skipped a beat.

"You have a daughter—with a good pair of lungs and a very strong heart."

"Give her to me. Let me hold her—" Charity released the stick, only to discover that she was too weak to stay upright. She slumped against Black Sun's shoulder, her blurred vision fixed on the tiny, squirming creature who rested between his knees. He was drying her off with a piece of soft leather, his hands huge and dark against the small, pale body. The baby was complaining at the top of her lungs, clearly giving him a piece of her mind. It was impossible to look at her without smiling in wonder.

"Lie down and rest," he said, nodding toward the buffalo robe he'd placed on the soft pine needles. "You'll need to feed this little wildcat right away to keep her quiet."

Even as he spoke, Charity felt the liquid surge in her swollen breasts. How strange, and yet how natural it seemed. She was already aching to hold her daughter in her arms.

Glancing down at the front of her scorched, mud-stained dress, she groaned in dismay. The faded chambray gown buttoned down the back. How on earth was she going to get it open, with the charred fabric all but fused to her skin?

Black Sun's eyes flickered toward her and she saw that he understood. "Lie down," he said again. "I'll help you."

Bone-weary, Charity stretched out on her side and waited for him to finish drying the baby. Her eyes followed his every movement as he cradled the small figure between his hands and placed her gently in the crook of Charity's arm.

The baby was still crying, kicking with her legs and beating the air with her tiny fists. Gazing down at the perfect little rosebud face, crowned by moon-pale hair, Charity felt her heart quiver and melt.

Black Sun bent over her. Charity's pulse skipped as she saw the knife in his hand. "Hold still," he murmured, reaching for the front of her dress. She gasped softly as the blade sliced downward, cutting through the worn fabric of her dress and shift, causing her breasts to tumble into view.

He withdrew his hands at once but did not avert his gaze. Charity felt a hot blush creep over her skin. Indian women often went bare-breasted, she reminded herself. They nursed their babies in the open air, within sight of anyone who passed. She had seen them herself near the trading posts. It would not occur to Black Sun that there was any impropriety here. And this was certainly no time to be modest.

Conscious of his eyes on her, she shifted the baby to her breast and brushed a nipple against the small, puckered mouth. Instinctively the baby clamped down and began to suck like a greedy little piglet. Charity's soul overflowed with love and she realized there was nothing on earth she wouldn't do for this tiny bit of squalling, kicking, hungry life.

Black Sun smiled—the first real smile Charity had seen on his somber face. "Your daughter is strong," he said. "One day she will grow up to be a strong woman, like her mother."

Charity gazed up at him. This man had saved her life and brought her daughter into the world. He was truly her guardian angel. She owed him everything.

Glancing down at the baby again, she thought briefly of Silas. She could see nothing of the grim, fanatical preacher in her daughter. The coupling that had conceived this spirited child had been a furtive, almost shameful act, performed in total darkness with both participants modestly clad in their nightclothes. Physical contact had been limited to the essential body parts—Silas had not even kissed her, she recalled now.

Why, then, did it feel so natural to lie bloodstained and bare-breasted in full sight of a heathen savage she had known for only a few hours—a man who already knew her far more intimately than had her own husband?

Something unreadable flickered in Black Sun's eyes. Abruptly, he turned away from her and moved toward the flat rock where he'd unrolled his pack. Picking up another buffalo robe, smaller and softer than the one Charity was lying on, he laid it carefully over her and the baby.

"Rest and keep her warm," he said. "I'll be close by."

Covered by the woolly robe, Charity was already beginning to feel drowsy. She opened her mouth to thank him, but by the time her thoughts could form words she was drifting into the soft, dark fog of sleep. The last thing she remembered was the heart-binding tug of her baby's mouth and the awareness that Black Sun was on guard, watching over them.

Black Sun took a moment to check the horses. Then he settled himself on the flat rock beside the pine tree that sheltered Charity and her baby.

He was exhausted, but he was too elated for sleep. In any case, it might be wise to stay awake. There was always the chance that the smell of birth blood could attract a wolf or a cougar, or that the *Siksika* had managed to pick up their trail in the moonlight. But his sharp instincts detected no such dangers tonight. There was nothing on the wind but the freshness of damp earth and the sweet peace of the canyon.

As his gaze drifted over the rocky ledges, Black Sun felt a quiet sense of welcome and forgiveness. He had come here in need, and the canyon had taken pity on him. It had blessed him with Charity's life and the life of her baby daughter.

Rising, he crouched beside the sleeping pair and tucked the buffalo robe around them. Charity lay on her side, the baby cradled in the crook of her arm. Her profile was soft in sleep, the fear and pain gone from her flower-like features. Her mouth was as innocent as a child's, her lashes like the vane of a golden feather against her pale cheek. Her hair spilled over the dark brown buffalo skin. Tentatively, he touched a stray lock. It curled around his finger like the tendril of a vine.

She had displayed a warrior's courage today, he thought. A woman of his own people could not have shown more bravery. The pride that surged through him was hot and fierce, almost possessive, as if she belonged to him.

Swiftly he willed the forbidden feeling away. This was no time for emotion. As soon as Charity was strong enough to ride, it would be his duty to get her out of the canyon and to deliver her safely to the nearest trading post. That accomplished, he would mount his horse and ride away—and he would not look back.

There could be no bond between them, no connection that would last beyond the day of their parting. She would go back to her people and find herself a new husband. He, in time, might even look for a new wife. His son needed a mother, and holding Charity's newborn baby in his arms had reminded him of how much he wanted more children.

Black Sun gazed up at the river of stars above the canyon walls. How small and unimportant he felt in this sacred place. Perhaps his quest to find the hidden power and become a medicine man for his people was nothing more than vanity. Perhaps he should abandon the dream, return home and settle down to an ordinary life. Was this the answer the spirits had given him? Was this why the vision had not come?

Black Sun's grandfather, Four Winds, had urged him to go on this quest. Four Winds had seen more than eighty winters and had wanted his only living grandson to take his place as medicine man. But Black Sun had not proven himself worthy of the gift. When he returned home, he would tell his grandfather to look elsewhere.

Closing his eyes, Black Sun listened to the sounds of the sacred canyon—the whisper of wind through the tall stands of pine, the rustle of a wood rat in the dry leaves, the cry of a night bird and the faint, distant rumble of retreating thunder. In the world beyond these rocky ledges there was danger, deceit, rage and bloodshed. Here he felt only peace.

When he opened his eyes, he saw that Charity was still asleep; but her infant daughter was awake and looking up at him. The blazing sweetness in that calm gaze tightened a band around his heart. A wise old woman had once told him that babies came from their creator knowing all the secrets of the universe. Only as they learned the ways of earth and began to speak did they forget.

Leaning toward her, Black Sun stroked her downy pink cheek. Her skin was as soft as the muzzle of a newborn foal. What would this small one tell him if she could talk? he mused. How would she answer the questions that gnawed at his soul?

An involuntary smile teased the corners of Black Sun's mouth as he imagined what this spunky little girl would say to him. He was a man, she would declare in a voice that would sound very much like her mother's. He had strong arms, skillful hands, an adequate brain and two people who could not survive without his help. It was time he pulled his head out of the clouds and did what a man is supposed to do—provide and protect.

And she would be absolutely right. With so much to do, there was no reason to waste time on idle thoughts.

At first light tomorrow, he would set about finding a safer camp, higher in the canyon, for this temporary family of his. While he was looking, he would gather more yarrow and prepare new poultices for Charity's burns. Once she and the baby were safe and comfortable, he would make a foray out of the canyon for meat to replace the small supply he'd brought with him in his pack. If he saw signs of the *Siksika,* he might need to create a diversion to draw them away from the canyon. In the next few days, while Charity regained her strength, he would scout the landscape for the safest way out of this dangerous country.

Easing himself to his feet, Black Sun massaged the stiffness from his lower back. The desire for sleep had long since left him, but he was too restless to sit and wait for dawn. There had to be some useful thing he could do without leaving Charity and the baby unguarded.

He took a moment to check the horses. The two ponies were drowsing contentedly where he had left them, their bellies sleek and taut with fresh spring grass. Nearby, screened by thickets of wild rose and willow, the creek splashed its way down the canyon to the valley below.

Black Sun was walking back toward the big pine tree when a stray breeze caused a willow branch to brush against his cheek. The touch triggered a chain of thoughts, ending in an awareness of something Charity's baby would surely need—something he could make while the two of them slept.

With a murmured apology to the canyon, he pulled his knife and knelt at the base of a willow clump. One by one, the blade sliced cleanly through the limber green branches, until the pile they made was large enough to fill his arms.

Feeling strangely lighthearted, he carried the willows back to the flat rock and set to work.

Charity awoke to the yellow brightness of sunlight slanting through the dark pine branches above her head. Her new daughter was already awake and squirming against her side. She was small and scrawny, but full of fight. As Charity turned toward her, feeling sore and sticky, the baby broke into a ravenous wail. Charity gathered her close and offered her a milk-swollen breast. The tiny mouth clamped onto the nipple, sucking eagerly.

Charity felt the flow of her milk as a deep, sweet ache, all through her body. Here, then, was the new center of her existence—this demanding little miracle. Misty with love, she gazed down at the perfect little pansy face.

"I'm going to call you Annie, after my mother," she whispered. "Hello, Annie. Welcome to the very first morning of your life."

A slight movement caught her eye. Charity looked up to see Black Sun sitting a few paces away, on a flat rock. The morning light cast his eyes into pits of shadow beneath his straight black brows. She could read no expression in their hidden depths, but his stern mouth was slightly curved, as if in a secret smile.

Only his hands moved. His long fingers worked with mesmerizing skill, weaving green willows around the frame of something that looked like a large basket. A baby-size basket, Charity realized, measuring it with her eyes. Black Sun was making her a cradleboard.

Gratitude washed over her, flooding her with emotion. She owed this man her life and little Annie's life. And as if that weren't enough, he was making her a gift that must have taken him most of the night.

"Thank you, Black Sun," she said softly.

"Thank you for saving us, and for weaving that fine cradleboard."

He glanced up at her, his features rearranging themselves into a scowl. "I don't expect your thanks," he said. "I did what was needed, as I do now. When we leave this place, you'll need a cradleboard to carry the baby. If we put her in it today, she'll become used to it, and she will learn not to cry."

As if in defiance of his words, Annie spat out the nipple and began to howl. Pulling the buffalo robe up to her collarbone, Charity switched the baby to the other breast, where the tiny mouth clamped on hungrily. "It's natural for babies to cry," Charity said. "All healthy babies do it."

He shot her a dark glance. "Perhaps all white babies cry. But among my people, a crying baby can mean death to a whole village. Before we leave this place, your daughter must learn to be silent."

His words chilled Charity's blood. She remembered a story Rueben Potter had told her about Indian women who'd smothered their newborn babies rather than let their crying betray their people to the enemy. Could she do such a thing to Annie? Her arms tightened around her tiny daughter. She had only been a mother for a few hours, but Charity knew she would die—or kill—before she let her little one come to harm.

A sense of helplessness swept over her. She had no clothes for her or for the baby, no shelter, no way to protect herself and no way to get home, wherever home was. Her survival, and her baby's, rested on the broad shoulders of this angry man who could walk away anytime he chose and leave her to die.

Black Sun hated her people. He probably hated *her*. But he was still here. He had watched over her and the baby all night—her untamed, brooding, reluctant guardian angel. That in itself was a small miracle.

Weaving the last of the willows onto the frame, he checked the rawhide lashings and laid the finished cradleboard on the rock. As he rose to his feet, his looming head and shoulders blocked the sun for a moment, casting a long shadow across her vision. An eclipse, she thought. A black sun.

"We can't stay in this spot," he said. "Now that it's light, we'll need to move you higher in the canyon. You may have to do some climbing." He shot her a questioning glance. Charity could almost read his thoughts. After giving birth, a woman of his own people would be strong enough to get up and do whatever was required of her. But could he expect the same of a white woman?

She returned his contemptuous look. "I'll do whatever I must to get my baby to a safe place," she said. "When do we start?"

"I'll need to scout a trail and find a good hiding place," he said. "It shouldn't take long. By the time the sunlight reaches that high ledge, I'll be back for you." He pointed to a shadowed outcrop, making sure she understood. Then he pulled his long buckskin shirt over his head and tossed it at her feet. "Put this on. And keep your baby quiet. The *Siksika* could be close by. They mustn't hear you."

He turned and melted like a shadow into the trees, leaving Charity alone. Annie had drifted into a light slumber. Placing her daughter carefully on the buffalo robe, Charity inspected the buckskin shirt Black Sun had given her.

It was a beautiful piece of work, made with skill and care. Its open front, which closed with a thin leather lacing, would make it easy for her to nurse the baby. Its fringed hem, Charity calculated, would be long enough to hang well below her knees.

Her own cotton garments were charred from the fire and soaked with sweat and blood. She peeled them off, down to her bare skin. What she wouldn't give for a bath! But this was no time to wish for what she couldn't have. She and her baby were lucky just to be alive.

Black Sun's shirt slipped easily over her head. His clean, smoky scent crept through her senses as she pulled it down over her arms and shoulders. The tanned buckskin was soft against her burned back.

Moving gingerly, she rose to her feet and pulled the long shirt down over her hips. Her legs were raw and caked with blood. Pain from yesterday's long ride shot down her thighs. Her worn high-topped boots and filthy stockings protruded below the buckskin fringe, looking as odd as a turkey's legs on a falcon. But there was nothing she could do about that now.

The baby's sky-blue eyes gazed up at her, round with curiosity. For all her discomfort, Charity could not help laughing.

"Well, what do you think of your mother, little Annie?" she asked. "Have you ever seen a sorrier-looking sight? And look where she's popped you out into the world! A wild, heathen spot in the middle of nowhere, with nary a roof over your poor little head! And you don't even know enough to be miserable!"

Annie's cherry-bud mouth blew a milky

bubble, as if to say that lying on a buffalo robe under a pine tree in the morning sunlight was perfectly fine. Charity's heart swelled with love.

"Don't worry, Little One," she promised her daughter. "We'll get out of this mess somehow. And when we get back to civilization, I'm going to dress you in ribbons and lace, and you'll be the prettiest little girl in all the land!"

Annie gurgled; then, as if on a whim, she wrinkled up her face and began to yowl like a hungry young bobcat.

Remembering Black Sun's warning, Charity scooped the baby up into her arms and cradled her against the hollow of her shoulder, kissing the downy hair and patting the bony little back with her free hand.

"There, my sweet," she soothed as Annie continued to wail. "Hush. Your mother's right here. Everything's all right."

But as Charity glanced upward, she realized, with a lurching heart, that everything was *not* all right.

From the plain beyond the mouth of the canyon, a thin trail of smoke curled upward, rising like a long charcoal smudge against the azure sky.

Chapter Six

Black Sun wound his way up the rocky canyon, following the course of the stream. His moccasins moved as lightly as the padded paws of a cougar, disturbing nothing that lived in the hollow between the sacred cliffs.

On his right he could hear the gurgling of water, but here the stream was overhung with a maze of vines and willows that had not been cut back in the memory of generations. To make a comfortable camp, he would need to find a level, open spot with easy access to water. There was no such place here. He would have to climb higher in the canyon.

Emerging from the trees at the top of a rock

slide, he came upon exactly the kind of place he was looking for.

Above him, a silvery waterfall cascaded down the cliff. When he climbed the narrow game trail to its top, he discovered that the water flowed from a shallow pool among the rocks. On its far side, a sandy hollow beneath an overhanging ledge offered a soft bed and shelter from the weather. Aspens and willows screened the view from below. It was perfect, like finding an unexpected gift. Even a pampered white woman like Charity could not fail to be pleased with its beauty.

Murmuring his apologies to the rocks, the trees and the water, Black Sun turned around to go back down the canyon. Only then did he see the long thread of smoke curling skyward from beyond the canyon's mouth.

Dread pushed his pulse to a gallop as he sprinted down the rock slide. He should never have left Charity alone, he berated himself. If the young *Siksika,* or others of their kind, heard the horses or the baby, their curiosity could make them reckless and bring them into the canyon. If they found her…

Black Sun forced the unthinkable images from his mind. In the eyes of his people, the woman was not even a human being, he told

himself. She mattered no more to him than a
white butterfly that had settled on his hand
and would soon fly away, and her baby mattered even less. But as he plunged downhill,
Black Sun knew beyond doubt that he would
give his life to save them.

"Hush...hush, Little One..." Charity rocked
Annie in the crook of her arm as her free hand
fumbled to unlace the front of the buckskin
shirt. The sky had darkened with roiling gray
clouds that hid the face of the sun. Charity
could feel her own taut nerves pulsing a subtle
current of unease through her body.

"Hush..." She pulled the lacing loose and
gathered Annie to her breast. The baby sucked
blissfully, her crying stilled for the moment.
But Charity knew she could not wait for Black
Sun to return. If the smoke was coming from a
Blackfoot camp, the ponies would be as much
of a lure as the baby. If the Indians found the
horses, they would find her and Annie, too.

Clutching the baby to her breast, she started
up the slope. Beneath her boot soles, the
ground was covered with layers of wet, decaying leaves. With each step, the surface threatened to slither away beneath her feet and send
her sliding back down to the canyon floor.

Her weight loosened a treacherous patch and she stumbled, scrambling and flailing. Her free hand closed around the slender trunk of an aspen. The shoulder-wrenching grip stopped her fall, but Annie lost her nipple and broke into an indignant wail.

Charity's boots dug into the earth as she clawed her way to a level spot and sank back against the hillside. The baby regained her place and chomped happily as they rested in the dappled shadows. A magpie scolded from an elderberry thicket.

Even here they were far from safe, Charity knew. It would be foolhardy not to keep moving. But she was so sore and tired. Her legs quivered beneath her with every step, and the buckskin shirt, as soft as it was, chafed her burned back every time she moved her arms. Only a moment, she promised herself. She would rest until her head stopped spinning and her heart stopped pounding. Then she would push on.

Looking back down the slope, she could see the trail her feet had gouged in the hillside. She could see the two horses and the sodden dress, the buffalo robes, the packsaddle and the cradleboard she had left nearby.

Charity groaned. In her panic, she'd ignored

the signs of her presence that were strewn all over the ground. Then she'd clambered up the hillside, leaving a trail that any child could follow.

What had she been thinking? Lying beneath the buffalo robe in the morning sunlight, she had promised Annie that she would get them both to safety. Then, as soon as she was on her feet, she had made a careless mistake that could get them both killed.

No more mistakes, Charity vowed. For her daughter's sake and her own, she would learn to survive in this wilderness. She would learn to hide her trail and to move through the trees without a sound. She would learn to find food and shelter and to fight, even to kill any enemy that threatened her baby. When Black Sun returned, she would ask him to be her teacher. Meanwhile, she needed to do something about the things she had left behind at the bottom of the canyon.

Annie had spat out the nipple and drifted off to sleep with a milky little smile on her face. Charity weighed the idea of leaving her in a cradle of leaves on the hillside, then decided it would be too risky. Whatever happened, she wanted her baby at her side.

Squaring her jaw, she gripped the nearest

sapling with her free hand and began inching sideways down the hill. She was not quite halfway to the bottom, still in the trees, when a slight movement at the edge of the clearing caught her gaze. Charity froze, afraid to breathe, as a tall figure emerged from the willows. Her heart began to beat again as she recognized Black Sun.

His gaze darted around the clearing. She knew he was looking for her, but only when his furrowed mahogany face flashed upward, catching the light, did she realize how worried he must be. Charity swallowed the shout that rose in her throat. She'd made one foolish mistake. She would not make another.

He saw her then. The relief that brightened his features swiftly darkened into annoyance. "What are you doing up there?" he snapped, reaching up to help her. "I told you to wait for me."

Charity nodded in the direction of the smoke. His breath released with a little catch, as if he'd decided that arguing would only waste precious time.

His big hand pulled her down the slope. Grimly silent, he led her across the clearing to the spot where he'd emerged from the willows. There she saw a narrow, winding path that bore faint imprints of delicately pointed hoof marks—a deer trail, she realized. Why hadn't she thought to look for one instead of blundering up the untracked hillside? One lesson learned, she told herself.

"Follow this," he said in a rough whisper. "I'll clear out the camp and catch up with you. If you get as far as the rock slide, stop there and wait for me—and keep the baby quiet."

As if on cue, Annie opened her eyes, crinkled her little red face and began to fuss. Black Sun muttered under his breath as Charity spun away from him and fled up the trail, clasping the baby to her shoulder.

Where the trail wound through the willows, the way was steep and overgrown. Branches lashed her face and arms as she climbed, gaining ground but tiring rapidly. Annie's mouth had found a fold in the buckskin shirt and she was sucking contentedly on the soft leather. The shirt would taste of salt and smoke, like Black Sun's skin, Charity thought. Because of the shirt, Black Sun's own unique smell and taste would become a part of Annie's deepest memory.

It would become part of her own memory, as well.

By the time the trail leveled out, Charity's

lungs were heaving. She leaned against a boulder to rest, fearful that if she sat she might not have the strength to stand again.

Through the screen of budding aspens, she could look down the slope to the hollow, where Black Sun had bundled up her dress, the buffalo robes and the packsaddle with its contents and placed them behind the flat rock. Now he was dragging a broken branch over the ground and up the hillside to cover their tracks. Another lesson learned, Charity thought, watching as he led the two ponies in circles over that same ground so that the prints of their hooves obscured the marks of the branch. By the time he was finished, the hollow that had been Annie's birthplace looked as untouched as when they'd come upon it.

She waited, expecting him to herd the horses up the trail and brush out their tracks behind them, but what Black Sun did next surprised and dismayed her. Standing on the flat rock, he called the two ponies to him. They came forward at the sound of his voice, snorting softly, their ears pricking forward.

Black Sun stroked each horse affectionately. Bending down, he slipped the braided tethers from their necks. At last, with a final murmured word, he slapped their hindquarters and sent them trotting toward the mouth of the canyon.

Charity stared after them in shocked silence. What had he done? They needed those horses. How else were they going to get away from the canyon and make the long journey home? Fear, distrust and exhaustion welled up in her and flooded over. By the time Black Sun caught up with her, she was beside herself.

"Why did you turn those horses loose?" she demanded. "Now we're stranded here with no way to leave!" Her throat jerked tight as a new fear struck her. She gazed up at him, clutching the baby protectively in her arms. "Am I your prisoner, Black Sun? Is this what you've intended all along, to keep me here and use me any way you like? Was that why you chased the horses away, so I couldn't steal one and escape?"

He glared at her, as tall and cold and angry as the thunder clouds that now filled the sky above the canyon. "Your fear is foolish," he said in an icy voice. "I turned the horses loose so the *Siksika* wouldn't hear them and come after us. When you're strong enough to leave this place, I will find them again or steal others. As for my taking you prisoner to use you—" He looked at her as if she had just slithered out from under a rotting log. "What use could you be to me? You can't hunt or dress skins. You can't make roots into stew or put up a teepee. And, believe me, I have no desire to sleep with a white woman."

Charity felt the color rise in her face, flooding her cheeks with hot crimson. His insult deserved a resounding slap in the face, but she could hardly afford to alienate the man at such a dangerous time. "In other words, I'm nothing but a burden to you," she snapped.

"Your words, not mine."

"Then why did you help me?"

"Because you needed help." Something flickered in the coppery depths of his eyes. "But if I'd known how much trouble you would give me, Charity Bennett, I might have gone away and left you for the ravens."

Charity lowered her gaze, feeling like a scolded child. This man had risked his life to save her from the Blackfoot. He had saved her again when he'd brought Annie into the world. Reason told her she had every reason to trust him.

But when Black Sun had turned the horses loose, all the old fears had boiled up inside her and she had lashed out at him. Even now, as he loomed above her, she felt those same fears knotting in the pit of her stomach.

Why? Charity asked herself. Had her strict upbringing and loveless marriage steeled her against trusting an act of simple kindness? Was she fearful because her good Samaritan was a member of the same race as the savages who had murdered her husband and companions? Or was it simply that she felt lost, helpless and at the mercy of this fiercely gentle giant of a man?

Whatever the reason, Charity had long since learned to trust her instincts. Now that she was a mother, with a child to protect, she could not lower her guard, even with Black Sun. Her first duty was to take care of Annie and to get her to safety. She could not let misplaced trust open them both to betrayal and harm.

As if roused by the thought of danger, Annie began to cry again. A pained look crossed Black Sun's face. Lowering the bundled gear to the ground, he held out his hands. "Give her to me," he said.

Charity's arms tightened around her baby as Rueben's story flashed through her mind—the Indians who'd smothered their babies to keep them still. She would be skewered alive before she would let such a thing happen to Annie.

With a sigh, Black Sun dropped to one knee and freed the cradleboard from the bundle. Folding the smallest of the buffalo robes, he tucked it into the willow frame to make a soft lining.

"*Now* give her to me." The sternness in his voice bordered on contempt, as if he were thinking, *Doesn't this white woman know anything about babies?*

Charity's legs quivered beneath the fringe of the buckskin shirt as she placed Annie into the bowl of his hands. Black Sun gathered the tiny, straining body against his shoulder, stroking Annie's back and chanting low, musical words in her ear—words that sounded more like chattering birds and the rush of water than human speech. Almost at once Annie stopped fussing and settled against his warm, golden skin. Her mouth stretched open in a drowsy little yawn.

Still crooning in his own language, Black Sun eased Annie away from his shoulder and lowered her into the cradleboard. She gazed up at him, mesmerized by his voice and his eyes as he packed a layer of soft moss around her legs and bottom, then pulled the edges of the buffalo skin around her and laced it tightly in place, all the way up to her shoulders.

When he had finished, Annie was so snugly

bound that only her head and neck were free. Strangely enough, she did not seem to mind. She lay contentedly in her tight wrappings, gazing up at the trees with serene blue eyes.

On her way west, Charity had seen Indian babies bundled in such a fashion and thought it a quaint but harmless custom. But seeing her own precious child trussed like a sausage was quite another matter.

"Merciful heaven, she has no room to move!"

"Did she have room to move in the days before she was born?" Black Sun retorted as if he were speaking to a backward child. "Look at her. Is she in pain? Is she crying? Babies are used to having no space around them. They feel safe when—" He broke off, raising a finger to his lips as a signal for silence.

Charity strained her ears, but she could hear nothing. It was then she realized that a hush had fallen over the canyon. The birds had stopped singing. Even the wind seemed to hold its breath.

Instinctively she dropped to a crouch beside the cradleboard, ready to snatch up her baby and run. But Black Sun's light touch on her shoulder warned her not to move.

Following the direction of his gaze, she

looked back through the trees, the way they'd come. Along the edge of the hollow where they'd spent the night, slender, naked brown forms were moving through the trees. Charity's heart lurched as she recognized the young braves who'd wiped out the wagon train.

Now she could hear them. Their voices carried up the slope—the precariously pitched voices of boys who were not quite men. Clearly they thought they had little to fear, for they were making no effort to be quiet. Two of them seemed to be arguing. Charity could make no sense of their language, but Black Sun, listening intently, seemed to understand enough to get the gist of what was being said. He glanced down at Charity where she crouched with her baby. "They found the ponies." He practically mouthed the words, his voice scarcely audible. "Some of the boys want to go up the canyon to see if there are more horses. The tall one is saying that this is sacred ground, that they should turn back." His hand fingered the haft of his long-bladed hunting knife. "Let us hope they listen to the voice of wisdom."

The air hung in stillness beneath the darkening sky, leaden and dangerous. Thunder rumbled faintly over the western mountains. Fear was a taste in Charity's mouth. If the young

Blackfoot picked up their trail, even Black Sun would be no match for a dozen reckless braves. They would fall on him like a pack of dogs, and once he was overpowered or killed, she and Annie would have no chance at all.

As if sensing her fear, Annie began to whimper. Black Sun shot Charity an alarmed glance. "Keep her quiet!" he whispered. But in spite of Charity's efforts to nurse her, the baby continued to fuss. For the moment, the voices of the arguing braves kept them from hearing her. But that, Charity knew, could swiftly change. And if the Blackfoot discovered their presence... Her blood ran cold at the thought of what they might do.

Gulping back her terror, she raised the cradleboard to her shoulder and began to hum softly in Annie's ear, much as Black Sun had done. But the tension had clearly affected the baby. Her whimpers grew more agitated, threatening to erupt into all-out howls.

"Can't you keep her still?" Black Sun's eyes glittered with desperation.

"I'm trying!" Charity muttered, struggling to maneuver the cradleboard so that Annie could nurse. She managed to work the front of the buckskin shirt open to offer her breast, but Annie would have none of it. Her head rolled back and forth in agitation. The color deepened in her puckered face. Her chest jerked in a rising crescendo of sobs.

Black Sun turned away with a sharp exhalation. Moving cautiously, he withdrew his bow and his quiver of arrows from the pack and slipped them over his shoulder. "Stay here and keep quiet," he hissed. "If they come for us, I'll try to draw them away. While they're busy with me, you run. Get as far away as you can, and don't look back!"

Charity's gaze followed him as he darted off through the trees, moving like a shadow across the rocky slope. He was risking his life for her and Annie, she knew. If the young braves heard the baby, or decided to venture into the canyon in search of more horses, he would stand against them alone with his arrows and his knife—all to buy time for her and her baby to escape.

How could she not trust such a man?

Annie was still fussing and refusing to nurse. Charity stroked her face, tickling and coaxing, but to no avail. She tried covering her lightly with the buffalo robe to muffle the sound, but the stuffy darkness over her face only frightened Annie and made her cry harder.

Black Sun had reached an outcrop of rocks. He crouched behind a boulder gripping his bow, one flint-tipped arrow nocked and ready to fly. He might kill one or two of the braves, but in the end there would be too many for him. Charity could only pray that, if they attacked, he might be lucky enough to die fighting.

If they survived this day, Charity vowed, she would make certain that Annie never forgot the man who had saved them.

Shadows deepened in the canyon as the clouds boiled above the ledges. The gloom only heightened the feeling of danger. In the hollow below, the young Blackfoot were still arguing. The braves had arrived only moments ago, but time had crawled at such an agonizing pace that, to Charity, it could have been hours.

She rocked Annie against her pounding heart. "Hush…" she whispered, sick with fear. "It's all right, Little One. Don't—"

Annie's howl split the leaden air, startling a dove from its perch above them. The bird shot upward in an explosion of fluttering wings.

In the hollow, the young braves had fallen silent. As Charity clutched the baby frantically to her breast, one of them pointed to the spot from which the bird had flown. With their bows, they moved up the hillside. Only the tall one who had argued for leaving the canyon hung back.

Hunkering close to the ground, Charity crawled beneath a chokecherry thicket. Branches scratched her face and arms as she moved deeper, one hand shielding Annie from harm. Her daughter had stopped crying, but the damage had been done. The braves were coming up the trail, straight toward their hiding place.

Through the tangle of budding foliage, Charity caught a glimpse of Black Sun in the rocks. The string of his bow was drawn back, the point of the arrow aimed at the warrior in the lead. As soon as that arrow found its mark, the Blackfoot would be after him, leaving her with no choice except to run. And run she would. Whatever the cost, she had to save her baby.

The braves were coming closer. Now, through the brush, Charity could see their faces. How young they were—no more than sixteen or seventeen, she estimated. But the blood of her husband and her companions was on their hands and, given the chance, they would not hesitate to kill again.

The darkened air was electric with danger.

Charity could feel the hair prickling on the back of her neck. Annie had begun to whimper. One of the warriors glanced up, alerted by the sound. Black Sun's arm tensed, pulling the bowstring back for release.

At that instant a huge lightning bolt struck a dead pine that jutted above the ledges. The accompanying boom shattered the air and shook the earth. Charity felt it all the way to her bones. She smelled it. She tasted the scorched air on her tongue.

As she cowered beneath the chokecherry bush with Annie clutched to her breast, only one thought, defying all reason, flashed through her brain.

The great Thunderbird's spirit has returned to the canyon.

Chapter Seven

The echo of the thunderclap ricocheted off the canyon walls, halting the young Blackfoot in their tracks. They stood frozen in shock as lightning forked across the sky a second time. The white-hot bolt struck somewhere above the cliffs, sending an electric ripple through the ground. Charity felt it pass through her body as she crouched under the chokecherry bush, clasping Annie in her arms and wondering if they were going to die.

She'd been intrigued by Black Sun's story of the great Thunderbird returning to the canyon every spring, but had dismissed it as a charming legend. In this terror-struck moment, however, she was prepared to believe everything she'd heard.

As a second deafening thunderclap rumbled down the canyon, the young Blackfoot wheeled and took to their heels. All their manly bravado evaporated as they fled the hollow like a troop of boys who'd just prodded a hornets' nest.

Charity lay still, protecting Annie with her body as the last rumble died away. The rain that followed was no more than a silken drizzle. The drops felt gentle on her skin, like the touch of a soothing hand.

Slowly she eased herself away from Annie and sat up. Across the slope, behind the rocks, Black Sun had lowered his bow. He was gazing up toward her, a stunned look on his face. He had been as frightened as she was, Charity realized, and he shared her amazement that they were alive and safe.

She struggled to stand, but he motioned for her to keep still. Sheet lightning danced through the clouds beyond the canyon as they waited to make sure the Blackfoot were really gone. Thunder rolled like a distant sigh above the canyon walls.

The rain had dissolved to a shimmering mist by the time Black Sun moved out from behind the rocks and made his way toward Charity's hiding place. Laying the cradleboard on a bed of soft leaves, Charity rose shakily to her feet. Through the mist, she could see him coming toward her, tall and broad-shouldered, powerful in face and form, just as the great Thunderbird would have been in the story when he took the shape of a man and came down to walk upon the earth. And the woman who waited for him here in the sacred canyon would have been beautiful—not burned and bruised and rain-soaked, her body stretched and sagging from childbirth and her hair hanging in colorless, dirty strings over her bloodshot eyes.

But it was only a story, Charity reminded herself. In her own reality, her appearance didn't matter. Black Sun was not the least interested in her as a woman. He had told her that much himself.

As for her feelings toward him, she was grateful, of course. But beyond that, he was merely her rescuer, the key to getting herself and her daughter back to the civilized world— the *safe* world, with solid walls, locked doors and warm beds, a world with proper meals served on tables set with plates, bowls, cups and utensils, a world where no dark-skinned savages lurked in the trees waiting to murder her and her loved ones.

That was the world she wanted for herself and for Annie—the world that Black Sun hated to the core of his being.

She waited in the thicket as he came up the hill, her mouth dry, her knees as treacherous as jelly beneath the buckskin fringe. His features were arranged in their customary scowl, but when Charity looked at him, she sensed—or perhaps only imagined—a faint luminosity radiating from his face, as if the lightning had passed through his body and left traces of its glow.

The illusion lasted no longer than the space of a heartbeat. Black Sun glanced down the hill toward the hollow, and when he looked back at her, the light was gone. Now he only looked tired and badly shaken. Charity gazed up at him, overcome by the thought of what this man had nearly sacrificed.

"If those Blackfoot had attacked, you would have died to save us," she said, fumbling for words. "I...don't know how to thank you."

Black Sun's scowl deepened. "Since they didn't attack, and since I didn't die, there's no need for your gratitude."

"Are you too proud to accept the thanks of a white woman?"

He scooped up the bundled gear. "Let's get

moving," he said. "Are you strong enough to carry your baby?"

"You didn't answer my question." Charity gathered up Annie's cradleboard and stood holding her. Black Sun shot her a withering look.

"Pride is a waste. I did what was required." He started up the trail, moving at a slow enough pace for her to follow, but not looking back at her. With a weary sigh, Charity trudged after him.

"Do you think the Blackfoot will come back?" She spoke to break the silence between them.

"Not if they were as frightened as I was."

His admission startled her. "It was only a thunderstorm," she insisted, taking refuge in reason now that the danger was past. "Wasn't it?"

He climbed in stubborn silence. Balancing the cradleboard on her hip, Charity watched silvery streams of rainwater trickle off his hair and down the curve of his sinewy back. Long moments passed before he spoke.

"With every step I take on this sacred ground, I ask forgiveness. I will continue to ask forgiveness until we are gone from here."

Charity's heart skipped. "Then it wasn't just

a story you told me, was it? The legend—you believe it's true!"

"True?" He sighed. "Not exactly true in the way I told you. But there's a guardian spirit here, a power that lives in the earth, the trees, the water and the air. I respect that power. So should you. Do you understand?"

"I...want to understand." Charity's breath came in ragged gasps as she toiled up the slope. "I'm trying to understand."

Pausing, he turned around, lifted the cradleboard from her arms and looped one of the carrying straps over his shoulder so that Annie dangled comfortably behind him, in full view of her mother.

"You and I have violated this place," he said. "It's only because of the spirit's forgiveness that we're allowed to stay. As soon as you're strong enough, we must go from here—and we must leave everything as we found it."

"And what about those Blackfoot? What if they ask forgiveness, too?"

He moved uphill, lost in thought for a few moments. "The fathers and grandfathers among the *Siksika* know enough to respect the spirit of the canyon. They know that to take a life, any life, in this place is a violation of its sacred power. But the young ones who came after us today are like foolish children who would stick their fingers into fire. We can only hope they've learned that this canyon is to be left alone."

"And if they haven't learned?"

Black Sun did not answer. Looking past him, up the slope, Charity could see a steep rock slide where a section of the canyon wall had caved in. Beyond the slide, a waterfall dropped in a glittering thread from a towering stone ledge.

"Is that where we're going?" She gazed up at the waterfall's dizzying height.

Black Sun nodded. "You'll be all right," he said. "It's not as steep as it looks. Come on, I'll help you."

Struggling upward, they reached the foot of the slide. In this part of the canyon, the rocks were a pale cream color, with darker streaks that sparkled in the emerging sunlight. Some of the rocks were as big as small houses and rested at odd angles as if balanced by some playful hand, but the gnarled trunks of the ancient pines that thrust upward between them attested to the fact that the slide had taken place long ago and was stable enough to cross.

"Mind your feet." Black Sun gripped Charity's hand as they moved upward, stepping from boulder to boulder. In her cradleboard, Annie was wide awake and clearly enjoying the bumpy ride. Charity, however, was exhausted. Her knees and ankles ached from twisting on the slippery rocks, and the rolled strip of petticoat she'd tied in place to stanch her bleeding had chafed her thighs raw.

There was no part of her that did not hurt. But she'd be hanged before she would utter a word of complaint, Charity vowed. She had seen the contempt in Black Sun's eyes when he'd spoken of her as a white woman. True, he had reason to feel as he did. But if he believed that all women of her race were weak, pitiful and whiny, he was sorely mistaken. Whatever it cost her in stifled groans and swallowed sighs, she would show the man how wrong he was.

By now they were nearing the waterfall. The splash of water on rocks was like the blend of a hundred musical notes underscored by the joyous *zeet-zeet* of a water ouzel. Spring-fed ferns and clumps of lush alum root hung from the face of the high, mossy ledge. Clouds of spray rose from the rocks at its foot, where the water coursed on down the canyon. The scene was breathtaking, Charity thought, forgetting her discomfort. The Garden of Eden could not have been lovelier than this.

The ledge itself, however, was another matter. Its vertical face was slick with moss and water, its mist-shrouded top so high that it seemed to vanish into the clouds. The thought of climbing all the way up, especially in her condition, was enough to rattle her heart and turn her knees to quivering stems that threatened to collapse beneath her.

"Do you need to rest?" Black Sun glanced back over his shoulder. Charity shook her head, ignoring her fear. "What's up there?" she asked.

"Safety." He stepped behind some spruces and onto a path that was no wider than one of her feet. It was more like a rabbit trail than a deer trail, she thought, her eyes following the route where it wound upward between the rock slide and the cliff. It was easy to understand, now, why Black Sun had turned the horses loose. There would have been no way to take a horse across the field of rocks or up the slippery, winding trail.

"You go first," he said, moving behind her. "That way I'll catch you if you slip."

"I won't slip," she said, forcing her feet, in their worn, rain-soaked boots, to take the first step. "Just mind yourself. You're the one who's carrying the baby." She glanced back at her child, who had slipped into a doze, her small head lolling against the side of the cradleboard. Why was it that Annie always seemed so comfortable with Black Sun? Was it because the little girl felt safer with him than with her own nervous, fearful mother? Never mind, Charity admonished herself. For now, she could only be grateful that her baby was safe and content with a man who had proven that he would die to keep them from harm.

"Oh—" Her foot slipped on a patch of wet moss. Black Sun's hands caught her waist, their grip solid and sure. A surge of heat flashed through Charity's body and she found herself wishing that, by some magic spell, she could be as beautiful as the woman in the legend— the woman who had kept the great Thunderbird here in the canyon and taught him everything he'd needed to know about men and women.

"Take your time." Black Sun's hands released her. "You don't need to show me how strong you are, Charity Bennett. I've seen enough of your courage to know what you're made of."

His words flooded her with warmth. But they were only words, she reminded herself. A man's fine words, telling her what she wanted to hear. "How can you say that?" she demanded. "I've been nothing but a burden from the moment you found me."

There was a long silence behind her, broken only by the squawk of a magpie in the tangled crown of a dead pine. "That may be true," Black Sun said at last. "But our burdens can bless us by becoming our teachers."

"Oh? And how could I bless you, Black Sun? What could you possibly learn from someone like me?"

"Patience."

His reply was so swift and terse that it triggered an unexpected welling of laughter. Charity felt that amusement bubble up inside her to emerge as a burst of emotion—a release so compelling that it poured out of her like a river breaking through a dam.

Her grandparents had raised her to believe that laughter was frivolous, and therefore evil. Silas, if anything, had been even more rigid in his views about laughter, music and the pleasures of the flesh. Now, suddenly, it struck her that she was free of them all. Silas was gone and her grandparents were far beyond reach. She was trudging through this vast wilderness under conditions that would make any proper lady reach for her smelling salts. She had traded her clothes for a buckskin shirt and entrusted her baby to a half-naked savage who had seen every intimate part of her. And she was giving him lessons in patience!

Her situation was ludicrous—and Charity laughed. She laughed until the tears ran down her face and she had to grip a sapling to keep from falling off the trail.

Suddenly it was as if her frayed nerves had snapped. What had begun as laughter became something dark and deep. Charity found herself convulsed by sobs as the fear and grief she'd held back found its release. Images of Silas, Rueben and the others, dying in a hail of arrows, swept over her. Her body jerked with emotion. Her breath came in tiny hiccups of anguish. Her body bent almost double, as if she'd just been kicked in the stomach.

Black Sun's hands closed on her shoulders, turning her toward him on the narrow trail. Charity's resistance was no more than a flicker as she sank against his chest and felt his arms close around her.

"I'm...sorry," she whispered between sobs. "I don't mean to be so much trouble. I've given you enough lessons in...patience."

His throat moved against her hair. "Let your

tears fall, Charity. You've lost your husband. Your spirit will never heal unless you mourn."

His tenderness only frustrated her. Was that what she was doing, mourning Silas? Silas, who'd treated her as a mindless possession with no more will of her own than a sheep or cow? Silas, who'd been as miserly with smiles and kind words as he was generous with blows and rebukes? Surely something in her must have loved him. But that meek, submissive part of her was gone. If she mourned Silas now, it was only for the useless, violent way in which he had died.

And what was she doing in another man's arms, savoring the feel of his strong, masculine body while the ravens picked the charred flesh from her husband's bones? Oh, she was wicked to have the thoughts that were stealing into her mind. Wicked, when she should be in mourning, to feel stirrings of carnal desire whenever Black Sun came near her. Not only wicked, but foolish. If he was holding her now, it was only out of pity. He was a good man, this savage who had saved her. He would be shocked and repelled to know what she was feeling in his arms.

Steeling her will, Charity pushed herself away from the smoke-scented hardness of his body. "I'm all right now," she said huskily. "I can go on."

He nodded, his mouth set in a thin line. Charity strode up the trail, willing herself not to slip. If she slipped, he might reach out and steady her. She would feel the clasp of his hands and the surrounding strength of his arms, and she would be torn in a way she had no right to be torn.

"Tell me about your son," she said, needing the distraction of talk. "You told me he was six years old. What's his name?"

"We call him Two Feathers." Black Sun's voice warmed slightly. "But that's only a baby name. When he's older, he'll be given another name, one he will earn or choose for himself."

"Oh? And did you have a baby name?" Charity tried to imagine Black Sun as a child. She pictured a serious, solemn little boy with a burning curiosity about everything around him.

"My people always called me Black Sun because of my birth," he said. "My white stepfather called me Johnny, but I threw that name away when my mother died and I left him." He fell silent as if passing through a shadow. When he spoke again, however, there was no bitterness in his voice. "If I live to be old, I may give my name to my son or another young man. Then he will be Black Sun and I will choose a new name for myself."

"You can't keep your own name if you give it to someone else? What a confusing custom!" Charity exclaimed.

"Is it any more confusing than your custom of giving a boy the same name as his father, while the father still lives, so that both their names are the same? Among my people, a name can only belong to one person. It is something to be earned or chosen or given as a gift. One who receives another's name vows to keep that name sacred and to never bring shame or dishonor upon it. Your people could learn from our customs, Charity Bennett."

His hand steadied her elbow as they crept upward along the edge of the waterfall. Charity was grateful for his conversation, which distracted her from looking down into the depths of the canyon. She had always been terrified of heights, and she knew that even a downward glance would trigger an image of losing her balance and plummeting onto the teeth of the sharp-edged rocks below.

The watery mist was all around them now, turning the cliffside into a hanging garden of ferns, mosses and the tiny, bunched white flowers. The trail was as slippery as ice, each step a new adventure in terror. Far above her, the top of the waterfall was lost in mist. For all she knew, it could be a mile above her head. Only trust kept her moving upward—the faith that the man behind her would steady her if she slipped, and that no matter what else happened, he would keep Annie safe.

"Your husband was a missionary. Isn't that what you told me?"

Black Sun's abrupt question startled her. "Yes," Charity answered, her mouth consciously forming the word. "We were going to build a mission in the Flathead country. It… was his dream. It was my dream, too. At least, I thought it was when I married him."

"Missionaries!" He spat out the word. "Isn't it bad enough for the whites to steal our land? Do they have to steal our spirits, as well?"

"Not steal them. Save them."

Surely she was right, Charity thought. Surely Silas had been right, and her grandparents, and all the good people who had donated money for their journey. The Indians of the West were lost souls, their spirits crying out for the light. It was the duty of Christian missionaries to bring them that light. Surely it was.

But why, then, at the missions where they'd

stopped on their way West, had the converted Indians appeared so wretched, begging for food and wearing ragged, cast-off white people's clothes? Why did the so-called heathen savages, like the man walking behind her, bear themselves with the splendid pride of free people?

"We did not ask for your religion or your rules." Black Sun spoke as if he had read her thoughts. "Our gods are wise and good as long as we honor them, and we treat our brothers with kindness and respect. As for our enemies, we do not love them as your missionaries say we must. That would be foolish. But if an enemy is brave in death, we treat his body with honor. What else do we need? Why should we care about people in a book who lived on the other side of the world?"

Charity winced and almost stumbled as her toe stubbed against a sharp stone. Between the height of the cliff and her own fatigue, she was beginning to feel light-headed. She imagined closing her eyes and floating off the trail into space, drifting downward like a fallen petal... how sweet it would feel.

"You have the freedom to believe whatever you wish," she said, wrenching herself back to reality. "So do I."

Black Sun chuckled under his breath. "Well," he said, "at least we agree about something."

"Thank goodness for that." The clouds were thickening again, casting a pall of darkness over the canyon. Charity dragged herself upward, driven by the fear that another swift storm would catch them on the trail and wash them off the cliff. Every move dredged the well of her strength. She moved on leaden feet, clutching at rocks and tree trunks for support. The sound of the falls swirled in her ears, white sound, like the sigh of gentle ocean waves. The waves flowed around her, lapping at her senses, cool and alluring. She swayed, drifting with the pull of the tide.

The last thing she remembered was the sensation of powerful arms lifting her above the waves, then the distant echo of thunder and the wetness of rain on her face.

Black Sun caught her as she fell, lifting her scant weight in his arms. Charity had climbed the dizzying trail with a warrior's courage, but now she had nothing left. She would need days of good food and rest before she was strong enough to travel back to her people.

Her head lolled against his chest, pale hair plastered wetly to her skin. She reminded him of the lynx kitten he had once rescued from a flood, tired and wet and battered, but still full of fight. He had returned the kitten to its hillside den, just as he knew he must return this small, golden kitten of a woman to her rightful home. She and her baby needed him now. They needed his strength and care. But they were not his family. They could not be part of his world, and he could never be part of theirs. Letting them creep into his heart would be the most foolhardy thing he could do.

Charity had collapsed near the top of the trail. Even so, carrying her the rest of the way, with the cradleboard slung from his shoulder and the bundle of provisions tucked under his arm, was not easy. Black Sun was breathing hard by the time he reached the glade with its rain-dimpled pool and sheltering rocks.

Lulled by the motion of the climb, the baby had fallen asleep in her cradleboard. She stirred and opened her sky-blue eyes, then settled into slumber once more as Black Sun let the carrying strap slide down his arm, lowering her to the ground.

Charity's lips were tinged with blue and her teeth were chattering. Black Sun carried her to the sandy hollow beneath the overhang of the rock. Supporting her with one arm, he spread the largest buffalo robe over the sand and shifted her onto it.

Her eyelids fluttered open as she came to rest. "Where are we?" she whispered, gazing up at him with worried eyes. "Where's my baby?"

"We're safe, and your baby's here. See?" Cupping the back of her head with his hand, he raised her so that she could see where he'd left the cradleboard. The tiny girl was awake now and beginning to fuss.

"Bring her to me." Her voice was edged with a mother's urgency. "I want—I *need* to hold her!"

Black Sun picked up the cradleboard and laid it beside her. Charity rolled onto her side beneath the buffalo robe. Her numb fingers plucked awkwardly at the lacings in an effort to free her child from the rigid willow frame.

"I'll do it." Taking pity on her, Black Sun untied the knots, folded back the leather wrappings and lifted out the squirming baby. At once Charity's daughter began to squall, kicking like a frog with her spindly little legs.

"Is it safe for her to cry?" Charity glanced up at him with wary eyes.

"No one will hear her in this place," Black

Sun said. "But still, she must learn to be quiet before we leave."

Charity fumbled with the front of the buckskin shirt. Instinctively, Black Sun averted his eyes. Among his people, mothers nursed their babies in the open without a second thought. But Charity was a white woman, and although there was no part of her moon-pale body he had not seen, he reminded himself that to look at her would not be proper.

While the baby sucked noisily, Black Sun busied himself with organizing the supplies he'd carried up the cliff. These included a large buffalo robe and a smaller one, along with some pieces of leather, several lengths of sinew and three amulet-size leather bags he'd brought along for collecting medicinal herbs. There were the bridles, hobbles and tethers for the horses and the long, coiled throwing rope he had braided from rawhide. There was also a spare knife, smaller than the one he carried, and the parfleche, which contained only a few scraps of dried meat—far too few, he realized.

Charity's stained, ragged dress and underclothes might be useful for wrappings once they were washed. He lifted the dress, surprised by its weight until he realized that the toy-size gun was still in the pocket. Removing the tiny weapon, he laid it in the palm of his hand. Without bullets, it was little more than a trinket. But it might do for trade later on. For that alone, it would be worth keeping.

Black Sun sighed as he surveyed their pitiful resources. What he had was adequate for his own survival. But keeping Charity and her baby alive would require much more. In the days ahead he would have to provide for all their needs: food, clothing, shelter and protection. Once they were strong enough to travel, they would need horses. And he would have to find a way through territory that was crawling with braves who'd look on a young white woman as a prized trophy.

His gaze flickered upward to the darkening clouds. He had fasted for four days and begged Heisonoonin to grant him a vision. What if *this* was his vision—the woman, the baby and the mysteries of the sacred canyon? What if the Great Spirit had something to teach him, some lesson he could learn only through experience? And what if Charity Bennett was to be the instrument of that lesson—this scrawny, argumentative creature who surprised him when he least expected it by tugging at his heart?

Had it been by chance that she'd survived

the attack on the wagon train, when the other whites had died?

Had it been by chance that she'd been discovered by the only person within many days' ride who could speak her language?

Had it been his destiny to find her—or had it been *her* destiny to be found by him?

Behind him, the sounds of blissful sucking had ceased. Black Sun turned his head for a tentative glance. He saw that Charity had fallen asleep with her tiny daughter in the crook of her arm. Her swollen breast, as smooth and pale as a wild rose petal, lay within reach of the baby's mouth. The nipple, elongated by sucking, was the deep mauve color of a ripening blackberry.

Again Black Sun felt the tug at his heart— that rush of emotion he'd battled from the moment he'd found her. He fought it still, knowing that to give in to his feelings would open the door to tragedy.

Crouching beside her, he folded the sides of the buffalo robe around her chilled and weary body. Unbidden, his fingertip brushed a lock of hair off her forehead. Her golden eyelashes twitched but did not open. She slept like an exhausted child, her expression shifting with the current of dreams that flowed through her mind—dreams that carried her to places he could never go.

Nestled against her breast, the baby stirred in her sleep, blowing milky little bubbles as she breathed. Black Sun found himself aching to lie down beside them, to gather them into his arms and drift with them in the sweet, warm world of their slumber. But that thought was no more than a fantasy. Wisdom required that he keep a proper distance between himself and this woman of the *Nih'oo'oo*—this woman he could never possess.

Wrapping himself in the remaining buffalo robe, he settled at the entrance to their rocky shelter, with his back against the sloping wall of the cliff. It was not a comfortable bed, but he had not rested for the past two days and his mind was as tired as his body. As rain clouds swept over the canyon, Black Sun closed his eyes and slept.

Chapter Eight

He was soaring above the mountaintops, his vast wings trailing black storm clouds across the sky. Each beat of those wings lanced the heavens with arrows of lightning and sent thunderclaps crashing off the peaks. But no life-giving rains fell in their wake. The plains and forests, the mountains and canyons, were parched and barren.

His eyes, sharper than an eagle's, saw the misery of the people and animals far below. He saw the buffalo pawing the earth for water in the dry beds where lakes and streams had been. He saw the people in their camps, the children crying with hunger, the women digging in the dust for withered roots, the men riding far in search of water and returning with despair etched across their faces.

Everywhere on the earth there was want and sadness. And yet the heart of the great Thunderbird felt nothing. He had many gifts and powers, but compassion was not among them. And only through compassion could he bless the earth with rain.

"What can I do to feel pity for the people and animals, that I may give them what they need?" he asked Heisonoonin, the giver of all life.

The answer came as a whisper inside his own ear. "To learn pity for the beings on earth, you must become one of them. You must live on the earth for a time and feel what they feel. Only then will your heart overflow with enough compassion to bring the rain."

The Thunderbird spread his wings and flew over the mountains until he found a high-walled canyon with a waterfall like a silver thread. The canyon opened onto a plain where there were people living in a village. *If I come to earth here, I can watch the people from the canyon,* he thought. *Then, when I am ready, I can come out and join them.*

He flew down into the canyon. As soon as

his feet touched the earth, he became a man, with a man's body. How strange it was to feel the ground beneath his bare feet. The rocks and thorns were sharp and pricked him with every step. He tried to fly away, but his wings were gone, and so were his feathers. He felt the wind on his bare skin. When he looked down, he saw the parts of a man's body, wonderfully shaped like some rare flower, between his legs. He touched them and was startled by the sweet, shimmering ache that arose from the merest brush of his fingers. His sharp eyes had seen naked humans from the sky, so he knew how their bodies looked. But this sensitivity to touch was a surprise, like no pleasure he had ever known.

A faint rustle reached his ears on the wind and he realized that someone was coming up the canyon. He was wondering if he should cover his nakedness, as humans often did in each other's presence, when he glanced down and saw a pair of moccasins and a length of buckskin lying at his feet. Hastily he put them on, working his feet into the moccasins and draping the buckskin around his loins. Then, because he was not ready to show himself, he moved back into the trees.

As he watched from his hiding place, the

bushes parted and a woman stepped into sight. He could see at once that she was not one of the women from the village, for her skin was as pale as moonlight and her hair was the white-gold color of winter grass. When she turned toward him, he saw that her eyes were the soft silver color of water on a cloudy day.

She was dressed much as he was, in moccasins and a short leather skirt. From the waist up she was bare except for a simple string of blue beads around her neck. The swollen globes of her breasts were as delicately colored as the inner surface of a shell, the nipples deep pink, like swollen buds.

Watching her, he felt an unaccustomed heat beneath the buckskin that wrapped his hips—a yearning so deep, so human, that it shook him to the center of his being. In his Thunderbird form, he had paid little attention to the differences between the bodies of men and women. Only now, as a man, did he understand what those differences meant; and he discovered that he wanted her in a way that caused his body to burn and swell with desire.

Heisonoonin had sent him to the earth to learn pity for humans. But it was not pity that he felt, only the deepest hunger he had ever known.

Driven by instinct, he stepped into the open and held out his hand. Her silvery eyes widened for an instant, inspecting him from head to toe. Then, with a shy smile, she slipped her hand into his and they walked, side by side, into the depths of the canyon.

He had never seen her before, but he knew she was no ordinary woman. She had come to be his teacher, to lead him to experiences he could only know as a man. The simple pressure of her fingertips rippled through his body like waves of liquid fire. Beneath the light buckskin wrap, his male parts were hard, swollen and so sensitive that the slightest movement caused him to bite back a groan.

From the distance of the sky, he had seen men and women engaged in a strangely sensual wrestling match, always with the man thrusting his hips between the woman's legs. Only now did he begin to have some sense of what it meant. The very thought of doing it made his blood run hot.

As they moved up through the canyon and wound their way to the rocky glade above the waterfall, he stole furtive glances at his companion. He ached for her touch against his skin, yearned to know the deep, sweet secrets of her woman's body and to perform that exquisitely savage dance of men and women.

She led him upward, to a sheltered cave in the ledges above the pool. This appeared to be her home, for she had covered the floor with thick buffalo robes and hung bundles of fragrant herbs from the ceiling to dry. A savory stew of meat and wild onion simmered over a bed of coals. As the Great Thunderbird, he had not required food, but now that he was a man, the aroma of the stew triggered a compelling growl in the pit of his stomach.

His greater hunger, however, was for the woman. The firelight shimmered on her skin. He fought the wild desire to seize her in his arms and fling her down on the buffalo robes. She was his teacher, he reminded himself. It was seemly that he show respect and wait for her to make the next move.

Something stirred in the shadows and he heard a small, mewling cry. He watched as she walked to a sheltered corner of the cave and lifted a squirming bundle out of a reed basket. Astonished, he saw that it was a baby, as pale and golden and beautiful as the woman herself.

Cradling the baby in her arms, she lowered herself to a cross-legged position on the buffalo robe. The nipple of one swollen breast hung above the baby's mouth. Rooting hungrily, the little creature found it and began to suck. The woman looked up at him, a peaceful smile on her lips.

Outside, darkness had fallen over the canyon. Instinctively he moved to the entrance of the cave to guard the woman and child against the dangers of the night. As he stood looking down on the two of them—the woman's golden head, the baby's tiny, rosebud mouth pulling at her life-giving breast, the sweetness that swept over him was unlike anything he had ever experienced. He felt the warm glow of the fire and smelled the mouthwatering aromas of meat and onions. He heard the soft hiss of the burning coals and the low, velvety voice of the woman as she sang a lullaby to her child. Her eyes gazed up at him, shining with the promise of what was to come.

A sense of absolute contentment flowed through his body, as if all he had ever wanted in his life was contained in the warmth of this cozy space, the presence of this woman and her infant, the peace of this small sanctuary in the night. To preserve this place and these precious people, he realized, he would do anything—work and hunt, fight, raid, kill, shed his own blood, even lay down his life.

It was the most powerful feeling he had ever known.

Satisfaction simmered in his soul as he looked around him. Take pity on humans? How could he? What could arouse his pity, when human bodies and spirits held such a capacity for joy?

The baby had fallen asleep at its mother's breast. Carefully she rose to her feet, carried the infant to the far side of the cave and eased it back into the reed basket. Then, turning, she glided toward him and held out her arms.

Without a word, he reached out and gathered her close. Her curves fit against his body as if one had been used as a mold for the other. He was utterly innocent, yet he knew instinctively that he was to touch her. How could he not touch her, when every sweet, warm, willing part of her invited his hands? He felt the swelling rush of heat in his loins as he cradled her breast in his palm, his thumb stroking the taut bud of her nipple. She sighed, arching her body against him. The pressure of her hips against his swollen manhood triggered a low moan that, this time, he could not hold back. He wanted more. He wanted that sensual, serpentine dance of male and female, with his body thrusting hard between her legs.

His hands slid beneath her deerskin skirt to find the small, plump moons of her buttocks. Instinctively he cupped them, pulling her against him until the pressure threatened to shatter his control. He could feel the jerky, pounding rhythm of her heart, hear the rasp of her breathing as she pushed against him. Her frenzied fingers caught at the buckskin wrap that circled his hips, pulling it loose. It fell away, leaving him naked against her. He gasped with the pleasure of it, understanding more and more.

Without needing to be told, he lowered her to the buffalo robe. She lay back, her hair spreading in golden waves. The eyes that gazed up at him were suddenly filled with tears.

Tears? Was this what the woman had been sent to show him?

He would have questioned her, but the need that drove him was too urgent, too strong. Parting her thighs, he found the place that, somehow, he had known would be there. With a cry of purest joy, he thrust himself into her, deeper, deeper, burying his shaft to the hilt. Dizzy with the wonder of it, he paused for an instant, savoring the warmth of her, the tight, welcoming, wet embrace.

And then, in a sudden flash, he knew.

He would lose all of this—the woman, the baby, the glowing sanctuary of their little home. However and whenever it was to happen, he would lose them all, just as humans did. Children lost parents; parents lost children. Husbands and wives lost each other. Friends lost friends, and lovers lost lovers. To feel such sweetness, such love, and then to experience the killing pain of loss—that was what it meant to be human.

The Thunderbird felt his heart burst inside him. As he thrust his manhood into her beautiful body, driven by love and anguish, his compassion opened the sky and the blessed rain began to fall....

Black Sun's limbs jerked as he tumbled out of the dream. Stunned by the memory of it, he lay back against the rock, listening to the rain drizzle over the lip of the sheltering cave.

Everything about the dream had seemed absolutely real—the sensation of flying on wings as broad as the sky, the sharpness of the ground beneath his feet, and the woman in his arms—her face had been Charity's face, and her ripe, sensual body had been Charity's body. Stirring now, he felt the slickness between his thighs. The dream had been all too real. But what did it mean? Had it been the vision he'd sought, or only the wanderings of a weary mind?

Still dazed, he sat up and rubbed his eyes. How long had he slept? Long enough for the sun to have set and twilight to have closed in. Beside him, Charity slumbered with her infant in the peace of complete exhaustion. He could hear her soft breathing in the darkness, its sweet cadence blending with the chirp of crickets and the faint, echoing cry of a wolf. The air was chilly, but he dared not make a fire. The night was filled with eyes and even a small blaze might be seen from a great distance.

Pushing away from the rock, he peered out through the rainy darkness. The canyon was shrouded in deep twilight, veiled by the mist that rose from the waterfall. A waning moon had risen to drift among the thinning clouds.

One silvery ray fell across Charity's face, casting her features into startling beauty. Black Sun gazed down at her, fighting the impulse to stroke her cheek with the tip of his finger. Burned, bloodied, filthy and exhausted, she was still the woman in his dream. But he was not the great Thunderbird. He was only a man, all too weak and all too human.

Loving her would be as natural as breathing. He knew that now. But the price of that love—the pain of losing her—was more than he was willing to pay. He knew that pain well. It had devastated him when he'd lost his mother. It had ripped him apart like a wild beast when his wife had died in childbirth. To feel the raging agony that would come when Charity turned her back on him and walked away to join her people—no, he had been through enough. To suffer that kind of loss again would be more than his heart could stand.

Rising to his feet, he stared out at the dwindling rain. He was wasting time, brooding about desire and loss, when there were more urgent concerns at hand. First thing tomorrow he would need to find food for this brief family of his. Killing was forbidden in the sacred canyon. To find game, he would have to leave and go into the hills or out onto the flatland, moving on foot. He would need to scout carefully for the young *Siksika,* to make sure they were no longer a danger to Charity and her child. He would also want to watch for his horses. Given the chance, the two ponies might escape their captors and wander back to where he had left them at the mouth of the canyon. If he found them, he could move them to a safe place and keep them there until he needed them.

For now there was nothing to do but watch, listen, rest and think. It would be three or four days, perhaps, before Charity was strong enough to travel. Until they cleared the territory of the *Siksika,* it would be wise to travel by night and hide during the day. Even then, danger would be their constant companion. Black Sun did not fear for himself, but imagining the things that could happen to Charity and her child made his heart shrink in his chest.

Being killed or captured by the *Siksika* would be their greatest peril. But they would also be dealing with wild animals, rough terrain, sudden storms, the chance of sickness. And the white men they encountered could be even more dangerous than the *Siksika*—bandits and renegades, capable of the most depraved acts.

Thinking of what lay ahead, Black Sun let his gaze linger on Charity's sleeping face. Her lips were full and pink and innocent, like a little girl's, but her eyes were shadowed with grief and exhaustion. Had she been dreaming of her husband while he'd been dreaming of her? Had she loved the dead missionary? Had she enjoyed the act that had conceived their child?

Questions like these were useless, Black Sun reminded himself. But he could not tear his eyes away from her where she lay in the moonlight, her baby nestled against the hollow of her shoulder. She had drifted off to sleep nursing her child. One creamy, swollen breast lay exposed, not quite touching the baby's mouth. The areola was a deep rose, darkening to russet brown at the nipple. Black Sun could see the faint blue tracery of veins that lay beneath her translucent skin. He ached to touch her, but he knew that if he allowed himself even the brush of a finger, he would be lost. The touch would become a caress. The caress would awaken her, and then he would see the fear in her eyes.

With a ragged sigh, Black Sun turned away from her, ducked under the lip of the low cave and walked out into the darkness. The rain had faded to a feathery drizzle that dimpled the pool above the waterfall, shattering the reflection of the moon. Crouching beside the pool, he dipped water in his hands and splashed it on his face, welcoming the cold shock of it.

He was alone—that was the one constant reality of his life. Fate had thrust him between two worlds, and he belonged to neither of them.

He yearned to be one with his people, but he had been raised by a white man. He had missed the vital connection of age groups, societies and rituals that guided young Arapaho boys to manhood. He could never get them back.

That was the reason he'd asked his wife's sister to raise his son with her family. He had wanted Two Feathers to grow up Arapaho in every respect. Now it was as if the boy was no longer his. But Black Sun's sacrifice had secured Two Feathers's place with his people. The child would never know the emptiness, the disconnection from his tribe that had haunted his father's life.

As for the *Nih'oo'oo,* Black Sun had learned to detest everything about them. The greed, selfishness and crude behavior of the whites he'd known had filled his heart with loathing.

Then, by pure chance, he had stumbled across Charity Bennett. Terrified, in pain and fighting for life, she had touched him in a way he had no wish to be touched. All he had ever wanted was to be Arapaho, his heart unsullied by the stain of the white world. Let Charity pull him back toward that world and he would lose everything he cherished. He could not, would not, let that happen.

So what had the dream of the Thunderbird

meant? *Nothing,* Black Sun told himself. Nothing but the stirring wants of a man who had been too long without a woman. His desire for Charity was natural. But desire could be controlled. He would keep his distance from her and deliver her safely back to her people. Once that was done, he would weigh the choice of giving up his useless quest and returning to his tribe to marry again and start a new family. If he could not serve the Arapaho as a medicine man, at least he might salvage a few years of happiness for himself.

His hand came to rest on the polished bone handle of the knife he had carried since the night of his mother's death. The weapon had become a symbol of his loathing for the white man. He had only to touch it or feel its weight at his hip to be reminded of the reasons for that hatred. But he had felt no such emotion when he'd used the blade to sever the baby's birth cord—or later, when he'd cut willows to weave the cradleboard.

Was the knife losing its power to keep his rage alive? Black Sun stared into the darkness of the canyon, his heart churning. Tomorrow he would be all right. He would be able to think and move, to lose himself in action. But this night would be long and sleepless, with

Charity and her baby lying in the shelter of the rock, warm, sweet and far beyond his reach.

Charity awoke to the piping call of a chickadee. Perched on a gnarled pine trunk that overhung the pool, the black-capped bird seemed to be curious. It flitted from branch to branch, cocking its head and scolding in a voice that seemed far too loud for its tiny body.

Annie stirred against her side, rooting for her breakfast. With a drowsy sigh, Charity shifted the baby in her arms and felt the strong little mouth close around her nipple. As the first rays of morning sunlight glimmered above the canyon, she felt a surge of strength and contentment. She was going to be all right. Annie was going to be all right. Black Sun would see them safely home.

Black Sun! Her heart lurched. Where was he?

Clutching the baby to her breast, she struggled to a sitting position. The clenched feeling in her chest eased as she saw him crouched on the other side of the pool, grinding something between two flat rocks.

He glanced up at her, then averted his eyes. Seeing that her breast was uncovered, Charity used her free hand to pull a corner of the buffalo robe over her bare shoulder and the nursing baby. Yesterday the danger had made modesty unimportant. Today was different— and so was the danger.

"What are you doing?" Even when she spoke softly, her voice seemed to echo off the cliffs. Startled, the chickadee took flight.

"I'm making a new poultice for your burns," he said without looking up. "Leave it on until tomorrow. It will help your back heal without scars."

Charity huddled deeper into the buffalo robe, aware of her matted hair, her smudged face and bloodstained legs. "I was really hoping to bathe," she said with a wistful glance toward the water. "Can't your poultice wait until after I've had time to get clean?"

"Not unless you can put the mixture on your back by yourself," he answered gruffly. "We need meat. Hunting is forbidden in this canyon, so I'll have to leave you here for a day or two, maybe longer."

Charity felt her heart drop. Only now did she realize how dependent on Black Sun she had become. Without him, she and Annie would be alone and helpless.

"You should be safe here," he said, reading her thoughts. "You'll have plenty of water, and I'll leave you the parfleche with the rest of the dried meat. If you run out or get hungry for something different, the bulbs of that lily plant by the cliff make good eating. You won't starve." He scraped the pounded, leafy mass off the rock, working it in his hands as he rose and walked toward her.

"Turn around and let me see your back," he said, crouching beside her. "You can bathe tomorrow. I need to treat your burns now, so I can be on my way before the sun fully rises."

Annie had finished nursing and drifted back into slumber. Charity laid her child in the cradleboard, then turned her back toward Black Sun and peeled the buckskin shirt down off her shoulders, baring her body almost to the waist. As he bent closer to examine her burns, her arms crossed self-consciously over her breasts.

"The blisters are looking better," he muttered. "Do you have much pain?"

"Only a little soreness." Her pulse rocketed as his fingers touched her skin. Her breathing seemed to take conscious effort. "My…grandmother always put mutton fat on burns."

"Fat is bad. It keeps the heat inside the burn." He pressed the cooling mixture onto her blistered shoulder blade, sending a little shiver down her spine. The aroma of his body crept into her senses. He smelled of rain and damp wood and warm, pungent maleness.

"I like your remedy better." Charity focused on the words with effort. "What is it?"

"Yarrow. Mixed with a little mud to make it stick." His voice was husky, as if he needed to clear his throat. His breath was warm on the back of her neck. She imagined him leaning closer, brushing her skin with his lips, kissing her hurts better, as her father might have done when she was a little girl. But there would be nothing fatherly about the feel of Black Sun's kiss, she sensed. Not when his slightest touch sent flickers of heat rippling through her body.

Back in Indiana, Charity had overheard a remark from a married neighbor, to the effect that nursing an infant often awakened a woman's yearning for a man. Merciful heaven, could that be what was happening to her? Could the tug of that little mouth on her breast trigger sensations that transformed her into a wanton when Black Sun was near? The very thought of it was enough to make her blush with shame. But she could not deny that her heart raced when she felt the warmth of his breath on her bare back. And the deep, secret parts of her body, still unhealed from the birth, tightened and throbbed whenever he touched her.

"Raise your arm a little." His voice was thick, as if he had just awakened from sleep. One burn, Charity knew, extended in a thin line along her rib cage to end at the edge of her left breast. With her upper arm pressed against her side, he would not be able to treat the burn. She hesitated, her heart pounding. To refuse his request would be to admit that his touch disturbed her, offending his fierce pride. It would only serve to heighten the tension between them.

"Charity, if you don't want—"

"No, go ahead." She raised her elbow outward, away from her body, leaving her hands crossed over her bare breasts. Black Sun would be exquisitely careful, she told herself. He would not allow the slightest impropriety to pass between them.

She held her breath as his gentle fingertips glided forward around her rib cage. The yarrow was cool and soothing, his touch like the brush of a feathered wing, as if his fingers were trembling. The shimmer of heat that stole through her body was as sweet and heady as forbidden wine.

Heaven help her, she did not want him to stop.

Chapter Nine

Black Sun could feel the slight ridge of her blistered flesh beneath his fingertips. The flame had etched a path through the worn fabric of Charity's dress, burning forward around her side before being crushed out as she'd dropped from the wagon and fallen against the earth. The burn was not serious, but it was in a tender spot. Until it healed, it would give her pain every time it came in contact with her arm. The poultice would speed that healing.

She trembled at his slightest touch. He could feel the ragged galloping of her pulse through the bones of her rib cage. Was she afraid of him? Repulsed? It didn't matter, Black Sun

reminded himself. Soon he would be finished
with treating her burns. Then he would take his
bow and arrows and leave her here in peace.

Black Sun spread the poultice along the
fire's trail, which ended where the soft, creamy
swell of her breast began. Acutely aware of that
breast, he pressed the herbal mix onto her skin
to make it stay. He could feel the warmth of her
flesh through the cool poultice. He could feel
himself rising rock-hard through his leather
loincloth. Mortified, he bit back a curse. It was
bad enough, the inappropriate thoughts he'd
been having about this white woman. Now his
own body was betraying him.

Was it that same betrayal that caused his
hand to move too far? Black Sun would never
know. He only knew that when his fingers
brushed the soft, swelling boundary of her
breast, liquid fire rippled up his arm and down
into his loins, and he could no more stop touching her than he could stop his heart from beating.

She moaned, her chest arching upward, her
body turning to press her nipple against his
palm. Something shattered inside Black Sun
as he wrapped his fingers around her, cradling
the wondrously soft, milk-swollen weight in
his hand. She whimpered with need and slid

her own hand over his to hold it in place. Her skin was baby-soft, warm with desire. His thumb stroked her nipple. She gasped softly as it puckered and hardened beneath his touch.

Lowering his head, he brushed his lips along her bare shoulder. She tasted the way she smelled, salty woman-sweet. Again she moaned, letting the damp tangle of her hair fall back against his shoulder. Her breath came in tiny, raw gasps. Dizzy with wanting her, he kissed her throat, her ear. Beneath the leather that girded his hips, his arousal throbbed, aching for release.

What are you doing? the voice of wisdom screamed in the back of his mind. This woman had just given birth. She was in no condition to be taken by any man, especially a man of his people, one who had sworn to keep his distance from everything white. Touching her like this was pure craziness. He had to stop now, before desire ravaged them both.

"I have to go." He tore himself away from her and stumbled to his feet.

"Black Sun—" She gazed up at him, her arms wrapping her breasts, her silvery eyes swimming with tears. "I'm sorry. I didn't mean—"

"No." He backed away from her, sick with

need. "We need to forget this ever happened. We can't speak of it again!"

Snatching up his bow and quiver, he strode toward the trail that led down the cliffside. At the spot where the narrow path dropped below the ledge, he glanced back over his shoulder. Charity was huddled beneath the shelter of the overhanging rock, clutching the buffalo robe in front of her. Her stricken look all but shattered him.

"Stay here," he said, forcing out each gruff word. "Whatever you do, don't try to leave. I'll be back as soon as I can find food for us."

Her lips moved, but she did not reply. Tearing his eyes from her soot-streaked face, Black Sun turned away and started down the trail.

Shaken to the core, Charity stared at the spot where he'd dropped below the rim. The poultice Black Sun had applied so gently was cool and soothing on her blistered back. But her conscience burned with the memory of what had just happened.

What had she done?

If she'd had time to think, she might have pulled away when his fingers skimmed her breast. She might have ignored the accidental touch, or even made light of it. Instead she had responded in the most imprudent way, groaning like a wanton and offering her body for more of the same.

What a fool she'd been!

In truth, she could not be angry with Black Sun. He was a man, after all, with a man's needs. Even so, he had taken no more than she'd been willing to give. And it had been his strength, not hers, that had pulled them both back from the precipice.

But how could she face him again? How could she meet the cold caution that would flicker in his eyes every time he looked at her? He had told her he wanted nothing to do with a white woman. She should have taken him at his word, not put that word to the test.

And what about herself? A few weeks from now, if all went well, she would be back among her own people. To ensure a respectable future for Annie, she would need to keep her own reputation spotless. Charity could imagine how so-called decent white people would feel toward a woman, especially a minister's widow, who had welcomed the attentions of an Indian. If they so much as suspected any impropriety, they would cast her out, and her innocent daughter with her. For Annie's sake, if not her own, she could not allow that to happen.

Black Sun was right. There was nothing to do but to put the encounter behind them and never think about it again.

Forcing herself to move, she eased the buckskin shirt up over her yarrow-coated back and onto her shoulders. She yearned to plunge into the icy water of the pool and scrub her whole body clean. But she wanted the herbal mixture to do its work. Tomorrow would be soon enough for a bath. Meanwhile she would not be idle. There were plenty of things she could do to improve this temporary home.

Picking Annie up, she ducked under the lip of the low cave, and stepped out into the open. Dazzled by the first rays of morning sunlight, she closed her eyes. As she opened them again, her mouth formed a little *O* of wonder.

She was standing in a hanging valley, about two-thirds of the way between the floor of the canyon and the highest point of its walls. Above her, glistening cliffs in shades of cream and buff jutted against a dawn-streaked sky. Springs of cascading water trickled from the ledges to join in the pool at her feet. These springs filled the pool, which fed the waterfall that splashed down the cliff to the canyon floor.

Once, when she was a little girl, her father

had told her how rivers of ice, called glaciers, carved canyons with hanging valleys out of the mountains. This place, she speculated, had been scooped out by a vanishing glacier. Its rocky sides still bore the marks of the ancient ice, but over the passing centuries, this miniature Eden had filled with life. Where the springs flowed downward, ferns and flowers festooned the cliffs. Velvety mosses carpeted the rocks and white lilies, the ones Black Sun had told her were safe to eat, sprouted along the ledges. Beside the pool, a gnarled pine tree stood like a sentinel over the little glade. Swallows darted among the ledges. A yellow butterfly hovered above the water, then fluttered out over the falls and vanished in the mist.

Charity moved cautiously, stretching her limbs, testing her strength. Her young body was recovering well from Annie's birth, and the yarrow poultice was doing its work on her burns. For the first time since the attack on the wagon train, it felt good to be alive.

Walking to the top of the cliff, she gazed down into the canyon. The trail where Black Sun had descended was lost in the waterfall's mist. That same mist would hide her small paradise, concealing any view of it from below.

She and Annie would surely be safe here until Black Sun returned from his hunt.

If he returned...

An icy dread crept over her. Black Sun had promised to come back with food. But he was walking into a world of danger, where anything could go wrong. He could slip and tumble off the slippery path or be taken by the Blackfoot. He could be attacked by wild animals, drowned in a bog or caught in the open by a late spring blizzard. Or he could simply change his mind and decide that a white woman and her child were not worth saving. Any one of a hundred things could keep Black Sun from returning; and if even one of them occurred, she and Annie would be stranded in this place.

For the past two days she had been completely dependent on Black Sun. Now that would have to change. Starting today, she would take stock of her resources. She would determine what she and Annie needed to survive and then prepare as best she could. She owed that much to her daughter, and to herself.

With Black Sun's help or without it, she vowed, she and her child would live to find their way to safety.

Black Sun had left their meager supplies

piled against the lowest wall of the shelter. The parfleche contained half a dozen strips of dried venison. It would be wise to save it, she knew, but if she denied herself nourishment, she would have nothing to feed Annie.

Weighing her choice, Charity tore off a sliver of meat and chewed it carefully. It was tough and salty, but nursing the baby had given her a roaring appetite. It took an act of will to replace the rest of the venison, close the parfleche and put it away. She would learn to eat the lily roots, as well, she resolved. That way, the meat would last longer.

Her sodden dress, petticoat and underclothes lay in a bloodstained wad on the ground. The clothes were beyond wearing, but if washed clean and dried in the sun, the fabric could have many uses—bandages, a makeshift tent for shelter, wrappings for the baby or for her feet.

Washing the clothes would be the first order of the day, she decided. She had no soap, but the flat rock at the far side of the pool, where the water streamed out toward the falls, would do as a scrubbing board.

She took the time to wipe Annie clean and replace the absorbent moss that served as a diaper in the cradleboard. Then, gathering the soiled clothes into a bundle, she picked up the baby and walked around the pool to the far side. A patch of yellow sand still bore the imprints of Black Sun's long moccasins. Charity gazed down at the tracks, color flooding her face at the memory of his hand on her breast, his lips searing a path up her shoulder. For a moment her heart clenched like a fist in her chest and all she wanted was to see him again, to feel his hands on her body, to taste his seeking mouth with her own.

No! She wrenched the forbidden thoughts from her mind. She could not think of him, could not yearn for him. She had her own future to think of and, more important, her daughter's.

With Annie propped safely nearby, she knelt beside the band of water that streamed toward the falls. Gripping the waistband of her petticoat, she rinsed it clean in the current, scrubbing out the stains against the rough rocks. When it was as clean as she could manage, she spread it on the rocks to dry, then started on her dress.

By the time the dress was clean, the weathered chambray fabric had been scrubbed full of holes. Charity twisted out the water, gave the garment a good shaking and spread it over a boulder to catch the sunlight.

Only her underdrawers—or her unmentionables, as her grandmother would call them—remained. These were badly stained, the cheap muslin fabric worn gossamer-thin. They hardly seemed worth saving, but in this place, she could not afford to waste anything.

As Charity leaned over the water, something in the graveled streambed caught a ray of sunlight, glinting so brightly that it dazzled her eyes. The drawers slipped from her fingers and floated away, drifting toward the waterfall.

"Oh, no—" She made a desperate lunge for them, but she was too late. Caught up in the swift current, the unmentionables bobbed into the mist and vanished over the edge of the falls.

With a sigh of resignation, she sank back onto her heels to rest. The sun was well above the cliffs now. Last night's storm had passed and the sky was as blue as the flash of a bunting's wing above the glittering ledges.

Fate had dropped her into a tiny piece of paradise. But even a paradise could become a prison, Charity reminded herself. She could not let herself be lulled by the magical beauty

of this place. If she and Annie were to survive,
she would need to think, to plan, to act.

Scooping her palm into the stream, she
raised her cupped hand to her lips and took a
cautious taste. The water was fresh and good,
and she was thirsty for more. Bending closer,
she made a bowl of her hands. That was when
she noticed the school of finger-length trout
swimming along the bottom of the stream. The
fish were tiny, but there were literally hundreds
of them. If she could catch enough of these
small trout and dry their bodies in the sun,
they would provide a nutritious, lightweight
food source on the journey home.

She grabbed for a fish. But the slippery creatures were too fast for her. She only succeeded
in scraping a knuckle on something sharp and
solid in the stream's graveled bed.

Charity withdrew her hand and stared down
into the crystal-clear water. That was when she
saw it—the same bright, reflected glimmer of
light that had caught her eye earlier.

Curious, she thrust her hand into the water
again. Her fingers groped in the gravel and
closed around an object that was about the
length of her thumb. Its chilled surface, unlike
the stream-tumbled rocks around it, was lumpy
and had a dense, metallic feel to it. Charity

worked it free from the surrounding stones. An instant later she had it out of the water.

Shaped like the rough head of an eagle, it lay heavy in the palm of her hand, glowing with yellow light, like a piece of the sun itself.

Charity's heart crept into her throat. She was holding a nugget—a precious lump of pure, solid gold.

By the time Black Sun emerged from the canyon, the *Siksika* braves had departed. Their campsite was empty, the bonfire blackened and cold, the ground littered with discarded bones from the deer they'd killed and eaten. He had hoped to find horses nearby, either his own or some he could take. But there were no horses to be found. He would have no choice except to hunt on foot.

Black Sun's hunting turned out to be even more onerous than he'd expected. The *Siksika,* being young and lacking in proper behavior, had made enough commotion to scatter all the game within a half day's ride. He spent the first day of his hunt trekking through the foothills with his bow, seeing not so much as a rabbit or grouse, let alone a deer, elk or antelope. That night he made a small fire in the shelter of a rock and used the coals to roast some roots he'd dug. Even cooked, the roots were tough and stringy, but they would nourish him until he could bring down some meat.

With the foothills barren of game, Black Sun had no choice except to venture out onto the flatland, where the animals could see across the open distance and places for a hunter to lie in wait were few and far between. Worse, he knew that without a horse, he was vulnerable. There was no way to outrun a mounted enemy or to outmaneuver a charging buffalo on foot. Only luck and alertness could keep him safe.

On the second day of his hunt, he came upon a herd of antelope, but their speed was like the wind and they bounded out of arrow range. On the third day he saw a distant herd of buffalo, but he was separated from them by a deep gorge. By the time he found a way across, he knew, they would be gone.

At night he lay under the stars, listening to the breath of the wind and the stirring of small animals around him. When he closed his eyes, Charity's face drifted above him like a pale moon in the darkness. It was all too easy to remember the feel of her soft breast in his hand and the taste of her skin against his seeking lips. Her husky little voice seemed to whisper in his ear—sensual, caressing words that had no meaning yet told him all he wanted to hear.

He worried about her, alone with her baby in the sacred canyon. There were times when it was all he could do to keep from abandoning this fruitless hunt and retrace his steps to where he had left her. But that, wisdom argued, would be the most foolish thing he could do.

Charity would be safe, he assured himself again and again. She was an intelligent woman, with the good sense to stay where he'd left her. By the time he returned she would have several days of rest. With luck, they'd be able to leave immediately. Until he found horses, they could make fair time on foot, keeping to the woods where they wouldn't be seen.

There were times when Black Sun could almost make himself believe that everything would go as planned. But he knew better. Fate had filled his life with tragic twists and turns. This encounter with the white woman would be just one more. Their journey would be dangerous and filled with uncertainty. But no matter what befell them, or when and how it happened, one thing was certain. In the end, he would lose her.

Maybe that was the reason for the dream. And maybe that was what Charity was meant to teach him.

On the tenth day of the hunt his luck finally

changed. From a low ridge, he spotted eleven antelope browsing in a hollow. The lay of the land, and the fact that he was downwind from the small herd, allowed him to belly-crawl within arrow range. The animal he brought down was in prime condition, its horns black and curving above its large eyes, its coat beautifully patterned in fawn and cream.

"Forgive me, child of the wind," he murmured, slitting the creature's throat to end its suffering. "And thank you for the gift of your life."

He skinned and butchered the carcass on the spot, wrapping the meat in the hide to keep it clean. He was several days from the sacred canyon, too far to carry fresh meat on foot without danger of it spoiling. He would need to find a safe location to build a fire, cut the meat into thin strips and hang them to cure in the smoke. That would mean more days away from Charity. But the delay was necessary. Black Sun could only hope she would stay where he had left her and that the spirits of the sacred canyon would keep her and her child safe until he returned.

Charity had searched every inch of the streambed in the hanging valley. She had dug in the gravel until her fingernails were worn to raw nubs. But she had found no more gold nuggets to delight her eyes and fire her dreams.

Never mind, she told herself. Where there was one piece of gold there were sure to be more. The gold was simply hidden away, out of easy reach. And it *was* gold, she was sure. On the journey west, Rueben Potter had shown her a chunk of fool's gold. Real gold was deeper in color, he'd explained. The look of it was so rich and bright that there could be no mistaking it for anything else.

While Annie slumbered in her cradleboard, Charity had explored the full circle of ledges. Trapped in the buff-colored quartz, she had seen tiny flakes of gold—thousands, perhaps millions, of them, glittering like tiny gems in the sunlight. There was gold all around her, she sensed. But it would take more resources than she possessed to bring it down from the canyon and smelt it out of the rock. Even so, when she held the nugget in her hand, it was impossible not to dream and plan.

Perhaps, once she was safely home, she could file a mining claim to the canyon. She could hold it until the country became less dangerous, or sell it to someone with the means to set up a mining operation. What a wonderful life the money could provide for Annie—

a comfortable home, a good education, even such luxuries as fine clothes and travel!

But the future was no more than a dream, Charity reminded herself. Right now only the nugget was real. She held it in her hand, savoring its solid weight. Her fingers traced the contours of its eagle-head shape. The nugget was too wonderful to think of selling, especially when she had just found a canyon full of gold. She would save it as a special souvenir for Annie.

Wrapping the nugget in a scrap of deerskin, she tucked it into the cradleboard, among the folds of the buffalo robe. "This shall be yours, Annie," she promised her blue-eyed daughter. "When you look at, it will remind you of the place where you were born."

And the Arapaho brave who brought you into the world, she thought, but she did not say the words out loud. She would tell Annie the story of Black Sun when the little girl was old enough to understand. But the memory of that unguarded moment when his hand lay over her pounding heart would be locked away, never to be shared.

For the first few days of Black Sun's absence, gold hunting provided Charity with a pleasant diversion. But as the days passed and he did not return, she grew more and more anxious. She understood that he might have to travel far in search of game, but surely he had not planned to be gone so long.

With each passing day, Charity had grown stronger. By now her burns were nearly healed. She was able to swim in the pool and to climb on the rocks wearing the moccasins she'd stitched from rawhide and deerskin, using the bone needle and sinew she'd found among Black Sun's supplies. On one foray, she'd discovered a larger, better protected cave higher in the ledges and had spent the rest of the day hauling bedding and supplies up to the new home.

The sun had sprinkled her skin with pale gold freckles and bleached platinum glints into the clean, windblown mane of her hair. She had no mirror except the sunlit pond, but it was easy enough to see that she was no longer the exhausted, frightened woman who had arrived in this mountain sanctuary.

From a forked stick and a piece of her petticoat she had fashioned a dip net. With this, she soon became adept at catching the fingerling trout, whose numbers never seemed to lessen. Her supply of sun-dried fish filled the parfleche where the venison had been, adding much-needed protein to her diet of roots and berries.

Annie, too, was thriving. Thanks to her mother's rich milk, her little stick-thin arms and legs were filling out. At the age of nearly two weeks she was plump, rosy and already showing signs of a stubborn streak.

All these blessings, however, were darkened by the shadow of Black Sun's absence. Within one day of his leaving, Charity discovered that the slightest sound from below the cliff was enough to make her race to the edge, grip the aspen that grew there and peer downward, eager for the sight of his tall, lean figure striding up the trail. At night she huddled beside the pool, gazing up at the sky and wondering if he was looking at the same moon, the same stars. Sometimes, when she slept, she dreamed of lying in his arms, her head pillowed on his shoulder, her bare legs tangled sweetly with his.

As the days passed, however, her dreams evolved into nightmares. One night she saw his lifeless body sprawled on the prairie, trampled by buffalo. Another night she saw him tied to a burning stake in a hostile Blackfoot camp. But perhaps the most haunting dream of all was the one where she saw him on horseback, riding away from her without looking back. Riding away, despite her pleas and calls, until he vanished into the twilight.

Anxiety clawed at her day and night. Her appetite faded and sleep, when it came, brought only bad dreams. Sensing her mother's worry, Annie grew tense and cranky.

Charity bore the strain until the morning of the fourteenth day, when she looked out over the canyon and told herself that it was time she faced the truth.

Black Sun would not be coming back.

Whatever she did next, she would have to do alone.

Squaring her shoulders, she walked back to the cave, where Annie was fussing to be fed. Sitting cross-legged with her back against the ledge, Charity nursed her daughter while her mind spun with desperate plans.

The sooner she left this place, the sooner she would be home, she told herself. She had seen no smoke from the camp of the Blackfoot braves since the day of the thunderstorm. With luck, they would be far away by now. She could work her way down the canyon and cut over into the foothills, using the sun to keep her directions straight. As long as she avoided the open flatland, she should have no trouble keeping out of sight.

Why not go now? she reasoned. Why wait another agonizing day for a man who would never return? She had as much food as she could carry. She had buffalo robes for sleeping and shelter. She had the small knife and the long, braided rawhide rope that Black Sun had left behind. She would never be better prepared than she was right now.

Annie had finished nursing. Charity patted the bony little back till the air bubble came up, then laced her daughter securely into the cradleboard. Next she collected the things she would need for the journey and bundled them into the buffalo robe. With Annie's cradleboard slung behind her shoulders, it would be all she could do to carry what they needed. But that couldn't be helped. She would grow stronger with each day of walking.

At last she was ready to go. She made one final check of the cave that had been Annie's first home. She had left it clean, with the odds and ends she wasn't taking bundled up and stashed behind a rock. Maybe someday Black Sun would come back here and find them. But she could not think of Black Sun now. If she imagined him returning to this place and finding her gone, she would never have the courage to leave.

Resolutely, she thrust her arms through the straps of the cradleboard and lifted it onto her back. Then, tucking the bundled supplies under her arm, she started for the path down the cliff.

She had almost reached the waterfall when she chanced to look out toward the mouth of the canyon.

Her heart dropped.

From the place where the young Blackfoot had camped, a thin column of smoke rose against the morning sky, then another, and another....

Chapter Ten

Black Sun saw the columns of smoke at dusk, as he was crossing the last ridge of wooded hills. With mounting dread, he stared at the sky, taking the measure of what he saw.

It was a whole village, perhaps twenty or thirty lodges, camped right at the mouth of the canyon. And although he could see little more than the smoke from their cookfires above the trees, he would wager his life that they were *Siksika*.

Keeping to the wooded slope, he plunged toward the mouth of the canyon. Fear pushed him on, shooting strength through his tired legs. Somehow he had to reach the hanging valley above the canyon. He had to find Charity and the baby—if they were still alive.

Pausing where a high boulder gave him a vantage point, he peered down through the leafing aspens. Yes, they were *Siksika*. He could see the camp now; not a war party, but an entire band, including women, children and elders.

Spring was a time when many tribes migrated up from their winter camps, following the herds of game that grazed on these high plains. But these *Siksika* did not appear to be on the move. They had put up their lodges and their meat-drying racks as if they meant to stay right here.

A tall, young man passed through Black Sun's view. Even at a distance, Black Sun recognized him as one of the youths who'd come into the canyon on the day of the thunderstorm. The young braves must have ridden home and told their elders about the big medicine in the sacred canyon. Now the entire band had come here to experience that medicine for themselves.

Had they ventured into the canyon? Had they found Charity and her child? There was only one way to know.

Slipping to the ground, Black Sun started

up the slope. There was only one ground-level entrance to the canyon, and it was blocked by the camp. To get to the place where he'd left Charity, he would have to go in higher up, then look for a place where he could work his way down the sheer ledges. If Charity and the baby were gone, he would search for them. If they were captives, he would rescue them at any cost. If they were dead...

But to dwell on the horrors that might have taken place would only paralyze him. He could only go forward one step at a time and act on whatever he found.

Searching his memory of the canyon, he remembered a deep, vertical cleft in the ledge below the falls. If he could find it, the cleft might be narrow enough for him to bridge with his body and climb down to the bottom of the canyon. Then he would have to mount the trail up the side of the falls to the place where he had left Charity.

The dusk was fading into moonless night. Racing with the darkness, Black Sun scrambled up to the rim of the canyon and, after some frantic searching, managed to find the cleft. It was narrow enough at the top for him to press his back against one side and his feet against the other. He could only hope the width would remain constant all the way down.

He could not climb with the bundle of smoked meat. Without hesitation, he tossed it into the blackness. For what seemed like a very long time, it ricocheted down between the ledges before coming to rest with a final thud. Black Sun followed, bracing his body in the cleft, working his feet, then his back, slowly downward over the face of the rock.

The effort was exhausting. By the time he reached the canyon floor, Black Sun was scraped, bruised and bleeding. Every muscle in his body quivered with strain. Barely stopping to catch his breath, he found the bundle and made for the trail that would take him alongside the falls. With every step he prayed to Heisonoonin that he would find Charity and her baby safe and well.

By now the canyon was pitch-dark. Even the waterfall, which caught every speck of light, was no more than sound in his ear and wet mist on his skin. Black Sun flinched, nearly losing his balance, as an insect-hunting bat brushed past his face. Vines and roots caught his feet, causing him to slip on the treacherous moss. Only the stars were constant. Glittering like a river above the canyon, they guided him upward until he reached the top of the falls and staggered onto level ground.

"Stop right there!" The voice was familiar, but the figure who leaped out of the shadows, brandishing a long, sharpened stick like a spear, looked like a ghost-creature in the starlight, all wild, pale hair, fluttering buckskin fringe and menacing limbs. Was this the woman he had left behind? The woman who'd wept when he turned his back and walked away from her?

The makeshift spear quivered as she raised her arm, ready to thrust the point into his chest and push him back over the falls to his death.

"Charity." He whispered her name, dizzy with relief at having found her alive. "It's all right. I'm here."

She froze, her arm still upraised, her eyes flashing defiance in the starlit night. Only then did Black Sun realize what it had taken to transform her into the savage female warrior he saw in front of him—the long, empty days and nights, the feelings of desertion and betrayal, the anger and the fear.

A woman of his own people would have simply waited, accepting his absence and return as she accepted the passing of seasons. But not Charity Bennett. Left alone and unprotected, she had taken on the desperation of a trapped animal, ready to fight to the death against anyone who threatened her or her daughter.

"Where's your baby?" he asked, bracing himself for her reply. If anything could have pushed Charity over the brink, making her hate him for his absence, it would have been the loss of her child.

Her head jerked ever so slightly toward the ledges. Then, slowly, her arm came down and the spear clattered to the rock. "Annie's all right," she said in a tired voice. "So am I."

He took a step toward her. Charity's eyes flashed like a wildcat's, warning him not to come closer. "You told me you'd only be gone a few days," she said.

"I know," he said without apology. "It took more time to get the meat we needed. How long have those people been camped at the mouth of the canyon?"

"Three…days." She swayed a little and he could see that she was exhausted. "I haven't slept in all that time. Whenever I close my eyes, I imagine them coming up over that ledge. I've been waiting right here, to drive them back before they could get to Annie."

He took another step. "I'm here now, Charity. I'll keep you safe. You can rest while I guard the cliff." Black Sun found himself aching to gather her into his arms and hold her. She had been so brave, and she was so tired. But after what had happened between them the last time, he knew better than to touch her.

"Have they been in the canyon?" he asked her.

She shook her head, her hair like a cloud on the night breeze. "Not that I know of. I've only seen the smoke from their camp. I haven't dared go down the cliff." She peered into the darkness. "What do you make of this? Were you able to get close?"

"As close as I dared. It looks like a village, whole families, not a war party or a hunting party. I saw one of the braves who came into the canyon before. My guess would be they're here for some kind of ceremony, some big medicine."

"How long do you think they'll be here?" She sounded unspeakably weary, and once more Black Sun fought the urge to gather her into his arms, hold her close and rock her like a child.

"Setting up that many lodges is a fair amount of work," he said. "They wouldn't have done it if they'd planned on moving soon."

"So we could be trapped up here." She

moved beside him, at the edge of the cliff, and stood looking out over the canyon. From the distant camp, the faint throb of drumbeats floated up through the darkness. "You got into the canyon," she said, fixing her eyes on him. "How did you do it? Can we get out the same way?"

Black Sun sighed and shook his head. "I climbed up to the rim and came down over the ledges. Even I couldn't make it back the way I came. It's too high and too steep. All we can do is watch and wait, and leave as soon as it's safe."

She stood in silence for a long moment, listening to the sound of the drums. "You didn't have to come back for us," she said.

"Do you think I would have left you here?" he asked, gazing at the sky, where dark clouds were spilling in above the canyon. The breeze carried the fresh smell of rain.

"It was what I'd begun to believe," she said. "Why should you risk your life to save a white woman and her baby?"

Black Sun avoided meeting her eyes. Should he tell her that she had been in his thoughts day and night? Should he tell her that when he saw her standing with her spear, alive and safe, his heart had come home?

"You're worn out, Charity," he said. "Get some rest while I keep watch. We can talk in the morning."

She exhaled, still tense. "Wake me if anything happens," she said. "I'll be up on the ledge with Annie, in the new cave I found."

"Fine. Go ahead." He glanced toward the low cave beside the pond, which was now clean and empty. That would be his sleeping place while they remained in the canyon, he resolved. She had not invited him to share the new cave and, even if she had, he would not risk the temptation of being so close to her.

Turning, she walked away without another word. He watched her climb the narrow, hidden path that led to a shadowed opening in the cliff, moving along the narrow ledge with the easy grace of a puma. An instant later she vanished from sight.

Black Sun stowed most of his supplies in the small cave. Armed with his bow and arrows, his hunting knife and Charity's clumsily fashioned spear, he settled himself on the flat rock above the falls, which offered him the best view of the canyon.

With his bow across his knees, he gazed into the darkness. From below, the drums beat out a driving, hypnotic cadence, punctuated by the shrill sounds of chanting. The wind that gusted up the canyon carried the pungent smell of burning sage. The *Siksika* were performing a medicine ceremony, he surmised. Such gatherings often took place in the spring, to ensure plentiful rain, rich grass and good hunting. Holding such a ceremony here, at the mouth of the sacred canyon, would lend added power to the songs, dances and rituals.

The drumming and dancing would continue far into the night. While it lasted, the canyon would be safe. No one in the village, except a few sleepy children, would leave the bonfire until the last dancer had dropped from exhaustion. Charity, alone with her baby, would not have known this. The sounds from below must have terrified her.

How long would they be safe here? There was no easy answer to that question. If they could keep the *Siksika* from discovering their presence, it might be possible to simply wait them out and leave after they were gone. But every day posed a greater risk that someone would see them or hear the baby. If they were caught, the penalty for violating the sacred canyon would be a slow and excruciating death.

Black Sun fingered the hilt of his knife, thinking of Charity and her baby and wondering whether, if it came to that, he would have the strength to spare them such a death. But no, he promised himself, their situation would never get that far. He would see to it—even at the cost of his own life.

Something stirred in the darkness behind him. Charity moved up onto the rock and sat at his side, her shoulder not quite touching his. "I couldn't sleep," she said.

"You should try," Black Sun said, aware that her simple nearness had triggered a quickening of his pulse. "You're tired," he said. "You'll need your strength later on."

She raised her knees, clutching them to her chest as she stared into the darkness. The drumbeats, sensual and compelling, floated up through the mist-shrouded canyon. Black Sun's heart drummed with a rhythm of its own. He could feel the heat rising in his body. He remembered the taste of her skin and the swollen softness of her breast in his hand.

"Every night since they arrived I've listened to them," she whispered. "What are they doing down there?"

"Making medicine," he said. "Dancing and singing to ask their gods for a good hunting season. They aren't monsters, Charity, in spite of what those young fools did to your people. All they want is to keep what belongs to them."

"And that includes this canyon, doesn't it?" She lifted her gaze to the sky, where dark clouds were racing in over the peaks. Sheet lightning flickered in the west, followed by a distant growl of thunder. "What will they do if they find us here?"

"I think you know. That's why we mustn't let them see or hear us." Black Sun flexed his tired shoulders. "To speak of such things invites the dark spirits, Charity Bennett. If you want to talk, ask me about something else."

"Very well." Lowering her feet to the ground, she turned back to face him. Her silvery eyes penetrated the darkness. Could she see how much he needed her—and how desperately he was fighting that need?

"Once, you started to tell me a story about the night your mother died and you left the white man," she said. "I want to hear the rest of it."

He shot her a startled glance. Until now, he'd forgotten what he'd told her on the trail. To tell her the rest of the story would be like ripping the scar off an old wound.

"It's not a pretty story, Charity," he said, hoping she would relent and change the subject. "Why would you want to hear it? I've never told it to anyone, not even to my own people." *Not even to my own wife,* he thought, but he did not say the words out loud.

Her hair seemed to float as the breeze swept it back from her face. Until tonight he had only seen her wet, dirty and in pain. She was beautiful, he realized. As beautiful as she had appeared in his dream. His throat ached with wanting her.

"I need to hear it all," she said gently. "There's a darkness in you, Black Sun, an anger that goes all the way to the depths of your heart. I felt it the first time I saw you." She laid her palm on his arm, sending a quiver of tension through his body. "Even now I feel it," she said, withdrawing her hand.

He stared down into the canyon, knowing she was right. Even with her, the anger was there. The knife he carried was a constant reminder of it.

For the space of a breath she was silent, as if gathering her courage before she spoke again. "When we leave this place, I'll be putting my life and my baby's life in your hands. You've already taken great risks to protect us, and I'm grateful for that. But you can't imagine what I went through during all those days and nights when you were gone. If I'm to trust you completely, I need to know you won't desert us or betray us. For that, I need to understand your anger and where it comes from. Let me see into your darkness, Black Sun."

Still reluctant, Black Sun fingered the polished bone handle of his hunting knife. Hearing the story he'd kept to himself for half his lifetime might help her understand him. But the truth would be more likely to shatter her trust than to strengthen it.

"You're not going to like what you hear," he said.

Her answer rippled through his senses like wind in spring willows. "I'm not expecting to like it. But if you can be honest with me about that night, you can be honest with me about anything."

Anything? The word triggered an involuntary tightening of Black Sun's mouth. He could lay his past bare for her to see. But the hunger he felt for her would have to remain his secret.

She was silent now, waiting for him to begin. Still, he hesitated, on the brink of pain.

"Your white stepfather was drunk and he was beating your mother," she prompted him gently. "You were only a boy, and when you tried to help her, he threw you out into the night and locked the cabin door. That's all you've told me."

Black Sun took a deep breath, feeling as if he were about to unravel his heart and pull the strands of it out between his ribs. He could refuse to tell her, he knew. But Charity was right about one thing. If he wanted her trust— and their lives could depend on that trust—he would have to give her what she wanted.

Reaching down, he pulled the hunting knife from its sheath and held it out, lying flat, toward her. "Hold it in your hands while I tell you," he said when she recoiled from the weapon. "You wanted truth. This is truth."

Black Sun laid the knife on her open palms. She accepted it gingerly, holding it in front of her like an offering as he took up the painful thread of the story.

"I pounded on that door until my hands were bloody. From inside the cabin I could hear the two of them fighting. I could hear the curses and screams and the sounds of things falling and breaking. Suddenly everything on the other side of the door went quiet. I thought maybe he'd passed out. That was how most of their fights ended—my mother would let me in and I'd help her put him to bed. But this time was different. The bolt slid open. My mother staggered out onto the porch and closed the door behind her. Her nose was broken, and blood from a cut above her eye was streaming down her face. 'Let's go,' she said. 'Let's get out of here.' I wanted to go back inside and get some food and blankets before he woke up, but she wouldn't let me. 'We have to get away now,' she said."

Charity had not stirred. Thunder echoed over the distant peaks, blending with the throb of drumbeats as Black Sun continued his story.

"It was dark and cold, and she was in so much pain that she couldn't walk far without leaning on my shoulder. Later I saw the bruises where he'd kicked her belly with his big boots. We got as far as the first ridge above the cabin. When we stopped to rest, she lay down on the ground and couldn't get up. 'I'm going to have this baby right here,' she said, 'and you'll have to help me.'"

Black Sun felt the anguish well up in his throat. He gazed down at his hands, choking it back. "I helped her as best I could. But by the time the full moon reached the peak of the sky, both she and the baby were dead. I built a platform in a tree and laid them on it and sang the death song over them—what I remembered of it. Then I started back for the cabin. I don't know what I planned to do. The only thing I knew for certain was that I wanted to leave and go back to my mother's people. With luck, I thought, the monster would still be passed out. I could gather up a few supplies and leave him there."

He glanced up to meet Charity's silvery eyes. In the darkness he caught the glimmer of tears. But the story wasn't finished. By the time he reached the end of it, her sympathy would be replaced by revulsion.

"I reached the cabin and opened the door. Inside, the lantern was still burning. I was hoping my stepfather wouldn't be awake—he was a big man, big enough to kill a boy like me with his bare hands." Black Sun swallowed hard. "I walked into the cabin and found him lying dead on the floor, with his own hunting knife driven into his chest."

Charity's eyes widened. "Your mother—?"

"Yes. She'd stabbed him with the last of her strength. He would never beat her again."

She stared down at the knife in her hands. Even in the darkness, Black Sun could sense that her face had gone white. "This—" she whispered. "This was his, wasn't it? This was the knife she used to kill him! You took it, you use it—"

"Yes, I took it." His voice had dropped to a hoarse rasp. "And I did more. After I pulled the knife out of his body, I stabbed him with it again and again and again, as I'd wanted to do when he was alive. It was pitiful revenge for what he'd done to my mother, but his spirit had passed beyond my reach. It was the only thing I could do." He gazed at her stunned face, knowing he had to finish. "After that, I gathered up the supplies I could carry and took them outside. Then I poured lamp oil over his body and set it on fire. When I walked away, I didn't look back."

The story had drained Black Sun of emotion. He felt as empty as he had on that night, when he'd walked away from the blazing cabin into the wilderness, drowning in a boy's helpless rage.

"And you kept the knife." Her voice was as fragile as the etching of frost on grass on a winter morning.

Black Sun tried to arrange his features into a mask of cold composure. "I keep it with me always, and every time I see it, every time I touch it, I remember what that white man did to my mother and how she used his own knife to kill him."

Her breath hissed out as if she'd been

punched in the stomach. She slumped where she sat, gazing at him with hollow eyes. He had shocked her. He had *wanted* to shock her, to repel her to a safe distance where she could not be touched by the heat of his desire.

"You wanted the truth," he said. "Now you have it. You're holding it in your hands."

She stared down at the knife, a visible shudder passing through her body. "Have you ever killed a white person?"

"Never," he answered truthfully. "But I would have found a way to kill my stepfather if my mother hadn't killed him first."

"You're not a boy anymore," she said. "Wouldn't it be better to throw the knife away and forget that terrible night?"

He shook his head, pushing the frightened boy back into memory. "I keep the knife to remind me of my mother's courage, and I keep it to remind me of how much I hate all whites for their greed and selfishness."

"Do you hate me, Black Sun? Do you hate my child?"

"Your people are my enemies. I know that if I live long enough, I'll see them sweep over the whole land, destroying everything fine and sacred. If I thought I could stop it from happening, I would go to war and kill them all. But the answer to your question is no, I could never hate you, Charity. I could never hate your child. All I want is to get you safely back to your people."

"I see." Her hands quivered as she laid the knife on the rock between them. "I asked you for the truth. You gave it to me."

"And does it change anything?" He picked up the knife and slid it back into its sheath. "Have you learned anything about me you didn't already suspect?"

He waited for her response, but she had turned away. A distant flash of lightning cast her face into stark profile. The need to be held and comforted in her arms was like a cry in him—a cry he willed himself not to hear.

"I want you to promise me something." He spoke above the thunder that rumbled over the peaks. Charity had turned back and was gazing at him with curious eyes.

"If I get you and your daughter to a white trading post, I ask one thing," he said, letting the anger creep into his voice. "I want you to go back East where you came from and stay there. If you ever return to this place, alone or with your people, you will return as an enemy."

Her gaze flickered to her hands, which were clasped in her lap.

"Promise me, Charity," he said. "Say the words."

Her gaze met his, but with a flash of evasion that made Black Sun wonder what she was thinking. She took a little breath. "Of course," she said. "Yes, I promise."

Lightning flashed above the rim of the canyon. The answering thunder was like the low growl of an approaching beast. A few raindrops spattered the rock where they sat. Charity rose to her feet, one restless hand brushing back her hair. "It's time I was getting back to Annie," she said.

Keeping his seat, Black Sun looked up at her, but her expression told him nothing. "Sleep well, Charity," he said.

She nodded farewell, then turned away. He watched her climb the narrow trail. Had he imagined the slight hesitation in her voice when she'd given him her promise? Was there something she wasn't telling him?

Inwardly churning, he gazed into the darkness. The light drizzle of rain had not stopped the drums. Their rhythm floated up the canyon, low and steady, like the pulse of the earth itself. Black Sun felt it moving through his body, stirring the loneliness, the raw need, that slumbered in the depths of his soul. Only

Charity, warm and soft and golden, could ease the pain of that need. But he knew better than to touch her. She was not for him. She would allow him to be her rescuer and her guardian, but she would always see him as a savage.

Would she trust him now? He had been brutally honest with her, but it had gained him nothing. She had looked into the depths of his savage heart and been repulsed by everything she saw.

And that was just as well, Black Sun told himself. The boundaries had been drawn. No matter how he might ache for her, he would never be tempted to cross them again.

The rain was falling harder now. It spattered against the rocks, drowning the sound of the drums. Rising to his feet, Black Sun moved under the lip of the shallow cave. No one would come into the canyon tonight. It would be safe to get some needed rest.

Stretching out on his side, he made a pillow of the bundled provisions and closed his eyes. But sleep was as elusive as the fleeing game herds he'd tracked on the plain. He lay with his eyes open, watching the raindrops splash into the pool and burning with hungers that would never be satisfied, wanting the sight of her face, the sound of her voice, wanting her in his arms and in his bed.

Charity.

A white woman.

Chapter Eleven

Charity lay awake, listening to the drizzle of the rain and the rumbling sigh of distant thunder. Her cave was warm, almost cozy. The entrance was sheltered from the weather, and she had covered the floor with the largest of the buffalo robes. Her supply of roots and dried fish was stored under a ledge, and bunches of herbs and flowers she'd gathered hung drying from a pole beneath the ceiling.

Against the inner wall, Annie slumbered in the cradleboard Black Sun had woven on the night of her birth. Illuminated by occasional flashes of lightning, the child was the picture of contentment, a fearless and serene little island in a sea of danger.

Sadly, Annie would not recall any of this time. She was far too young for that. But maybe when she heard the story of the sacred canyon where she'd spent the first weeks of her life and the tall Arapaho warrior who'd brought her into the world, a few buried impressions of this place, and of Black Sun, would awaken and remain.

Charity shivered as she remembered the cold weight of Black Sun's knife lying across her hands. That knife had been used to cut Annie's birth cord, giving life as it had once given death, she reminded herself. A weapon was not innately good or evil, only the intent with which it was used.

Black Sun's honesty had stunned her. His act of boyish rage, shocking as it had been, was easy enough for her to understand and forgive. But the fact that he'd kept that fury inside him, as he had kept the knife, continued to trouble her. Black Sun had never shown her anything but kindness. But she knew that the anger was there, simmering below the surface, waiting to strike.

Raising up on one elbow, Charity gazed out at the gray rain. There was little danger that anyone would climb the cliff in such weather. Knowing that, Black Sun would have taken shelter by now. But the shallow cave by the pond would be damp and cold, the night miserably long.

Should she ask him to come up and join her in her own warm, dry place? Would he understand that her invitation was meant only as a kindness?

A kindness? Would she really expect him to believe that? Did she believe it herself?

If you ever return to this place, alone or with your people, you will return as an enemy.

Charity lay back on the buffalo robe. Black Sun had meant to repel her. He had made it clear that, despite the desire that had flashed between them, he wanted no part of any white woman.

But even as he had been telling his terrible story, even as he had been telling her how much he hated the white race, she had wanted only one thing: to be in his arms.

When had she discovered that she loved him? There was no easy answer to that question. She only knew that when she was with Black Sun the earth sang beneath her feet. He had awakened her to the warmth of the sun, to the sweetness of the wind and to the world of womanly sensations that had slumbered, untouched, in her own body. He had taught her courage and selflessness. She would never forget him.

But she had no illusions about the future. Black Sun had weakened for a moment, but there was no place for a white woman in his life, and no place for an Indian brave in hers and Annie's. She had to go forward, doing what was best for her daughter.

If you ever return to this place, alone or with your people, you will return as an enemy.

She heard his words again, as if he had burned them into her memory. Did Black Sun know about the gold in the canyon? Had he guessed that she would find it? Was that why he had given her an ultimatum that was tantamount to a threat?

She had promised him that she would go back East and never return to the sacred canyon. She planned to keep that promise. But why should it prevent her from filing a mining claim that she could sell to the highest bidder? The nugget would provide enough evidence to dazzle any buyer. Charity didn't care about being wealthy. She only wanted enough money to raise herself out of poverty and to give her daughter a respectable future. The gold in the canyon was her best hope of doing that.

And that, Charity reminded herself, was one more reason why she should distance herself from Black Sun. He would be outraged if he discovered her plan, and he would do everything in his power to stop her. Then they would truly be enemies.

Her plan to exploit the gold was a betrayal of everything she owed him. Charity was well aware of that, and she had agonized over her decision. But when she weighed her daughter's welfare against her hopeless love for Black Sun, there was no question of where her duty lay and what she must do.

All the same, it tore her apart. As she lay staring up into the darkness, Charity knew that it was Black Sun's love she wanted most of all. A happy life with him would be worth more than all the gold in the world. If only it were possible…

She was drifting into a fitful sleep when the storm struck in its full, squalling fury. Lightning hissed out of the sky. Thunderbolts crashed off the canyon walls, echoing like a cannonade. The drizzling rain became a torrent that gushed down the ledges, flooding the pool and turning the waterfall brown with mud.

Below, in the Blackfoot camp, the drummers and dancers, their bodies likely streaked with ceremonial paint, would be trembling in their lodges.

The Great Thunderbird was walking in the canyon.

And in the hidden cave, his woman was waiting.

Black Sun had abandoned the low cave when the floor became flooded with water. Now he stood in the shelter of a rocky overhang, holding the bundle of smoked antelope meat between his body and the face of the rock in an effort to keep it dry. He had no fear of storms and had spent many nights in the rain. He would not be hurt by a little water. But the meat was too precious to risk spoiling.

A bolt of lightning crackled down the canyon, chased by a deafening boom of thunder. Water coming off the high slopes was funneling down through the canyon in a muddy river that covered his feet and swirled around his ankles. He would be foolish to stay here when Charity's safe, dry cave was only a short climb above him. Still, he hesitated. She had not invited him to share her shelter, nor had he asked her permission to do so.

Both of them knew the reason why. Even though they had never spoken of it, the memory of his hand caressing her breast hung between them in the tension-charged air. He wanted to touch her again, and he wanted more. He wanted her naked on the buffalo robe, the liquid heat of her body flowing beneath him, her legs parting to offer him the place where he knew he would fit as perfectly as a knife in its own sheath.

Did she know the hunger was still there inside him, tormenting him every time he thought of her? Did she feel a hunger of her own?

He could not afford to take the risk of finding out.

When he'd touched her before, she had responded with an ardor that left him breathless. He was the one who had pulled away, Black Sun reminded himself. He had heard the warning voice in his head and he had listened. Facing temptation a second time, would he hear the voice again or would he will it into silence?

Thunder crashed above the ledges as lightning struck a towering pine tree. It was dangerous here in the open, but even more dangerous in the place where his legs wanted to carry him. Wiser to stay here, he admonished himself. Before the night was over, the storm would end. But the consequences of being alone with Charity in the dark cave could pain him for the rest of his life.

"Black Sun!" He heard her voice, calling above the sound of the rushing water. "Black Sun! Where are you? Are you all right?"

"I'm here!" he shouted in reply. "Don't worry about me, I'm used to storms! But take this meat and keep it dry—"

She made an odd sound that could have been either a moan or a laugh. He saw her then, ghost-pale in a flash of light, standing on the ledge below the cave. "Don't be so stubborn!" she shouted. "You have to get out of the storm! I'm not going back until you come with me!"

Thunder crashed again, shaking the ground beneath his feet. Black Sun needed no more urging. Clasping the bundle, he followed her up the path and through the sheltered slit that marked the cave's entrance.

As he put the bundle under shelter and stepped into the darkness, a bolt of lightning flashed across the sky. For the space of a heartbeat, its blue light illuminated the inside of the cave. Black Sun saw the buffalo robes on the floor, the baby slumbering in the corner, the dried herbs bunched and hanging below the ceiling.

His throat jerked, cutting off his breath for an instant as the sense of destiny washed over him.

It was the cave he had seen in his dream.

They moved beyond the entrance and into the cave's shadowy embrace. The air was warm and vibrant, as if it had taken on a life of its own. Charity felt its movement on her damp skin. The sound of Black Sun's breathing mingled with her own, echoing like soft wind in the hollow space. Behind them the cave's opening, partly concealed by the ledge, was a broken rectangle of pewter-colored rain, lit now and then by blue-white flashes of lightning.

"Give me your hand. I'll guide you." She groped for Black Sun's fingers. "It seems dark when you first come in, but soon you'll be able to see a little."

Black Sun's hand found hers. His chilled fingers curled around hers, seeking warmth. The contact was so subtle, yet so intense, that Charity felt it as a sensual explosion all the way through her body. Her hand stirred. Her fingers skimmed his wrist. She felt the quickening of his pulse, heard the catch in his throat, as if he already knew what was destined to happen.

She had spent the past hours wrestling with the demon of common sense. She had reasoned and rationalized, tying her mind and her conscience into knots. They were enemies, the two of them, from different worlds. Soon those worlds would tear them apart.

Only by staying apart could they prevent the anguish of separation. Only by denying love could they avoid the pain that would come when their time was over.

She had called him into the cave with the purest of intentions—or so she'd told herself. She had only meant to give him shelter from the rain. But as the two of them moved through the entrance, a sense of peace had stolen over her, as if some knowing, invisible hand had swept through her mind, clearing away the clutter of doubt and leaving one simple truth.

She loved him.

The floor of the cave was rough and uneven. Her foot struck a high spot in the darkness and she stumbled forward. He caught her from behind. His hands curved around her ribs as he pulled her back against him to rest against his chest. For a long moment they simply stood there, her warmth flowing into his chilled body. She could feel the pounding of his powerful heart, its rhythm echoing the racing beat of her own.

Black Sun had insisted that he would never want a white woman, but Charity felt his tenderness in the way he cradled her against him, his lips pressing into her wet hair. Had the cave cast its spell on him, as well? Had the labyrinth that separated them become as clear and simple for him as it had for her?

Her hands moved upward and found his, where they rested against her ribs. Arching slightly, she moved them upward so that his palms covered her swollen breasts through the buckskin shirt. He gasped, then moaned low in his throat, holding her close as they swayed in the darkness. Where her hips nested against his thighs, she felt him stir and harden, pushing against her in a long, jutting ridge. Charity's legs went liquid. Her head fell back against his chest, eyes closed, lips parting, as she drifted in the delicious sense of anticipation. She was his woman. She wanted him in the most intimate way a woman could want a man. She wanted his flesh against hers, wanted to feel his powerful body pushing inside her, filling her.

Slowly he pulled her around to face him. His hands moved upward, framing her jaw. His eyes studied her face in the dim light. "Charity," he murmured, his voice thick with emotion, "there are things I can't understand, let alone explain. It's almost as if we were meant to be here. If you're afraid—"

She raised a finger to his lips. "No," she whispered. "I don't understand it, either. But if something happens to us, if we don't make it out of here alive, I want to remember this time with you. I want to be with you while I can."

Pushing up onto her toes, she kissed him— tender, nibbling, greedy little kisses that tasted like rain on her tongue. His arms went around her, pulling her close against him. His lips responded, caressing her mouth, her face, her throat with a slow, sensual hunger that turned her molten inside. Black Sun had not mentioned the future. Neither would she. For them, no future could exist. There was only this secret place and the strange enchantment of this night.

Lightning forked in a joyful leap above the canyon as he eased her down with him onto the buffalo robe. Thunder trembled in the air around them as his hands slid the buckskin shirt off her shoulders, tasting her skin, stroking and nibbling her exquisitely sensitive breasts. "We have time," he murmured against the hollow of her throat. "Time enough to pleasure each other as much as we like."

A vague fear seized her. She had married a man to whom pleasure was a sin. Black Sun would soon discover that she was woefully lacking in experience.

"What is it?" He raised himself up on his elbows to look at her, a worried frown on his face.

She felt herself blush in the darkness. "I've never—I don't know how to give you pleasure."

"You don't?" He laughed, a low, delighted rumble. "Then let me teach you."

What had she expected of love? Her daughter had been conceived amid layers of proper nightclothes in a fumbling, furtive, painful act she only wanted to forget. Now she lay naked and shameless in the arms of a glorious man. The feel of his skin, gliding silkily against her own, awakened shimmering currents that rippled through every nerve in her body. For the first time in her life, Charity felt completely alive, completely free—and suddenly she knew there could be no going back to the woman she'd been before she'd met him. Not ever.

Touching him was as natural as breathing. They lay on their sides in a loose embrace as her hands explored his broad chest, finding tiny nipples that shrank and hardened just as her own did when she stroked them. Her fingers traced the long, clean line of his backbone, flanked by steely bands of muscle. They found the hard little diamond shape at the base of his spine and brushed the leather thong that held his loincloth in place, then hesitated.

His thumb stroked a path along her cheek. "Where do want to touch me, Charity? Touch me anyplace you like."

She felt herself blushing again. Her fingers tugged lightly at the thong. With a deft twist, he released the knot and the loincloth slipped to the buffalo robe.

The heat surged into her face. "Oh…" she murmured.

Capturing her hand, he lifted it to his face and pressed a kiss into her palm. "Don't be afraid," he whispered, moving her hand down along his smooth-muscled belly. "Nothing will hurt you, I—"

He gasped as her fingers closed around him. He was as hard and smooth as polished hickory, cloaked in the softness of a rose petal. She could not get enough of touching him, holding him, hearing his breath quicken when her fingers moved. Bolder now, she explored lower, balancing his hanging weight in her palm. He groaned, lifted her hand away and kissed it again. "Enough for now," he muttered. "Lie still, Charity."

Shifting, he leaned above her. His long hair had come unbound. It hung down over his shoulders, the ends of it brushing her breasts. A lightning flash illuminated his body, casting the scars that streaked his golden chest into stark relief. She yearned to know the story behind each and every one of those scars, but there would be no time for that—no long, lovely days and nights together, no years of growing old in each other's company.

She loved this man to the depths of her soul, but she knew better than to speak of love now. Words could not bind him to her. They would only cause more pain when the time came for them to part.

Black Sun bent and kissed her mouth. She pulled him down to her, hungry for all he could give her. His hand eased lower, stroking her belly and gliding down to her moisture-slicked thighs. Sensing what he wanted, she let her legs part. His fingertips explored the hidden folds and hollows to find the swollen center of her need. She moaned as he caressed her, floating on waves of bursting sensation. She arched against his hand, gasping, needing more, needing all of him.

Breathing deeply, he shifted his body over hers, then paused, lingering above her in the darkness. "The baby—" he rasped, as if suddenly remembering. "Are you healed, Charity?"

"Yes..." she whispered frantically. "Yes!"

He glided into her in one long, smooth thrust. Charity had expected pain, but there was none, just the wonder of their joined bodies and the feel of moving with him, deeper, deeper, until the whole world seemed to shatter into rainbows. Black Sun gasped, shuddered and gathered her close. They lay quietly, holding each other as the storm passed from the canyon, leaving the sky washed clean and swimming with stars.

Black Sun lay still until first light, cradling Charity in his arms as she slept. They had come together three times in the night, each joining more tender and poignant than the last. Deliciously spent, she had finally drifted into slumber. But he had remained awake, his senses alert, his thoughts churning.

Destiny, it seemed, had brought them to this place and made them lovers. But they could not depend on the canyon to protect them. Their time of safety was running out. If the *Siksika* discovered them here, they would be trapped, with no escape.

The sooner he got Charity and her baby out of here, the better. But should they try to slip past the *Siksika* in the darkness, or would it be wiser to wait for the camp to break up and move on? It would be up to him to weigh the risks and make the choice.

Easing his arm out from under her, he sat up. With the storm gone and the new day approaching, there was no time to waste. First he would scout the mouth of the canyon for signs that anyone had entered, even though he wasn't apt to find anything after the storm. Then he would circle the camp to look for his horses and check for fresh hides and meat, to see if the braves had found good hunting. If game was as scarce for them as it had been for him, they'd be more likely to move on.

His loincloth and leggings lay tangled beneath him on the buffalo robe, where they had fallen in the night. He reached for them, then hesitated, looking down at Charity's sleeping face and remembering the sweetness of their loving. Her lips were soft pink in the waxing dawn. The memory of those lips and that warm, willing body triggered a rush of heat to his groin. Even now, he was hard and ready, aching to have her again.

Last night had held a curious magic, as if their bodies had been possessed by spirits other than their own. But this morning, Black Sun was fully himself. He wanted her with a raw need that had nothing to do with dreams or destiny or sacred caves and thunder spirits. He wanted to hold her every night of his life, to fill her with his seed and to cradle their children in his arms, to grow old with her in the wonder of each passing day.

But even now, in the softness of dawn, Black Sun knew that he would lose her.

Even if the dream hadn't told him, he would know the truth from simple, cold reasoning. Charity could no more live as an Arapaho than a fish could live as a bird. And he would not join her people to suffer a life he already knew and despised.

As for this morning... A resigned smile tugged at Black Sun's lips as he heard the baby stirring in her cradleboard. Soon she would be fully awake and squalling for her breakfast. It was just as well that he had not acted on his earlier impulse.

He lingered long enough to brush a stray curl back from Charity's warm, pink cheek. She smiled and sighed at his touch but did not awaken. For the space of a breath he gazed down at her, aching with gratitude for what she had given him. Then, shifting his thoughts to the day ahead, he gathered up his clothing, rose to his feet and walked out onto the ledge.

Last night's rain had drenched the canyon. The aspens sagged under the weight of dripping water, the lower rocks were slick with mud that would flake off in the sun, and the shallow cave was soaked to the top. Lightning had struck an ancient pine on the upper rim of the canyon. The huge tree stood splintered and naked, a pair of ravens perching on one broken limb.

The trail down the cliff was slippery but passable. Black Sun moved with care, scanning the canyon as he descended. Where the canyon widened, the storm had spread a fan of muddy water. If the camp had been flooded, that might give the *Siksika* reason to leave early.

Cutting up a side slope, he reached a van-

tage point where he could look down on the
camp. His heart sank as he realized the flood
had missed the high ground where the lodges
stood. Except for some meat racks that had
been broken and scattered by the wind, the
camp appeared undamaged. But at least he
could see no signs that the hunters had brought
down game. If meat was scarce here, or if the
Siksika meant to hunt elsewhere, they might
not be staying long.

Except for a few shaggy dogs rummaging
for food scraps, the camp was quiet. Along
the edge of the trees, Black Sun could see the
horses, bunched in a makeshift corral. His own
two animals, securely hobbled, were among
them. Black Sun weighed the wisdom of taking
them now and decided against it. It was nearly
daylight and the dogs might bark an alarm. He
would plan another, earlier foray tomorrow,
after he had scouted out a hiding place.

For now, there was little to be done except
to return to Charity and wait. The thought
of being with her again lightened his steps
as he zigzagged down the slope toward the
creek bed, avoiding open ground where the
mud would show his tracks. Danger was everywhere now, but the time that remained for
them in the refuge above the waterfall would

be treated as a precious gift. They would fill the days with good talk and the nights with tenderness, and he would carry the memory with him forever.

He reached the creek and stepped into the water, leaping from stone to stone to hide his trail. The willows were flattened and coated with mud from the storm. But the sun would soon warm them back to life. By the end of the day, the canyon would be fresh and green and alive with birdcalls.

In the camp, the *Siksika* were beginning to stir. The wind carried sounds to his ears—the wail of a baby, the shrill, scolding voice of an old woman, the yelp of a dog.

Black Sun's foot slipped on a wet stone. Adjusting his balance, he glanced down at the bank where the flooding creek had washed up a scattering of leaves and sticks. That was when he saw it—an object half buried in the mud. Heart racing, he reached down and worked it free.

It was a miniature arrow, no longer than his forearm. Clumsily fashioned, it consisted of little more than a feather tied to the end of a sharpened stick—the sort of toy that would be made by a child who wanted to play at hunting.

A child in the canyon.

Chapter Twelve

A chill crept over Charity as Black Sun told her about finding the toy arrow. There was no need for him to explain what it meant. The canyon might be forbidden to the adults in the band, but to an adventurous child it would hold all the allure of a secret playground. And where there was one child, there would be more.

"They'll be back." Charity watched a thread of mist curl above the waterfall. The morning was sunny, the rocks by the pool warm and pleasant to lie on, and until a moment ago she'd been floating on a tide of happiness. But Black Sun's news had drained the brightness from the day.

He sighed wearily. "Yes, unless their elders stop them, they'll be back. And if they come as far as the falls and find the trail up the cliff, they might not be able to resist climbing it."

Charity shifted the wriggling Annie from her lap to the cradleboard. In the long days of Black Sun's absence, she had imagined herself charging painted warriors with her spear and forcing them back over the cliff. But she couldn't imagine doing the same thing to a child.

"If the children are small—and they must be, judging from the size of the arrow—they won't be likely to venture this far from the camp."

"We can't be sure of that," he said. "And even small children have eyes and ears."

She met his somber gaze across the distance that separated them, thinking how much she loved him. Last night his loving had transformed her. She would have been content to spend a lifetime sharing this little corner of heaven with him; but, even now, their heaven was becoming a place of danger.

"I'm going back down to do some more scouting," he said. "Take Annie up to the cave and stay there until I get back. If you hear anything, just stay where you are and keep quiet."

The knot of worry tightened in Charity's throat. She suppressed the urge to run to his arms for what might be a last embrace. Black Sun was a warrior. The last thing he'd want would be for her to fuss over him. But her eyes clung to him as he disappeared down the path, and she knew she would not take an easy breath until he returned.

The kind of love they'd known last night wasn't meant to last, she told herself. Like other exquisitely perfect things—a flame, a blossom, a rainbow, a sunset—it had been doomed even as it came into being. One way or another, it was bound to end. But please, God, she prayed, not like this, with him simply going off and not coming back, leaving her to imagine the awful things that might have happened to him.

What would she do if he didn't return? The question tormented her, but for Annie's sake she knew she had to have a plan. The safest thing would be to stay where she was and hope the Blackfoot wouldn't come after her. She had food and water, and the weather should be warm for months to come. But sooner or later she would have to start for home, walking with the cradleboard on her back and her provisions in her arms.

Oh, but what was she thinking? Black Sun had been surviving danger all his life. She'd be a fool to worry herself sick over him. He would be back. Surely he would.

Sensing her mother's tension, Annie began to wail. Shushing her frantically, Charity hurried up the ledge to the cave, where the stone walls would muffle the sound.

Although she'd tried every trick she could think of, she had yet to discover the secret of keeping her daughter silent. When Black Sun returned, she would ask him how Indian mothers managed it. But she feared she might already be too late. Teaching an infant not to cry would take time, and with danger closing in around them, time was running out.

Black Sun moved along the creek bed, his body flowing through the shadows. He was still in the canyon but was so close to the camp that he could smell the stew that simmered over the cookfires. He glided closer, scarcely daring to breathe.

Through the willows he could hear the children's voices, laughing and shrieking their make-believe war whoops. He wanted a look at them, but he would need to be excruciatingly careful. Adults moved in ways that were easy to anticipate, but children were as unpredictable as sparrows. If they had dogs with them, the danger would be doubled.

Edging closer now, he could see them on the far side of the creek. He counted three children, all little boys, even younger than his own son. The tallest among them could be no more than five winters old.

One boy had made a bow from a curved stick and a scrap of sinew. As Black Sun watched, the child shot a crude miniature arrow—a match for the one he'd found earlier—into the bushes. Laughing, the boy raced to find it.

Exhaling through clenched teeth, Black Sun slipped back into the shadows. The boys were too young to be allowed far from camp. But if they were to venture deeper and lose their way, or if some anxious parent were to come looking for them...

He suppressed a shudder at the thought of what could happen. He would rather die than harm a child. But what if these little ones saw something and raised the alarm? The canyon was forbidden, but if the *Siksika* knew that strangers had violated their sacred ground, they would not hesitate to swarm in after the intruders.

Only one thing was certain. He could not wait long days for the camp to break up and move. He needed to get Charity and her baby out as soon as possible.

A woman's voice shrilled from the edge of the camp, breaking into his thoughts. Black Sun understood enough of the *Siksika* language to surmise that the woman was calling the boys out of the canyon and giving them a hard scolding in the bargain. He heard the childish mutters as the boys left their playground and returned to the cluster of lodges. The scolding faded as he made his way back through the trees. The canyon might be safe for the rest of the day, but from what he knew of small boys, the youngsters would return as soon as their elders' backs were turned.

Still preoccupied, he climbed the slope to his vantage point for a last look at the camp. At first it appeared that little had changed since dawn. Then he noticed that the women were taking down their drying racks and bundling up their scattered household tools. The hunters had not found meat. The band was preparing to move.

Elated, he watched long enough to be sure of what he was seeing. The *Siksika* would most likely spend the night here in their lodges. At dawn the next day, the women would take the lodges down, load the poles, skins and other possessions onto travois, and then the band would trudge off in a long procession, the men riding, the women and children walking, as they followed the migrating buffalo herds.

Tonight he would need to retrieve his horses and hide them in the foothills. After that, there would be little to do except to keep watch and wait for the *Siksika* to dismantle their camp and leave.

Even the clouds that drifted in over the peaks could not dampen his spirits as he climbed the cliff to the hidden pool. A storm would be welcome. The rain would give him cover while he moved the horses, as well as keep the canyon safe from intruders. It might even give him time to spend in the dark warmth of the cave with Charity in his arms.

The journey ahead would be long, dangerous and miserable. They would be sleeping in the open, living on their meager supplies and whatever they could forage off the land. He was accustomed to such a life, but the hardships would push Charity to the breaking point. By the time they reached safety— *if* they reached safety—she would likely hate him. And maybe that was just as well. It would make their parting easier.

But meanwhile, they had the time that remained to them in this secret canyon. He would do his best to make it a time of tenderness. They would need a few good memories to help them survive the days ahead.

Charity was nursing her baby on the buffalo robe, in the small patch of sunlight that slanted through the cave's entrance. A tall, familiar shadow fell across the floor and she looked up, almost fainting with relief, to see Black Sun watching her.

His warm gaze was like a caress on her bare skin. Yesterday she would have jerked the buffalo robe over her naked breast. Today she warmed beneath his gaze, knowing that the sight of her was giving him pleasure.

He was, she thought, the most beautiful human being she had ever seen. His golden skin glistened with moisture from the waterfall, and his long hair, hastily bound and blown by the breeze, was like a tangled skein of black silk floss. But it was his face that captured her gaze and held it—the fierce, aquiline bones, the flawlessly chiseled mouth that could be both stern and sensual, the eyes like dark pools with coppery glints that flashed below the surface.

His face was gentle now, the features re-laxed, the mouth molded into an easy smile, but worry flickered in the depths of his eyes. He was troubled, she realized, but he was making a show of good spirits for her sake.

"Good news," he said. "They're getting ready to move the camp. Judging from what I saw, they'll be taking down their lodges and packing up tomorrow morning."

"And the children? Did you see them?"

He nodded. "Three little boys, right at the mouth of the canyon. They were no taller than this—" He demonstrated their height with his level hand. "Somebody called them home while I was watching and gave them a good scolding into the bargain."

"So you don't think they're a danger?"

"We'll need to be careful, of course, but with the camp about to move, they shouldn't give us trouble."

Again she read the worried look in his eyes. She knew him too well not to see it. He was thinking of all the things that could go wrong and doing his best to spare her. She loved him for that, but what she really needed from him was the truth.

Annie had finished nursing and fallen into a doze. Charity slipped the leather shirt back onto her shoulder as Black Sun came inside the cave and walked to the low wall where his supplies were stored. "Among my people, it's customary to give every newborn child a gift," he said, rummaging in the bundle. "I have something here that I want to give your Annie."

He reached into the bundle and came up with a small deerskin medicine pouch, no bigger than the span of Annie's little hand. It hung on a soft leather thong. When he laid it on Annie's chest, Charity saw that it was decorated on one side with a sun design, rendered in beadwork so delicate that it made her breath catch.

"This is a treasure, Black Sun," she protested. "How can we ask you to part with such a beautiful thing?"

"Because I give it with respect," he said quietly. "If Annie were Arapaho, it would hold her birth cord to remind her of where she came from. But since that's not your custom, I thought you might want to choose something from this canyon—a stone or a flower, or a bird's feather, whatever you think she might like—as a remembrance of her birthplace."

Because she will never come here again—

that was the promise, wasn't it? The words hung unspoken in the silence until Charity willed them away. Black Sun meant this to be a happy occasion and she didn't want to spoil it.

"Think well about what you choose," he said. "Whatever you put in the medicine pouch will be sacred to her. No one else should touch it or look at it. When you close the pouch, hang it from the hood of the cradleboard where she can see it. As long as she keeps it with her, she will never forget who she is and she will never lose her way."

Charity gazed up at him, struck by something she had failed to notice before now. "Where is your medicine pouch, Black Sun?" she asked. "I've never seen you wear one. Did something happen to it?"

A bitter smile flickered at the corners of his mouth. Sadness and anger smoldered in his eyes. "My white stepfather tore my medicine pouch from around my neck one night and threw it in the fire. My mother tried to save it, but she burned her hand before he knocked her away." His mouth tightened. "Without it, I've lost my way more times than I can count. And I've spent half my lifetime trying to remember who I am—or who I should be. Let's hope your Annie will have better luck."

Charity sat speechless as Black Sun's simple story sank in. Since the day of their first meeting, she had struggled to understand the silent rage that smoldered inside him. Even last night, when he'd told her the story of his mother's death, she'd sensed that, for all the grief and pain, the heart of his anger lay even deeper. Now, at last, she had her answer. Not only had the white man abused Black Sun's mother, he had also taken away the boy's most precious right—the right to grow up as one of his people.

Black Sun had spent his life looking for the man he would have become if he had not been taken away from his tribe. In his solitude he had reached out for her, but no matter how much she loved him, she would never be able to give him what he needed. If she were to try, she would only make his life more painful and confusing.

Was this what he'd been trying to tell her all along? Even last night, as he was making love to her, she'd sensed that he was holding something back. Now, at last, she understood.

She fingered the beautiful pattern on the medicine pouch. "Thank you," she said. "I'll find something special to put in it before we leave this place."

He shifted his weight uneasily, like a stallion about to wheel and race away. "I need to go down and watch the canyon until it's safe to move my horses," he said. "After I've got them hidden, I'll come back here. Stay out of sight as much as you can. We don't want to take any chances."

"Be careful—" She failed to bite back the words this time. He was going into danger and concern for his safety overshadowed all her other misgivings.

Without speaking, he reached out and brushed a knuckle along her cheek. Then he turned away.

I love you. She could never speak those words to him out loud, but her heart whispered them as he stepped out onto the path that led down to the waterfall. *Come back to me.*

She watched him until he disappeared from sight. What would she do when he was gone for good? she wondered. How could she go back to the white world and behave as if she'd never known him—as if she had never loved him, never lain in his arms? How could she live a lie, when her most precious memories were here, in this canyon, with a man she would love for the rest of her life?

After he had gone, she tucked Annie into

her cradleboard. Only then did she remember that she hadn't asked Black Sun how Indian mothers kept their babies from crying. But as long as they didn't have to sneak past a sleeping camp, it probably wouldn't be important. The fact that the Blackfoot were leaving would make tomorrow much less dangerous.

It was good that they would have tonight, Charity thought—one last night in each other's arms before they left their refuge and descended into a world of hardship and danger. She would give him all her love, knowing it would probably be the last time. Like the Great Thunderbird and his mortal lover, they could only come together in this enchanted place.

Annie had discovered the medicine pouch that Black Sun had laid on her chest. Her exploring fingers fluttered over the beaded surface to tangle in the fringe that decorated the lower edge. Working the pouch loose from the baby's tiny fists, Charity held it up for her to see. Annie's sky-colored eyes widened. She gave a contented little belch and blew a bubble.

There was no question of what would go into the pouch. For days, Charity had wrestled with the problem of where to keep the gold nugget. Now, in her hand, she held the answer.

Reaching beneath the buffalo skin that lined

the cradleboard, she found the nugget. The eagle head shape glittered seductively as she lifted it into the light. Its solid weight in her hand was the weight of Annie's future and her own.

Loosening the drawstring, she slipped the nugget into the medicine pouch. It fit perfectly, as if the small deerskin bag had been created to hold it. Charity pulled the drawstring tight and knotted it. Then she wove the ties through the overhanging headpiece of the cradleboard, so that the beaded sun would dangle in Annie's view. Annie responded to the new object by waving her hands and staring up at it.

Yes, Charity thought, sometimes the best hiding place was in plain sight. The nugget would be safe as long as Annie was safe. And she would have the added advantage of always knowing its whereabouts.

Was hiding the nugget in the medicine pouch a treacherous use of Black Sun's gift? The question troubled her more than she cared to admit. But her first responsibility was to provide for her child. Without the gold, she would have no choice except to move back home with her grandparents and hire herself out as a servant—or, worse, marry another grim old man like Silas. With the gold, if she could sell the mining rights to the canyon, she'd be able to buy a cheerful little home of her own. Annie would grow up in a happy place, with music, dancing and books. She would go to school and have fun with friends her own age. When the time came for her to marry, it would be for love. And she would have every chance to fall in love with someone who could give her a happy life.

Tears blurred Charity's eyes as she fingered the medicine pouch, hefting the weight of the gold inside. There could be no other choice. She loved Black Sun to the depths of her soul. But her first duty was—and would always be—to her daughter.

Black Sun made his way down the canyon, keeping to the shelter of the trees. He had hoped for rain to drive the *Siksika* into their lodges and to cover his presence while he moved the horses, but the dark clouds he'd noticed earlier still hung above the western peaks.

Nerves strung taut, he settled himself behind a deadfall to keep watch while he waited for darkness. He had been feeling edgy since his conversation with Charity in the cave. He'd left with the feeling that something wasn't right between them, almost as if she were holding back some secret. Maybe tonight they could reason things out and come to some kind of understanding.

Black Sun picked up a piece of bark and crumbled it in his fingers. Reasoning only seemed to make matters worse between Charity and himself. When they spoke with their minds, using reason, all their differences came to the surface. It was only when they spoke with their hearts that they became as one. His heart told him he loved her. His heart told him he wanted her at his side forever. But reason told him, again and again, that what he wanted was impossible.

If only he could speak with his grandfather. Four Winds had lived more than eighty winters and was almost blind in the one eye that remained to him. But his mind was still keen, his wisdom as deep and true as the sky itself.

It was Four Winds who had advised Black Sun to undertake this vision quest. What would the old man say when he learned that his grandson had been given, not a vision, but a lost *Nih'oo'oo* woman to care for, and that the two of them had spent a night of love in the sacred cave of the Thunderbird? Would he have the wisdom to understand what had happened? Would he know the words that would heal his grandson's wounded heart?

Glancing up through the pine branches, Black Sun studied the sky. The clouds were moving in now, blown by a fresh wind that smelled of moisture. But it could be long after dark before the storm arrived, if it arrived at all. He could not count on the rain to give him cover while he moved the horses.

How long should he wait here? He was being impatient now, Black Sun cautioned himself. Impatience was never a good thing. He would wait as long as necessary for the best chance to get his horses away from the herd. Only when the animals were safely hidden in the hills would he think about returning to Charity and the night ahead.

Meanwhile he would mount the ridge to the vantage point among the rocks where he could look over the camp. He could wait there until he was sure the *Siksika* had settled down for the night.

He had started up the slope when he heard the babble of childish voices from the creek bed near the mouth of the canyon. The youngsters again. Black Sun sighed. To venture near them would only heighten his risk of being seen. Why not just go on up the ridge and leave them to their play? It would be dark soon. Their parents would be calling them home before they could do any harm.

He struck out for the ridge again, then hesitated, warned by a shrill note in the children's voices. They weren't just playing now. Their cries sounded as if they'd found something— something that excited and alarmed them.

Keeping low, he crept through the underbrush until he was close enough to see them through a screen of willows. The three little boys he'd spotted earlier were there, along with a fourth, older and taller. They were clustered on the bank of the creek, where the water slowed and widened into a deep hole, ringed by tree roots and willows.

The older boy was using a forked tree limb to probe at something in the water. They'd found a fish, Black Sun surmised, or maybe a frog. But they weren't going to catch it with that sweeping, twisting motion of the limb, unless—

The boy gave a shout and pulled his prize out of the water. Black Sun's stomach clenched. It was not a fish, not a frog, but a sodden rag of white cloth that hung dripping from the forks of the limb.

Chattering, the three younger boys crowded

around as the older boy untangled the rag, shook it, and held it up for inspection.

Black Sun's legs weakened beneath him as he recognized Charity's white underdrawers.

Chapter Thirteen

Charity was sitting on the ledge outside her cave, watching the purple shadows of dusk steal over the canyon, when Black Sun emerged at the top of the trail.

"You're back early!" she exclaimed, hurrying down to meet him. "Were you able to get your horses?"

He shook his head. Only then did she realize that he was out of breath. His sides were heaving and his face was ashen.

"Get the baby—and anything else you can carry—" he rasped. "We have to get out of here—now!"

She stared at him in shock. "What—?"

"The children. They found a piece of your clothing in the water!"

"But I didn't—*oh, no!*"

Her stomach lurched as she remembered the day she'd washed her soiled clothes in the stream that flowed out of the pool. The glint of the nugget had distracted her for an instant and she'd let go of her underdrawers. They'd floated away and vanished over the falls. In her excitement over finding gold, Charity had not given them another thought.

"When I left the children, they were running back to camp with their prize," he said. "The *Siksika* know that only white people make cloth. As soon as they realize a white person has violated their sacred canyon, they'll be hot for vengeance. If they follow the stream, it will lead them right to the base of the waterfall!"

The blood had drained from Charity's face. She raced back to the cave, her heart shooting jets of fear through her body. Her fingers shook as she laced Annie into the cradleboard and yanked the carrying straps over her shoulders. She had already bundled most of their provisions in preparation for leaving. Black Sun used the strips of her old petticoat to tie everything together.

Glancing sideways, Charity saw him testing

the strength of his long, braided rawhide rope, jerking sections of it between his hands before coiling it and slinging it over one shoulder. She wanted to ask what he was doing, but there wasn't time. Even now, the Blackfoot could be racing up the canyon, following the course of the creek.

Thunder echoed from the rainless clouds as they hurried down the cave ledge and skirted the pond. Black Sun carried all their provisions, leaving Charity to manage the cradleboard on her back. Only as they reached the top of the cliff trail did the question strike Charity with a force that halted her in her tracks.

"Black Sun," she whispered to get his attention. "How are we going to get out of the canyon?"

"Keep moving," he said. "We've got to get down before they reach the waterfall, or they'll have us trapped. We can talk on the trail."

He led the way along the steep, slippery path that had frightened Charity when she was climbing upward in broad daylight. Climbing down in near-darkness was an exercise in stark terror. Only the awareness of Annie dangling behind her in the cradleboard kept her feet inching safely over the rocks and moss. Where she could, she gripped jutting tree trunks for support. More often than not, her hands were empty.

Black Sun paused to let her catch up with him. "When they come in after us—and believe me, they will—my guess is they'll go straight up the creek to the falls, probably even climb this trail to the cave. When they see that we're gone, they'll likely spread out and search the rest of the canyon."

"But isn't it forbidden for them to enter the canyon?" Charity asked, grasping at straws.

"Not if they think the canyon's been violated by an enemy. And the darkness won't stop them, either, even though they fear the ghost spirits at night. They'll light their torches and stay together, but they won't be stopped." He glanced back at her. "I could be wrong. But do you want to take that chance?"

Even as he spoke, a stray breeze carried the sweet, smoky aroma of pitch pine to her nostrils. Gripping a tree root for balance, Charity looked toward the mouth of the canyon and saw the moving points of light.

"Hurry!" was all she said.

They reached the bottom of the path and crossed the creek without bothering to hide their tracks. There was no time for that now.

They could only hope the Blackfoot wouldn't pick up their trail before morning.

Without a pause, Black Sun headed up the slope toward the high ledges that rimmed the canyon. Charity followed him, breathing hard now. "They've got us trapped! There's no way out of here!" she gasped.

"There's one way—the way I climbed in."

"But you said that was impossible!" she protested, her lungs screaming with effort. "You said no one could get out that way!"

"Yes, I know." His voice was flat and grim. "Pray to your Christian God that I was wrong."

By the time they reached the foot of the ledges, the line of torches was weaving along the creek bed. The canyon was wide at this point and, with the slope factored in, the Blackfoot were a good two hundred yards away. Even so, Charity lived each moment in fear that Annie would cry and be heard. So far, her daughter had been remarkably quiet. But that behavior, Charity knew, could change at any moment.

"Here we are," Black Sun announced in a low voice.

Charity looked up to see that the dark streak she'd dismissed as a shadow had opened into a long, vertical fissure in the ledge. The walls were sheer and smooth, and the opening at the top seemed to touch the sky. That Black Sun had bridged his way down this natural chimney was wonder enough. That he expected to climb to the top, then bring her and Annie up after him, was beyond belief.

Impossible! she thought, though she did not say the word out loud. This was their only hope of escape. The mouth of the canyon was blocked by the camp and tonight that route would be closely guarded. They could look for a hiding place in the canyon, but the Blackfoot, with their superb tracking skills, would be almost certain to find them.

Black Sun had uncoiled his rawhide rope and tied the end of it around his waist. "Hold on to this," he said, passing the coil to Charity. "Play it out as I climb."

She nodded, knowing better than to ask what she should do if he fell. One slip, and all their lives would be over. She could only do what he'd so bitterly suggested—pray.

Her lips moved silently as he braced himself into the crack, his feet against one wall, his naked back against the other. She thought of the rough rock, scraping away his skin. "Take the shirt," she offered. "It will spare your back."

"No." He spoke through clenched teeth as he inched his way upward. She realized then that the layer of leather between his body and the rock would increase his chance of slipping. Only bare skin would give him the purchase he needed.

Little by little he crept upward, bracing with one foot while he slid the other upward, then bracing with both feet while he slid his body into balance. Drops of perspiration stood out on his face and body, gleaming in the faint light. His labored gasps echoed down the hollow space. Charity breathed with him as he disappeared into darkness. Only the slow unwinding of the braided coil in her hand and the darkness of his body blocking out the stars told her he was still climbing.

Seconds and minutes crawled by. Tears trickled down Charity's face as she imagined the pain of his screaming muscles and raw back. Somewhere behind her in the darkness, the torches were weaving their way up the creek. Had the searchers reached the foot of the falls? Had they found the cave?

Lightning flashed above the canyon, followed seconds later by a roll of thunder. She added rain to her prayer. Rain to hide their escape, wash away their trail and douse the torches.

The rain did not come. But the tension on the braided rawhide remained steady as the coil unwound inch by inch.

Suddenly the rope jerked upward and the stars came back into view through the top of the fissure. Charity's knees went liquid beneath her. Black Sun had made it! He had reached the top!

"Now for Annie." His hoarse whisper floated down through dark space. Panic welled in Charity's throat. Since the moment of her birth, Annie had rarely been out of Charity's sight. The thought of sending her baby up into that blackness left her sick with dread.

"Tie her on, Charity!" Black Sun's voice was urgent. "Hurry!"

Charity glanced back down the slope. She could see the moving torches like a procession of fireflies along the creek.

Lowering the cradleboard, she tightened the lacings that held Annie in place. Then she looped the rawhide rope around the headpiece, passed it through the carrying straps and kissed her daughter's golden head. "Ready!" she whispered.

Her fingers clung to the cradleboard until

it rose out of her reach and vanished into the black passage. The upward trip was swift and easy. Annie gurgled all the way, clearly enjoying the adventure. By the time the rope came back down empty, Charity had the bundled provisions ready to be hauled to the top.

A thread of nervous sweat trickled between her shoulder blades as she waited for the rope to come down one last time. She had always been terrified of heights. The thought of hanging in the darkness, suspended on a leather rope no thicker than her finger, was enough to make her stomach roil. She did not have the reach or the body power to brace her legs and back against the rock and inch her way up as Black Sun had. She would have to depend on the strength of the rope, her ability to hang on and his ability to lift her.

She remembered his hands, testing the braided rawhide as he coiled it, pulling it section by section through his strong brown fingers. Would he have done that if he'd had full confidence that the rope would hold her?

When, after nearly a minute, the rope had not come down again, a new fear began to curl its tendrils along her nerves. What if something had happened to Black Sun and Annie?

Or what if he'd simply taken flight from the danger and left her here alone?

But she was being foolish now. Black Sun had earned her trust by taking care of her and Annie. Then, when she'd asked him for more, he had opened the door to the darkness in his soul. How could she not trust such a man? He would fight to the death before he'd desert her.

Seconds later, the rope dropped from the rim of the canyon. Charity saw that he had fashioned the end of it into a sling to support her hips. "Get it around you! Hurry!" His voice was an urgent whisper down the black chimney of rock. Charity glanced over her shoulder to see that half a dozen torches had separated from the rest and were moving up the slope, coming fast. Had they heard something? But the answer to that question was pointless, Charity told herself. If she lost her courage now, she would never see Annie or Black Sun again.

Looping the sling around her hips, she sank into it. The rope stretched and sagged. How could it hold her all the way to the top? She would never make it as dead weight, Charity realized. Somehow she would have to use her own strength to support herself against the rock.

"Don't worry, I've got you." Black Sun's voice was calm. Too calm, she thought. "Put your feet against the rock," he said. "Walk your way up while I lift you. Use your hands, too—easier to move you that way—" His voice grated with effort. The rope stretched and quivered as he pulled it upward.

Charity felt herself moving. She pushed her feet against the sheer wall of rock, trying to imagine herself walking upward like a fly. Where she could reach and find the minuscule handholds, she used them to support a little of her weight. Every ounce of strain she could spare the rope might make the difference between life and death.

Up, up, she inched in total darkness, with only a patch of stars at the top. The hammering of her heart seemed to echo off the walls of the fissure. She could not see Black Sun. Most likely he had passed the rope around a tree or rock to create a pulley. He would be standing off to one side of the opening, unless—

The rope slackened for an instant. Charity gasped, all but screaming as it dropped her several feet before it jerked tight again, spinning her in a slow circle before she caught the rock with her feet.

Out of the corner of her eye she glimpsed the torches moving up the slope. The Blackfoot must have picked up their trail. Minutes, even seconds from now, they would reach the fissure. If she was still on the rope when they arrived, she would be a helpless target for their arrows. And even if she made it to the top in time, the Indians would see the footprints and know where their quarry had gone. It wouldn't take them long to climb the fissure, as Black Sun had done, or to circle around the mouth of the canyon and mount the outer slope to the rim.

What if they were already there? What if they'd taken Black Sun and Annie and were pulling her upward, ready to seize her, too? Images of brutal, brown hands flashed through her mind. She began to shake uncontrollably, hanging helpless on the rope.

Sheet lightning whitened the edge of the sky. Thunder, still distant, rumbled in its wake. Oh, if it would only rain. Sweet, pouring, drenching gray rain would be so welcome. But her life had been short on miracles, Charity reminded herself—unless she counted Black Sun's finding her beneath the burned wagon.

And Annie—she was her own kind of miracle. Both of them were up there waiting for her. She had to believe that and climb up to them.

Her feet found the rock and pushed off. Her hands found invisible holds that could only be detected by touch. Slowly, inch by inch, she moved toward the top of the crack.

The starry space above her head grew larger and opened. She was clambering up the rocks now, no longer dependent on the rope. Black Sun's strong hands seized her wrists, pulling her up beside him. He was all right. Annie was all right. Charity sank to the ground, her legs like jelly.

Black Sun gave her a few seconds to rest while he coiled the rope. Then he lifted the cradleboard and held it so Charity could slip her arms through the carrying straps.

"Come on!" Scooping up their provisions, he headed up the ridge. Still breathless, she scrambled after him. He kept to the rocky outcrops, where they were less likely to leave tracks. For Charity it was an agonizing effort, but Black Sun did not slow down and she didn't ask him to.

"Where...are we...going?" she panted, stumbling as her foot slipped.

"There's a rock slide this way. We can go

down without leaving a trail. When we get to the bottom, you and Annie will need to hide while I go after the horses."

Charity swallowed hard. As long as Black Sun was nearby, she felt protected. But he would be leaving her alone in a night filled with enemies—alone with a baby who had never learned to be silent.

Black Sun's last sight of Charity, huddled with her baby in the darkness, had all but torn him apart. He had concealed them in a hollow, beneath the tangled roots of a massive pine that had blown partway over in last night's storm. She had looked so frightened and yet so trusting as he'd laid branches in place to conceal the entrance to the hiding place. Both of them had known that her life and her child's life depended on his swift return with the horses. He could not bear to think about what would happen to them if he failed.

Crouching low in the trees, he peered through the darkness at the shifting forms of the ponies. He would have to move quickly, but first he needed to make sure the herd wasn't guarded. With luck, the excitement in the canyon had drawn all the braves and young men into the chase. But Black Sun had learned never to depend on luck.

Moving as fast as he dared, he made a cautious circle of the herd. The ponies were corralled in a small grove of aspens. No one was standing guard, but a waist-high circle of rope around the grove kept them together. The leather hobbles on their legs prevented them from jumping over the rope and going off on their own.

Edging closer, Black Sun picked out his own dun buffalo pony among them, as well as the sturdy, spotted packhorse. He had broken and trained them both, and he would do his best to get them back. But if things got dangerous, he would take any animals he could lay his hands on and make a fast retreat.

For a moment he hesitated, weighing his choices. He had planned to take the horses so discreetly that the *Siksika* wouldn't notice their absence until morning. But that was before they'd discovered the invasion of the canyon. Now, he calculated, the more damage he could inflict, the better.

A moist wind raked his hair as he withdrew his knife and slipped toward the rope barricade. Thunder rumbled above the canyon as he hacked through the barrier rope and let it drop to the ground, creating a wide gate for the escaping ponies. Separating his own horses, he freed their legs and tethered them to a sapling while he used the blade to slice through the hobbles of any remaining horses he could reach. If he let them scatter quietly, they would have time to travel farther and take longer to round up. But creating a commotion now would lure the braves out of the foothills and—he could only hope—away from Charity's hiding place.

The decision took him no more than the space of a breath. Seizing a fallen limb in one hand, he sprang onto the back of his dun buffalo horse. With his knees gripping the horse's flanks, he charged into the milling herd, shouting a war cry and brandishing the limb like a whip. The ponies shrieked and bolted as he lashed at their rumps, driving them in a wild stampede, straight toward the *Siksika* camp.

As the leaders crashed into the outermost lodges, Black Sun wheeled his cat-footed mount and raced back toward the place where he'd tethered the packhorse. He would be faster with the buffalo pony alone, but he would need both animals for the long journey east with Charity and her baby.

Snatching up the packhorse's lead rope,

he pressed himself low over the dun horse's neck and headed for the wooded foothills. He knew better than to go directly back to the spot where he'd left Charity. If anyone was following him, his trail could lead them right to her. Instead he would make a circle up the slope and cut back down along the rock slide, only approaching her hiding place when he knew it was safe.

He was just swinging the horses uphill when the arrow struck him from behind. He heard the singing sound of it and, almost at the same instant, felt it strike and enter the flesh above his shoulder blade. The deep, searing pain was so intense that he almost fainted.

Somehow he managed to stay on the horse. He could no longer guide the animal, but he tightened the grip of his knees and wrapped his arms around the surging neck. Gritting his teeth against the pain, Black Sun hung on with all his waning strength as they galloped into the night.

The darkness was alive with small, scurrying sounds. Crickets chirped in the tangled undergrowth, their chorus a high-pitched drone that grated on Charity's nerves. From its perch on an overhanging limb, an owl called again and again, its voice like the cry of a lonely ghost. A coyote yipped mournfully from a distant hilltop.

Charity shivered beneath the buffalo robe she'd unfolded to keep herself and Annie warm. Her hand felt for the small knife she had bound to her leg, within easy reach. How much time had passed? An hour? Two? The minutes had crawled by so slowly that it could have been days. She had nursed her daughter twice while she'd waited, and still Black Sun had not returned. Now Annie was growing fussy again.

Charity opened the buckskin shirt and put the baby to her breast. What was happening out there in the night? Had Black Sun been hurt or captured, even killed? Could he be leading the enemy away from her, or was he still waiting for the right time to free the horses?

And where were the Blackfoot? Had the moving torches swarmed to the ridge where they'd climbed out of the canyon? Had the trackers found their trail in the darkness?

Charity shuddered beneath the buffalo robe as she remembered the stories Rueben Potter had told around the campfire. The Blackfoot, he'd declared, could track a beetle over sheer rock by moonlight. And once they picked up a trail, they never lost it, not even in a storm.

Surely Rueben had been exaggerating. But that didn't mean she and Annie were safe. Even now, the warriors could be out there in the darkness, picking up the signs—a broken twig, an overturned rock, any small thing that would lead them to the hiding place beneath the tree.

Rueben had told other stories about the Blackfoot, as well—tales so gruesome that Silas had ordered the women into the wagons where they couldn't listen. But even then, Charity had pressed her ear to the canvas, unable to tear herself away. The mountain man's descriptions of unspeakable torture had given her terrifying dreams. Now, if she and Annie were taken, those nightmares would become real.

Thunder boomed overhead like the laughter of some malicious spirit, teasing her with the promise of rain that never came. Oh, where was Black Sun? Why hadn't he come back for her?

He had told her to stay in her hiding place and not to come out for any reason. But what if he never came back? What if he was lying somewhere out there, injured or dead? Or worse, what if the Blackfoot had taken him alive?

Stop it! she ordered herself. Black Sun would come back. And if he didn't, she would find a way to get herself and Annie to safety. She was strong and resourceful, and she knew enough about the sun, moon and stars to find her way east. If she had to, by heaven, she would walk all the way to the Missouri River with her baby on her back.

But her heart would ache for Black Sun every step of the way.

Annie had stopped nursing and was lying awake, sucking her thumb. Charity laid her back in her cradleboard and tightened the lacings. Everything would be all right, she told herself. She had to keep believing that or she would die of fear.

She settled back against a massive tree root. Only then did she realize that she could no longer hear the crickets. She could no longer hear the owl or the coyote, or the faint rustlings among the leaves. Except for the sound of Annie's contented sucking, the night had fallen into absolute silence.

Charity felt gooseflesh prickle along her arms and raise the hair on the back of her neck. Wild creatures, even the smallest, had senses that told them when danger was near. Their silence was a warning.

Straining her ears, she listened. At first she heard nothing. Then the sound of voices drifted down the slope toward her.

They were young men, she guessed from the pitch of their voices, maybe the same ones who'd attacked the wagon train. They were talking and laughing, making no effort to be still. Judging from what Charity could hear, there were no more than two or three of them. But there might as well be a hundred. If they found her hiding place, their numbers would make no difference.

Closer and closer they came, their careless talk punctuated with hoots and giggles. Clearly they hadn't picked up her trail. But they seemed to be headed straight for her hiding place.

Stretching upward, she could make out the glow of a guttering torch as it bobbed closer through the trees. Scarcely daring to breathe, she covered her own head and Annie's with the buffalo robe so their pale faces and hair would not catch the light. The sound of Annie chomping on her thumb seemed to fill the darkness around them. Charity weighed, then rejected, the idea of trying to quiet her. The small sucking noise blended with the night. Heaven willing, the rowdy young men would not even notice it. But if Annie were to cry…

Charity could not even bear to finish the thought.

The braves were near the uprooted pine tree. She could hear them teasing each other as they stumbled over one another's feet. One of them paused to relieve himself. Charity could hear the steady stream splashing into the dead leaves that covered the ground. Her hand slid the small knife out of its wrappings. She gripped its hide-wrapped haft, ready to fight to the death for her baby if they discovered her. She did not dare uncover her eyes to look, but her ears told her they were close enough to reach down among the tree roots and seize her hair.

Her pulse thundered in her ears, filling the dark space beneath the buffalo robe. Annie's little chomping noises sounded as loud as the snort of a horse. She was sucking harder now, frustrated, perhaps, that the thumb gave her no nourishment.

The braves, however, did not appear to notice. Their voices were fading. Yes, thank heaven, they were walking away. Charity felt the cold sweat of relief break out on her skin.

The danger had passed! She and Annie were safe! Now if only Black Sun would get here with the horses…

Annie chose that moment to spit out her thumb and break into a full-bodied wail.

Chapter Fourteen

Charity's hand clapped instinctively over her daughter's mouth. Rueben Potter's stories flashed through her mind—the Indian mothers who'd suffocated their crying babies to keep their people from being found and massacred. Now, as never before, she understood the fear—and the love—that would trigger such a desperate act.

But she had no intention of smothering her own child. There was no one else here to save but herself, and she would fight to the death before she would let the Blackfoot touch one hair on Annie's golden head.

"Hush...hush..." she whispered, clutching

the squirming, fussing baby to her shoulder. "It's all right, Little One. Don't cry."

But Annie had sensed her mother's fear. She began to squall in earnest, butting her head against Charity's shoulder. Charity pressed the tiny face against her breast, hard enough to muffle the sound but not to block Annie's breathing. Straining her ears, she could hear the two braves coming back toward her, speaking now in short, jerky exclamations. They had heard, of course. How could they fail to hear such a racket?

A cold breeze swept down from the ridge, filling her nostrils with the smell of moisture. Thunder echoed along the peaks, but Charity knew better than to hope for rain. Tonight, the clouds and thunder had offered nothing but unfulfilled promises. Once she had almost believed Black Sun's story about the great Thunderbird. She had viewed the storms in the canyon as a sign that some mysterious spirit was watching over them. But no longer. Her miracles had deserted her in this dark forest, leaving her with nothing to depend on but her own pitiful resources.

Peering from under the edge of the buffalo robe, she could see the reddish glow of the torch. It was no more than twenty paces away.

Seconds from now, they would find her hiding place.

With her free hand, she clutched the knife Black Sun had left with her. It wasn't much of a weapon, and she wasn't very strong, but she had the ferocity and determination of a mother protecting her baby. They would have to kill her to get to Annie.

Annie's crying had subsided to a mewling whimper—too late to make any difference. Charity laid her gently in the cradleboard, covered her with the smaller buffalo robe and eased her back among the roots, where the shadows would hide her. Then, knife ready, she shifted to a crouch that would allow her to leap at her attackers. She could only hope that, if they took her, Black Sun would return in time to find Annie and get her to safety.

The glowing torch moved closer and stopped. Like a malevolent red eye, it probed the darkness, moving along the trunk of the tree, toward the roots. Charity's muscles tensed as the light moved closer. Her hand locked around the knife, ready to strike.

From somewhere in the trees, an owl hooted. The torch swung abruptly in the direction of the sound. Charity heard a nervous laugh from one of the young men, followed by the distant rumble of thunder. Raindrops began pattering down, softly at first, then in a sudden torrent. Rain poured from the sky, dousing the torch and plunging the forest into darkness.

Charity could no longer see the two young braves, but she could hear them. They were shouting at each other in an effort to be heard above the storm. Although Charity didn't understand a word of their language, it was clear enough that they'd decided to abandon their search. She slumped against a tree root as their voices faded into the rainy night. The knife tumbled from her limp fingers.

Annie was whimpering. Charity picked her up and hugged her fiercely. Another miracle had occurred, or so it seemed. She and Annie were alive because of the rain. But Black Sun was still out there somewhere in the storm—hurt, maybe, or even dead. She needed one more miracle to bring him back to her.

But what if that miracle failed to happen? She would wait here until the storm ended, Charity resolved. After that, her hiding place would no longer be safe. She would have to take Annie and leave before the Blackfoot returned with torches to search for them.

How would Black Sun find her then?

Pressing herself into the deep shadows, she

held her daughter close. Silently she prayed to Black Sun's gods and to her own—to all who would listen. *Please, please bring him back in time....*

Black Sun awakened in a haze of pain. Ice-cold rain hammered against his back, streaming down his arms where he gripped the horse's neck. His wounded shoulder burned like fire.

What had happened? The last thing he remembered was the arrow striking him and his horse racing away into the darkness. He must have blacked out, for he remembered nothing else, not even the rain, until now.

Biting back the agony, he forced himself to sit up and to look around him. It was deep night, so dark that even the rain was invisible. But the ground appeared flat and open. And he recognized the sound that the rain made when it trickled into long, dry grass. The dun buffalo pony had carried him out onto the plain.

Something moved off to his left. His heart lurched before he heard the snort and recognized the spotted packhorse standing a few paces away. Even when he'd dropped its lead, it had stayed with its companion.

What to do now? Black Sun struggled to

clear his pain-fogged mind. The arrow had gone most of the way through his shoulder. He could feel the hard point of it in front, just beneath his skin—a good thing, which would make it easier to remove when the time came. But for now, the bleeding would be far less with the arrow in place. While he could still ride, he needed to get back to Charity and the baby.

The sky was a mass of roiling black clouds that veiled the moon, the stars and even the mountains from sight. Somewhere in the wooded foothills was the uprooted tree where the two people who had, strangely, become the center of his world were hiding. But with no way to get his bearings, he could lose his sense of direction and wander all night. Morning could find him even farther away from them than he was now.

The wind. As it struck his face, he remembered how it swept down the canyon during storms. If he headed the horse into the wind, that would at least take him toward the hills. With luck, the storm would pass soon and he would be able to find his way back to Charity and her child.

If they were still alive.

He kept the horse to a walk, unable to stand

the jarring pain of a trot or gallop. The sturdy little pack pony, its spotted coat barely visible through the rain, followed behind as if tethered to its trail mate. Time crawled as they plodded through the streaming rain. Every moment's delay, he knew, increased the danger to Charity and Annie. He could only hope that the rain had washed out their trail and kept the searchers under cover. But for all he knew, the rain had come too late.

He peered ahead, trying to see the hills and the canyon, but his vision was beginning to swim. Maybe he was losing more blood than he'd thought. With the rain streaming down his back, there was no way to know. But he sensed that he was getting weaker, to the point of drifting in and out of consciousness.

In desperation he nudged the horse to a trot, then a canter. The pain that flashed outward from his shoulder almost made him scream, but Black Sun clenched his jaw and bore it. The agony was keeping him awake, he told himself. He had to stay awake until he found Charity. His love. His heart. Somehow, if she lived, he would find her. And if she was dead, his spirit would find hers in the rushing wind above the canyon, in the spring, when the great Thunderbird called them home.

He was growing dizzy, losing the strength
to grip the horse with his knees. Through the
thinning curtain of rain he sensed the black
horizon looming ahead of him, a jagged shape
against the sky. The hills—he was almost
there. Soon he would be in the trees, where
he could rest and look for Charity...

His senses were clouding over, his limbs
growing so feeble that he could no longer cling
to the racing horse. As the black mist closed
in, he sagged to the left, slid down the horse's
flank and tumbled to the ground. Jutting from
the back of his shoulder, the arrow caught his
weight with a force that drove the barbed head
upward and outward through the flesh below
his collarbone.

From the edge of unconsciousness he heard
himself scream. And then there was only wind,
rain and long, dark silence.

The sky was still dark when the rain began
to ebb. Gazing up through the dripping tree
roots, Charity could see a sprinkling of stars.
Daylight, she reckoned, was two or three hours
off. By then, she and Annie would need to be
safely away from here.

Hoisting the cradleboard onto her back,
she gathered up the bundled provisions and

climbed out of her hiding place. Before leaving, she found a fallen branch and rubbed out all signs of her tracks. Then she tossed handfuls of dead leaves over the earth beneath the tree to look as if the wind had blown them there. If Black Sun returned to this spot later, he would know from its condition that she had gone of her own free will. It was the only sign she dared leave behind to let him know that she and Annie were alive.

Picking up the bundles again, she set off through the misting rain. Leaving without Black Sun tore at her, but saving Annie had to be her first concern. She could not risk having the braves return and find them.

Every few steps she turned and brushed out her tracks, as she'd seen Black Sun do. She'd learned many things from him in their brief time together—things she must use now to get her daughter to safety. If Black Sun was dead—and her hopes had bled away with each excruciating hour of the night—she would always remember that he had given his life for her and for Annie. She would make sure that Annie remembered it, too.

Grief and fear stalked her like gloomy monsters that would leap on her and tear her to pieces if she turned around to face them. Later, she would try to sort out all that had happened. For now, she had no choice but to keep moving.

The sky had begun to pale by the time she reached the open plain. She would head east, keeping to the edge of the trees, Charity resolved. And she would make herself believe that Black Sun was alive and that somehow they would find each other. Otherwise, she would never have the courage to go on.

An hour into her journey, as the sky was fading to silvered rose and the birds were stirring from sleep, Charity saw the horses. The sleek dun and the stocky little pinto were standing side by side in the grass, about a dozen paces beyond the trees. They raised their heads, their sharp ears pricking forward as they saw her.

Where was Black Sun?

Heart pounding, she crept toward them, fearful that they would bolt before she could catch them. "Easy," she murmured. "Easy now."

The dun horse snorted, showing the whites of its eyes, but neither of the animals moved. They stood as if rooted to the spot, almost as if they were guarding something. Scarcely daring to breathe, Charity edged forward.

The first thing she saw was the point of the arrow thrusting above the seed heads of the tall grass. Then, as she came closer, she saw Black

Sun, his eyes closed, his dark hair spilling like blood on the rain-soaked ground.

Was he alive? Setting the cradleboard and provisions close by, she crumpled to her knees beside him. Pressing her ear to his chest, she heard the steady throb of his heart, beating in counterpoint to her own skittering pulse. He groaned softly, as if aware of her touch, but his eyes did not open.

His shoulder was bleeding where the arrow emerged from his flesh, but only a little. The arrow itself was likely stopping the blood. She could remove it by cutting off the arrowhead and pulling the shaft the rest of the way out. But that could trigger serious bleeding, something she dared not risk until she could move him to a safe hiding place.

But she could at least cut off the arrowhead and remove the chance of his falling or rolling on it. Taking out her small knife, she braced the barbed bone arrowhead with her fingers and hacked through the shaft below the sinew that bound it in place. There was no way to do it without putting painful pressure on the wound. A shudder went through Black Sun's body as the tough, smoke-cured reed snapped and parted. He groaned again and opened his eyes.

Charity bent forward and brushed his chilled lips with her own. "Listen to me," she murmured. "I've cut off the arrowhead, but we need to get you someplace safe before I can take the shaft out. I can't carry you, and I can't drag you without hurting your shoulder. Can you get up?"

His lips moved, straining to form each syllable. "Horse...little one...here."

The horses had backed off, but neither of them had gone far. Charity caught the packhorse's tether and led the sturdy animal close to his side. The little pinto snorted and twitched its ears but didn't try to pull away.

"Help me up..." Black Sun mouthed the words. He struggled to rise, rolling onto his uninjured side and pushing his elbow beneath him. As he wrenched himself upward, Charity worked her shoulder beneath his good right arm and helped him. Gasping, he staggered to his feet and sagged against the side of the packhorse.

Charity moved behind him, freeing his arm to circle the horse's solid neck. Only then did she see the blood that had streamed and clotted down his back. The arrow had done far more damage than she'd realized. There was no way of knowing how much blood Black Sun had lost.

The blazing rim of the sun edged above the horizon, casting long fingers of light across the rain-glimmered grassland. There was no time to lose. Even now the Blackfoot could be moving along the foothills, their sharp eyes scanning the plain. Getting into the trees and out of sight was an even more urgent task than tending his wound.

Shouldering the cradleboard and provisions, Charity moved close to Black Sun. By leaning heavily on the packhorse, he was able to stay on his feet and walk. But his face was deathly pale and his jaw clenched against each jarring movement. Nickering anxiously, the dun horse ambled behind them.

Black Sun listened in grim silence as Charity told him how close the braves had come to finding her hiding place. He said little in return except to relate, in labored phrases, how he'd come to be shot while he was escaping with his horses. Only the storm had kept his pursuers from finding him in the darkness.

"We have to get away from here," she said. "Now that it's light, they could already be looking for us. Can you ride?"

"I can—once we get this arrow out and the

bleeding stopped—won't be much good till then."

Charity nodded. "Then we'd best start looking for a place to do it."

The next few hours passed in a blur. There was the frantic search through the wooded foothills that ended, finally, beside a gurgling stream overhung by a thicket of willows. There was Black Sun's gasp of restrained agony as she pulled the arrow shaft out of his shoulder, and the nightmarish spurt of blood—so much blood.

It had taken a small eternity to stop the bleeding. Even with Black Sun trying to soothe her fears by telling her the blood flow was cleaning out the wound, Charity had been terrified that he would bleed to death. She had closed her eyes and prayed as she'd held compresses of herbs and cloth tightly against both sides of his shoulder. She had come so close to losing him last night. She could not lose him now.

After the wound had been packed with crushed elder bark and tightly wrapped with strips salvaged from Charity's petticoat, Black Sun had rested only for as long as it took for her to nurse Annie. Then he'd insisted that they move on.

Now, as the sun rose in the sky, she rode behind him on the tall dun horse, her arms wrapped around his waist to keep him awake and upright. He was still in some pain and so weak that he swayed with every turn of the horse. She gripped him tightly, holding him close to her, as if she could will her own strength to flow into his body. It was all she could do to keep herself from tracing a line of kisses down his taut, golden back. Soon, when they parted, she would lose him for good. But for now he was her own, and she would savor every moment of their time together.

He smelled of rain and blood, but the warmth and color had returned to his skin. Black Sun was strong, Charity reassured herself. He would heal in no time at all. By the time they found a place where he could safely leave her, he would be entirely well. The thought was bittersweet.

Their senses were on constant alert for signs of the Blackfoot, but aside from the distant smoke of their morning campfires, there was no sign of them. Had the braves given up the chase and decided to move on with the rest of the band? There was no safe way to find out, but Black Sun pushed the horses as if he expected the warriors to appear on the horizon at any time.

He pushed himself, as well, so hard that Charity worried about him. He needed rest, but until they were safely out of Blackfoot territory, there could be no rest for either of them.

Trussed in her cradleboard and lulled by the motion of the horse, Annie was remarkably content. Charity nursed her on horseback, cradling her against Black Sun's solid back. The moments passed sweetly then, with the three of them riding close together, fitted like spoons. Charity etched the details into her memory—the green-gold hues of spring sunlight and fresh sprouting grass, the motion of the horse, the tug of the baby's mouth at her breast, the warm nesting of her knees against the backs of Black Sun's legs.

Late in the day, they skirted a valley where the charred remains of five wagons stood in a blackened circle, with fresh spring grass already sprouting up around them. Charity's breath jerked in surprise as she realized she was looking at her own wagon train. She had pushed the massacre so far into the hollows of her memory that, until now, it was almost as if it had never happened. But the sight of those wagons brought it all back—the screams, the smoke, the terror. She began to tremble.

"Don't look," Black Sun said, turning the horse away from the scene. "It's over. There's nothing you can do."

But Charity did look. She could not help but see the debris that was scattered in the grass—tools, burned books, odds and ends that the Blackfoot hadn't judged worth taking. However she glimpsed no bodies, not even bones. Either they'd been dragged off by wild animals or some kindly soul had come along and buried them all. That, or the well-nourished grass had simply grown up and covered them.

"Did you love your husband?" Black Sun asked. They were riding away from the scene of the tragedy now. "I know I have no right to ask, but—"

"My husband was almost a stranger to me," Charity said. "Now that he's gone, it feels as if I never knew him. He was old enough to be my father, and very strict. He didn't allow me to laugh or wear bright colors or sing anything but hymns. And he could be…harsh, especially when I didn't obey him fast enough."

"He hit you? Beat you?" His voice echoed the horror of his past, and she knew he was thinking of his stepfather.

"Not...the way your mother was beaten, no. Just enough to put me in my place, or so he said. Silas had very strong ideas about a woman's place and how to keep her there." A broken sob escaped Charity's throat and she began to tremble again. How many times had she told herself that her marriage to Silas was a proper one—that she needed the discipline, deserved the punishment he meted out? How long had she denied, even to herself, that she was miserable?

"It's my turn to ask the questions now," Black Sun said. "Tell me about your life, Charity. I need to know what brought you here... to me."

As the sun crept westward, she told him everything—her happy childhood, the tragic accident that had killed her parents and the dreary adolescence with her fanatical grandparents that had led, ultimately, to her marriage. "I wanted happiness again," she said. "I wanted love. But those things were too much to ask of a man who belonged only to his God."

By now they had left the valley of death far behind. The sun lay low above the peaks, its slanted rays touching the clouds with flame. Black Sun was silent—resting, perhaps, or waiting for her to tell him more.

But the remainder of the story was more than she could put into words. Her time in the wilderness with Black Sun had opened her to the strong, self-reliant, loving woman she was meant to be. She could never go back to the person she'd been, or to the bleak life she'd led before coming west. And she could never go back, Charity realized, to the confines of so-called decent society with its rules, prejudices and expectations of women. Not even gold would buy her the freedom she wanted for herself—and ultimately, for Annie.

How could she say those things to Black Sun, after the promise he'd forced her to make? How could she tell him that she wanted to stay with him, to share his days and nights and to raise their children here, in his country, surrounded by the sweep of open sky and towering mountains?

If you come back, it will be as an enemy.

His words echoed in her memory, haunting in their bitterness. How could she reach beyond his hatred for whites and show him that she was not the enemy? There were so many things to resolve, and they had so little time left together.

Black Sun's muscles tensed, snapping Charity's thoughts back to their present danger. His attention, she realized, was fixed on something in a grassy clearing beyond the trees. Nudging the horse to a trot, he moved closer. Through the deepening twilight Charity could see the recent remains of a small camp, with circles of flattened yellow grass where the teepees had stood. Her pulse leaped in alarm, but Black Sun did not appear to be worried.

"Cheyenne," he said, reading evidence that meant nothing to Charity. "Allies and brothers of my people. We can rest here in safety."

"And the Blackfoot?" Charity asked, scarcely daring to believe him.

"They won't enter Cheyenne hunting territory. It's too risky for them. We can make camp right here."

They tethered the horses and spread the large buffalo robe on the ground beneath a thicket of alders. While Charity nursed Annie and put her to sleep in her cradleboard, Black Sun kindled a small but cheerful fire, the first they'd enjoyed in all their time together.

They were too weary to prepare a meal. To keep up their strength, they chewed a few slivers of the smoked antelope meat. By then it had grown dark outside the circle of their firelight.

Black Sun's face was lined with fatigue. He made a final check of the horses, then stretched out on the buffalo robe and fell instantly asleep. Too agitated to close her eyes, Charity sat cross-legged next to the fire, savoring its warmth as the flames flickered down to glowing coals. Windswept clouds drifted across the face of the waning moon, shadowing a night that was quiet except for the silken rustle of leaves, the whispery music of insects and the deep, even cadence of Black Sun's breathing. He was alive, they were safe, and they were together. For those three things, she was grateful to the point of tears.

Giving in at last to her own weariness, she stretched out next to him on the buffalo robe and pulled the smaller, softer robe over the two of them. His body was warm in the chilly darkness. She nestled close, fitting her own curves and hollows against his. He stirred, sighed and pulled her closer. It was heaven, she thought, lying here in the darkness, enfolded in his sweet masculine strength, protected and protecting. For tonight, it was everything she could wish.

As she lay with her hips curving into his, she felt the hard, swelling rise beneath his loincloth. Instinctively her hand found him beneath the soft leather. She touched him in wonder, feeling her own moisture flow as she stroked him, wanting more of him, all of him.

He groaned, pushing upward against her touch.

"No," she murmured, pressing his chest down with her free hand. "Your wound—"

"I want you, Charity." His voice was raw with need.

Rising above him, she bent down and kissed his mouth. "Lie still, then," she whispered. "I have an idea."

His shaft jutted upward, hard and quivering, the moist, sculpted head catching a glint of moonlight. Straddling his hips with her knees, she lowered herself onto him. He gasped as he slid inside her. His hands seized her hips, pulling her all the way down, filling the place that was made for him. Feeling the contact in every exquisite nerve, she began to move. There was no thunder here in the peaceful darkness, no sacred cave, no legend; only a man and woman who needed each other, loving, moving and thrusting until their spirits spun together and burst in an explosion like a sky full of shooting stars.

Black Sun awoke shuddering in the dull gray light before dawn. For the space of a long breath, he lay still, struggling against the dream that had gripped him with the clarity of a vision.

In the dream he had returned to the sacred canyon to find it utterly changed. The cliffs had fallen into heaps of rubble that lay on the canyon floor. The sacred cave and the waterfall had been blasted away, the creek diverted into channels that were banked with ugly heaps of washed gravel.

The animals and birds that had once found safety in the canyon had either fled or died. In their places, white men swarmed like ants, armed with picks and shovels and kegs of exploding powder. Like ants, they had tunneled into the canyon walls, blasting away hunks of the glistening buff-colored stone and carrying it off in their wagons.

The stench that rose above the canyon was the stench of greed as the whites scrambled for gold, hoarding it, fighting for it, dying for it.

Still in shock, Black Sun sat up. He had known, of course, that there was gold in the canyon. But since gold was of no value to his people, he had given it little thought. White men, however, were crazy for gold. If they learned there was gold in the canyon, they would come swarming from all directions. And they would destroy everything.

Was this his vision? This horror that had been as real as anything he had ever experienced?

Taking care not to wake Charity, he eased himself to his feet. His shoulder was stiff and sore, but he felt no sign of fever in the wound. It would heal soon enough. The dream, however, haunted him as if it had been seared into his brain. He had fasted and prayed for a vision that would bind him to his people. Was this his answer—this nightmare of the future, connecting him not to the Arapaho but to the canyon?

Still dazed, he crossed the clearing and checked the horses, seeking comfort in their simple, solid presence. If the dream had been his vision, what did it mean? Was it the canyon's destiny to be destroyed by gold-seeking whites—or would it be his own duty to save it?

Charity was still sleeping when he returned, her sun-colored curls spilling across the buffalo robe. He studied the rose-gold beauty of her sleeping face, remembering the courage and resourcefulness she had summoned to save his life yesterday and the unbridled passion of last night's loving. She was the most magnificent woman he had ever known, and he could no longer imagine life without her. Somehow, Black Sun thought, he had to find a way to make that life possible.

The cradleboard was propped against a nearby log, where Charity could easily reach it in the night. Annie was awake, not fussing, but lying contentedly, her round blue eyes gazing at the fringed amulet pouch that dangled a handbreadth from her little flower-bud face.

Black Sun dropped to a crouch beside her. Reaching out, he extended his forefinger and felt a surge of warmth when her tiny pink fist closed around it.

"Good morning, Annie," he greeted her solemnly. "Are you ready for another day on the trail?"

Her pure eyes studied him, innocent but strangely knowing. To amuse her, he nudged the amulet pouch, lifting it slightly to make it swing.

Its dense weight astonished him. What could Charity have put into the pouch that would be so heavy?

Black Sun's spirit darkened as he hefted the deerskin pouch in his palm while his fingers explored the object inside. It was oddly shaped, like the head of a bird—and small, not much bigger than the end joint of his thumb.

Custom forbade him to untie the knot and look inside the pouch. But that would not be necessary. Only one thing could possibly be that heavy for its small size.

It had to be gold.

Chapter Fifteen

Charity opened her eyes to see Black Sun kneeling next to the cradleboard. He was looking down at Annie, his fingers toying with the amulet pouch that had been his birth gift to her.

Still basking in the warmth of last night's love, Charity stretched and yawned. "You'll spoil me, letting me sleep so late," she said with a happy little laugh.

He looked up at her then and she saw the expression on his face. Her heart turned leaden.

"Why didn't you tell me you'd found the gold in the canyon, Charity?" His voice was like the brittle ice that covers water after a sudden freeze.

She gazed at him, unable to answer. In the past day and night, she'd given no thought to the nugget, or to what she would tell him about it. Now she realized that, in not telling him, she had made the worst mistake of her life.

"Did you think I'd stop you from taking it?" He spoke softly, his tone more damning than if he'd screamed at her. "Is that why you kept it from me? Is that why you hid it in the one place where I'd told you I would never look?"

His eyes stabbed into her like sharpened flints. She knew he was waiting for her answer. But how could she explain that the gold meant nothing to her now, that all she wanted was to stay in the West—with him? After what he'd just discovered, he would never believe her.

"The gold was for Annie," she said. "From the very beginning, when I found the nugget in the water, it was always to be for Annie."

"But you never meant to keep the secret of the gold to yourself, did you? If you had, you'd have told me about it."

She shook her head, feeling sick and trapped but determined to tell him the truth. "Not at first. I was planning to return to the East, as I'd promised, and I knew I'd need money to provide for myself and Annie. The nugget would have given me enough evidence to file a mining claim and sell that claim to the highest bidder."

"You would have sold the canyon? The gold meant that much to you?" His face looked gaunt, almost gray in the pale morning light.

"You knew about it, didn't you?" she asked. "You knew the gold was there all along."

"All the people who call the canyon sacred know the gold is there," he said. "But what good is gold to us? Can we eat it? Can it keep us warm? Can it make medicine to cure us? No, we leave the gold in the rocks and streams, where it belongs. We would never destroy sacred ground to get it, as white men would."

He rose to his feet, turned and walked away. Then, as if he'd decided on another attack, he spun around to face her again.

"I had a dream last night," he said. "A dream about the canyon and how the whites had destroyed it in their greed for gold. Now I believe it was more than a dream. It was the future I saw, and it has already begun. I began it myself when I took a white woman into a sacred place."

"No!" Charity clambered to her feet, reeling as if he'd struck her. "Take the nugget back, Black Sun! Things have changed—*I've changed since I took it! I don't want it anymore!"*

He shook his head, his eyes cold and sad. "What's done can't be undone, Charity. The nugget belongs to Annie now. And even if you swear to keep the secret forever, we both know the gold in the canyon will be found in time, as more whites move west." He sighed, his shoulders drooping in resignation. "Keep the gold. Use it as you planned, to make a new life for yourself. If someone's going to profit from the canyon, better you and Annie than some stranger. As for the rest, I can forgive you for wanting the gold and taking it, but not for trying to hide it from me."

With a final shattering look, he turned his back on her and strode off to tend to the horses.

Charity stared after him, feeling as if every drop of her blood had been drained away. *I love you!* she wanted to shout after him. *The gold doesn't matter! Nothing matters except having a life somewhere with you and Annie!* But those words, she knew, were the last ones he would want to hear from her.

Annie had begun to fuss for her breakfast. Charity fed her while Black Sun, avoiding her gaze, cleared the camp and loaded the horses.

Today he shared the bundled gear and provisions between the two animals, making it clear that Charity and Annie were to mount the packhorse while he sat his tall dun gelding. From now until he left them, he would ride alone.

The sunrise that morning was a glory of amber sky and rose-tinted clouds, crossed by a skein of white snow geese flying north in their elegant *V* formation. The spring grass was a green-gold tapestry, glittering with crystal beads of dew. For Charity, however, there was nothing in her vision but the sight of Black Sun's rigid shoulders, veiled by his wind-tangled raven hair, moving along the trail ahead of her.

She ached to nudge the pinto to a trot, to catch up with him and force him to listen. But what could she say, when the very core of truth condemned her? She had indeed taken the nugget with the idea of filing a claim and selling the mineral rights to the canyon. And she'd kept it hidden for the exact reason Black Sun had stated—the belief that he would try to stop her.

That she'd since changed her mind, that she no longer cared about the gold, meant nothing to him now. She had betrayed his trust, and he would never forgive her.

The days passed in uneasy silence as they followed a path that wound alongside the Oregon Trail. Charity was beginning to recognize things she'd noticed on her way west with the wagon train—a fast-running river with a graveled ford, a rounded knoll, a stand of dead, beetle-infested lodgepole pines.

Even when they made camp, the tension stood like a wall between them. He spoke to her as little as possible, giving brusque answers to the questions she asked. He was never harsh or angry, just so remote that he might as well have been a hundred miles away. *Look at me!* she wanted to shout at him. *Scream at me! Call me names! Anything but this awful silence!* But that, she knew, was not Black Sun's way.

With every day the chance increased that they would meet a wagon train or come to a white outpost where he could leave her and Annie. Their parting would come as a relief, Charity told herself. Anything would be easier to bear than this miserable standoff.

She knew better than to believe such thoughts. But self-deception was easier than facing the truth—that when Black Sun rode away from her for the last time, her heart would begin to die.

The day she'd dreaded came sooner than either of them had expected. Late in the afternoon of the fourth day, they crested a rise that overlooked the Oregon Trail. There, some distance below them, rolling along in single file, were four covered wagons.

Except for its small size, the wagon train looked ordinary enough. When she shaded her eyes and squinted into the afternoon sunlight, Charity could see the teams of big bay draft horses that pulled each wagon. She could see the mounted outriders moving along ahead of the train and behind it. On the seat of one wagon, she glimpsed a figure in a sunbonnet.

Charity had been staring at the wagons for more than a minute before it struck her they were not moving westward. These travelers were headed east.

Why? she wondered with a flicker of uneasiness. Had they parted company with a larger wagon train and decided to turn back? Were they the survivors of an Indian attack, limping their way to the nearest outpost? Or were they simply traders, out to bargain with whomever they met on the trail?

Black Sun had stopped beside her. He gazed down at the wagons, saying nothing.

"They're headed in the right direction," Charity said, trying to sound flippant. "Do you think they'd have room for a woman and a baby?"

At first he did not reply, and for a moment her hopes soared that he would forgive her and ask her to stay. Then he exhaled. "We need to make sure you'll be safe first," he said.

Charity's spirit plummeted once more. "You musn't go down there with me. My husband shot the first Indian he saw out here. These people could do the same."

"And they won't take kindly to seeing you ride in with me, either." Black Sun's words sounded as if they'd been dipped in lye. "It might be best for you to tell them you were captured by murdering savages and managed to escape."

Charity watched him, too heartsick to speak, as he scowled down at the wagons. "We'll keep our eyes on them until they make camp. If things look safe enough, I'll send you and Annie down to them on the packhorse. If you feel comfortable going on with them, turn the horse loose and send him back to me."

"And if I don't?" Charity's voice emerged as a hoarse whisper.

His throat moved as he swallowed. "If you think you should leave them, just mount up and ride the pony back to me. Either way, I'll stay close by until he comes."

She nodded her understanding and they moved down the slope together, keeping to the trees. He was taking great care to see that she and Annie would be safe. Charity knew she should be grateful for that, even though the thought of leaving him tore her apart.

Viewed at closer range, the wagon train looked even more promising. The travelers appeared to be families. Women in faded sunbonnets drove three of the wagons while the men trotted their fine-looking mounts alongside. Charity even glimpsed a long-eared tan hound loping along behind the horses.

Charity kept her silence. She could hardly plead to stay with Black Sun if he didn't want her. It was time she grew up and accepted reality, she told herself. She did not belong in Black Sun's world. Like the Thunderbird and the mortal woman, they could not live together. But unlike the lovers in the legend, there could be no reunion for them in the sacred canyon. There could be no children who would grow up to enrich the earth. Their time together was over.

One thing only was left in her power. She had long since decided not to exploit the gold. She would honor their love with a promise to keep the canyon's hidden riches a secret. That promise would be her final gift to Black Sun.

Dusk was closing in by the time the wagons pulled into a circle and halted for the night. Neither Charity nor Black Sun spoke. It was time to say goodbye.

Black Sun had already divided up the things that each would take. Except for the buckskin shirt, which she needed, Charity had wanted only her own rags and the cradleboard. But he had insisted she take one of the buffalo robes and the smaller knife. He'd also returned Rueben's tiny one-shot pistol, which she'd agreed might be worth something in trade. She had tucked the weapon under the padding in the cradleboard for safekeeping.

Now they faced each other in the twilight. Both of them were mounted, which prevented any attempt at an awkward and heart-rending embrace.

"I'll never forget you," Charity whispered, fighting tears. "You gave me back my life."

"Then live it well," he replied huskily. "Good-bye, Charity Bennett."

He gave the rump of her horse a light slap and before either of them could say another word, Charity found herself moving downhill through the trees, toward the open plain.

Black Sun watched her vanish into the dusk, her pale hair catching the last glint of sunset. He had known all along that this moment would come, that he would lose her, but he had not known that watching her ride away would be like the slow rupturing of his heart.

He would wait and watch, of course. But he knew Charity would not come back. She had too much pride for that, and he had wounded her too deeply.

He'd had every right to be furious with her, Black Sun told himself. After all her talk of trust and honesty, Charity had betrayed him and hidden the truth. When he'd declared that he could not forgive her, he'd meant every angry word. But even then, he'd been wrong. In the days since their quarrel, his heart had forgiven her a hundred times over.

He would remember her with nothing but love.

As for her claiming the gold, it was a battle

he had stopped fighting. He had seen enough
of white people to know that, by the time Two
Feathers was a man, the land would be overrun
by them. If his dream had been a true vision
of the future, the canyon was doomed. Knowing that Charity had used its wealth to make a
better life for herself and Annie would at least
give him some consolation. But it could never
be enough to fill the emptiness in his heart.

During their days on the trail, riding in silence, sleeping apart, he had yearned to take
her in his arms and love away the bitterness
between them. But that would only have made
things more difficult. In taking the gold, Charity had proved that she belonged with her own
kind. He'd had no choice except to send her
back. His pretense of anger was the only thing
that had made it possible to let her go.

Now she was gone, swallowed up by the
darkness. Where the wagons had circled for
the night, he could see the flicker of a campfire. Soon she would reach the white travelers.
A missionary's widow with a fair, blue-eyed
baby—if they were decent people, they would
surely take her in. The packhorse would come
back riderless and he would never see her again.

Easing his tired body off the horse, Black

Sun stretched his limbs, then settled himself on the trunk of a fallen tree to wait.

Charity slowed the horse to an ambling walk as she neared the camp. She needed time to collect her thoughts and to calm—outwardly, at least—her churning emotions. There was also one final task she needed to perform before sending the little packhorse back to Black Sun. She would do that now, while she had time.

The cradleboard hung against her back, suspended from her shoulders by the carrying straps. Slipping it free, she swung it around to where she could reach it with both hands. Annie opened sleepy eyes, gazing up at her in the darkness.

"Someday you'll understand, my little love," Charity murmured as her fingers loosened the knots that fastened the laces of the amulet pouch to the cradleboard. "You and I were never meant to be rich. But that doesn't mean we can't be happy. We can dance and sing for free, and if we work hard, we'll have everything we need, I promise you."

The pouch dropped into her hand. For a moment Charity cradled it in her palm, feeling the rich, seductive weight of the nugget it contained. Then, with an odd lightening of her spirit, she wove the leather laces into the tangled locks of the pinto's mane and tied the pouch securely where Black Sun would be sure to find it. That done, she shouldered the cradleboard once more, blinked away her tears and nudged the horse's flanks.

The aromas of bacon, beans and coffee drifted on the evening breeze as Charity neared the circle of wagons. She could hear faint voices and the sound of laughter. She swallowed the choking fear that rose in her throat. A whole new life lay ahead for her and Annie. She could not turn back now.

Something was spooking the pinto. It snorted and laid back its ears, balking and dancing with every step. Too many unfamiliar smells and sounds, Charity thought. As soon as she knew it was safe, she would dismount and let the stalwart little horse go back to its master.

If only she could go with it.

Outside the circle of wagons, a lantern bobbed in the darkness. As she rode closer, Charity could make out the form of a woman stooping to gather buffalo chips for the fire. Watching her, Charity could not help remembering how many times she'd performed that same task herself.

Not wanting to startle the woman, she slipped off the horse, caught its tether in her hand and then walked forward. "Hello!" she called softly.

The woman raised the lantern and peered into the darkness. The dancing light revealed a plain, middle-aged face crowned by a bristly knot of hair. "Who's out there?" she demanded. "Show yourself afore I sic the dog on you!"

"It's only me and my baby." Charity moved into the edge of the light. Her voice quavered as she forced herself to mouth the words she'd rehearsed. "I—we got away from some Indians. I was hoping we could join you. I'm willing to work for my keep."

"Work, eh?" The woman raised the lantern higher. "That'd be a nice change. Ain't nobody else much inclined to work 'round here exceptin' me. Come on in closer, so's I can have a look at you."

Heart pounding, Charity took a tentative step forward. The nervous horse, however, was in no mood to follow her. Snorting and dancing, the pinto jerked the lead out of her hand and, finding itself free, wheeled and bolted away.

Charity swallowed a cry. The little pinto had been her last link to Black Sun, and now that link was broken. When the horse returned to him, he would go his own way. She would never see his face again.

Now there could be no turning back. She would have no choice but to ingratiate herself with these strangers and hope they would give her shelter.

"Guess that pony of yours didn't like the looks of me!" The woman laughed coarsely as she brought the lantern nearer. "Well, never mind. Some of the boys can round him up in the morning. Here, let's have a look at you, girl. Is that Injun garb the only dress you got?"

"The only one that isn't in rags." Too late, Charity remembered that her old clothes had been rolled up in the buffalo robe on the back of the horse. The garments were unwearable, but their condition might at least have given credence to her story.

"You say you run away from the Injuns? Is that there papoose you're packin' a half-breed?"

A tide of outrage swept through Charity, dizzying in its ferocity. If Annie had been Black Sun's child, she would have been proud of her daughter's heritage and would never have tolerated such language. But the truth was simple enough, and she could not afford to alienate the woman.

"My husband was a missionary," she answered calmly. "He was killed when the Blackfoot attacked our wagon train. This child is his daughter."

"A preacher's widow! Well, I'll be!" The woman snorted with laughter. Holding the lantern close, she peered at Annie. "She looks white enough to me. And you look like you could use a hot meal and a good night's rest. My name's Mamie Sloan, and them that's with me are my boys and their women. Come along and warm your bones at the fire, girl, and you can tell us your story."

Murmuring her own polite introduction, Charity followed the bobbing lantern toward the circle of wagons. There was nothing to fear, she assured herself. Despite her coarse manner, Mamie appeared to be a good-hearted soul. The other travelers were likely the same. They would treat her and Annie with the kindness accorded any stranger in need.

Still, as they neared the wagons, she found herself glancing back toward the wooded hills where Black Sun would be waiting for the pinto to return.

What would he feel when the little horse came trotting riderless up the slope? Relief? Regret? Would he understand when he discovered the pouch with the gold nugget tied into the horse's mane?

Would he forgive her then?

The baby had begun to cry. It was too soon for her to be hungry, but something was clearly bothering her. Charity eased the cradleboard off one shoulder and shifted it to the front of her body, where she could hold it in her arms. Annie's small face was the color of a radish. Her eyes were flooded with baby tears and her nose needed wiping. Charity made do with a scrap of petticoat she had tucked among the folds of the buffalo skin.

"That young'un had better not cry all night," Mamie said, scowling back over her shoulder. "Folks here don't take kindly to being kept awake."

"She's just tired," Charity said, her uneasiness mounting. "She'll sleep fine once she's fed and changed."

"Well, gettin' her out of that papoose carrier might help," Mamie said. "And one of the girls should have a dress that'll fit you. You been livin' with them Injuns too long, missy. We need to get you lookin' like a white woman again. You'll be right pretty once we get you fixed up."

Something about her words struck Charity as strange, but she shrugged off a sense of foreboding as she followed Mamie into the ring of firelit wagons.

She was greeted by a circle of curious eyes. Three slick-looking men with similar wolfish faces sat on a log by the fire. They were passing a jug back and forth among them. When they lowered it, their lips gleamed wet and red.

"Hey, Ma!" one of them shouted. "When's them beans gonna be ready? My belly's growlin' something fierce!"

Mamie raked a string of dirty gray hair back from her face. "Let it growl, Abner!" she snapped. "I can't tend to all of you at once!"

Two younger women lounged against the side of a wagon. They might have been pretty except for the hard-looking lines that framed their eyes and mouths. They wore matching calico dresses with the bodices unbuttoned to display their ample bosoms. One had a mole on her cheek and tight wine-colored curls. The other, a sultry brunette, was smoking a long black cigar. They gazed at Charity with eyes that were oddly glazed, saying nothing.

Charity found herself glancing around almost desperately for children. If there were children, surely there would be some trace of innocence in this place. But there was no sign of children to be seen. Only the sad-eyed hound, who thumped its tail when she looked at it, showed any sign of true good will.

"Well, now, what we got here?" The man called Abner grinned as he looked Charity up and down. "Appears you brung me a present, Ma. You know I like 'em blond. And that Injun outfit's right clever."

"Leave her alone, Abner," Mamie snapped. "She's offered to earn her keep, and she'll do it just like the other two, soon as she's had a chance to rest and clean up a bit."

"But that ain't to say I can't break her in first an' ride her whenever the fancy suits me." Abner unfolded his lanky body and sidled over to where Charity stood clasping Annie in her arms. He smelled of sweat and whiskey, and his grin showed a mouthful of rotting teeth. "You don't look like no squaw to me, sweetie. Where'd you git that yellow-haired papoose, eh?" He reached out a hand to touch Annie's hair, but Charity jerked the cradleboard out of his reach.

"Don't you touch her!" She spat the words at him.

Abner laughed. "Feisty one, eh? Well, you won't be so high and mighty when you're earnin' your livin' on your back, girlie. Wait and see. You'll beg me to be nice to you then."

Charity stumbled backward, fear and rage swirling like bile through her body. Beads of cold, sick sweat broke out on her skin. She had overheard talk about rolling brothels that plied the wagon trails, luring men with whiskey and women. The tales of debauchery, often followed by robbery and murder, had been so gruesome that she'd refused to believe them—until now.

"No!" The word exploded out of her. "I won't do this! You can't make me!"

Wheeling, she made a dash for the nearest break in the circle of wagons. But the other two men had left the fire and moved to block her way. With grinning mouths and pitiless eyes, they surrounded her. The two younger women looked on, making no move to interfere. Their expressions remained vacant, as if they might be drunk or drugged.

The man called Abner pulled an ugly, long-bladed knife from the sheath at his belt. His eyes glittered as he used the tip to clean the filth out from under his thumbnail. He took his time, toying with her fear, knowing she was trapped.

"You'll do whatever we tell you to, girlie," he said with a smirk that was pure evil. "And don't you drag your heels or try to cross us. You do and, by the time we get through with her, that sweet little baby of yours won't look so pretty anymore."

Chapter Sixteen

The sound of hoofbeats reached Black Sun's ears where he waited in the twilight. Rising to his feet, he sprinted down the slope to the fringe of the woodland, where the aspens thinned into scrub. His eyes scanned the flatland, straining to pierce the dusk.

Anxiety gnawed at his vitals. In spite of the coldness between them, hope still flickered that Charity would return with the packhorse. Their separation had come too soon, like an early, killing frost. He hadn't been ready to let her go. The truth was, he would never be ready. Whether he liked it or not, she and Annie had become part of him. They had become his family.

He could see the little pinto now, trotting up the slope through the brush. Something shattered inside him as he realized there was no rider. Charity had decided to stay with the wagon train.

He shouldn't have been surprised by her decision, Black Sun told himself. He had treated her with cold contempt, telling himself it was for the best. Now there was nothing left but the emptiness of knowing how wrong he had been.

If Charity and the baby were here, he would gather them into his arms, hold them close and let the healing begin. But it was too late for that now. They had already passed beyond his reach. He could only wish them a safe journey and a happy life.

As his eyes caught the flash of the mottled hide through the shadows, something struck Black Sun as strange. The pinto had barely been gone for the time it would take to reach the wagon train, turn around and trot back. Somehow that didn't seem right. He imagined Charity riding up to the circle of wagons, dismounting, glancing around, and then immediately turning the pony loose. She had made her decision quickly, he thought. Almost too quickly.

By the time the pinto reached him, Black Sun had already begun to worry. When he saw that the buffalo robe, with her old clothes inside, was still rolled up and tied to the horse, his gut clenched with the premonition that something was wrong.

Had the horse spooked and bolted before she could unload her things, or had she simply decided she didn't want them? He couldn't assume either answer until he knew more.

The pony edged closer and nuzzled his chest, wanting attention. Black Sun stroked the sturdy neck, his thoughts elsewhere until, suddenly, the back of his hand brushed something solid and heavy.

His pulse jerked as his fingers closed around the amulet pouch.

The nugget was still inside—there could be no mistaking the shape or weight of it. And it had not caught on the pony's neck by accident. When Black Sun tried to tug it free, he discovered that the ties had been braided into the tangled mane and securely knotted into place. He puzzled over this as he freed the pouch and looped it around his own neck. Charity had obviously meant to return it to him. But was it a peace offering, a farewell gift or a cry for help?

Leaving the pinto to graze, he sprang onto the tall dun horse, swung it toward the wagon train and kneed it to a gallop. He would never rest, he knew, until he'd made certain Charity was safe.

As he rode, Black Sun's mind spun out a tentative plan. He would tether the horse a short distance from the wagons and try to get close enough to see Charity. If she appeared safe, he would watch from a distance until the camp had settled into sleep. Then he would find her and quietly tie the amulet in its rightful place on Annie's cradleboard.

Would Charity understand the return of the amulet and see it for the token of forgiveness it was meant to be?

Would she realize what he truly wanted to say—that he loved her, and that if she chose to come back to him, he would welcome her with an open heart?

He was nearing the wagons now. Dismounting, he tethered the horse to a clump of sage. Except for the whisper of windblown grass, the night was eerily silent. Too silent, he thought.

The horse snorted, flattening its ears and pulling at its tether. Black Sun had always believed that animals, with their pure spirits and keen instincts, had a strong ability to detect evil. Maybe that was what had sent the pinto bolting away, leaving Charity on foot.

Black Sun felt his own instincts prickle as he crept forward. The evil, he sensed, was there in the wagon train, surrounding Charity and her baby. He could only pray that he'd arrived in time to save them.

He had covered less than half the remaining distance to the camp when he heard a sound that made his heart stand still.

It was the faint, frenzied crying of a baby.

Charity slumped against the wagon wheel where Abner Sloan had tied her. The women had taken Annie away and put her in one of the wagons. As far as Charity knew, no one had harmed the child. But Annie had never been left alone before. She was getting hungrier and more frightened by the minute. Her pitiful baby wails tore at Charity's heart.

"Oh, please!" she begged her captors. "Won't you at least let me feed her?"

Sprawled around the fire, the Sloans and their two women looked up from their plates of beans and Dutch oven biscuits. "You'll get your chance, sweetie," Abner said, leering at her. "After you've been nice to me and my brothers here, you can feed your little brat to your heart's content. We'll even give you a bite of supper, won't we, Ma?"

Mamie Sloan did not reply. Was she remembering how it had been to have babies of her own? Was she thinking about how much they'd needed her and how she would have done anything to protect them? Or was the woman long past recalling or caring?

"You're a mother, Mamie," Charity pleaded. "You know what it's like to love a child! Please, in the name of decency, tell your sons to let me have my baby!"

Mamie gazed at her with empty dishwater eyes. "My boys is grown men," she muttered. "They do what they want."

Annie was screaming her heart out now, as only a hungry, abandoned and terrified baby can scream. Charity twisted against the ropes that bound her to the wheel until her wrists were slimed with blood, but the knots had been tied from the inner side of the wheel and they held fast. Even if the Sloans hadn't found her small knife and taken it away, she could never have cut herself loose.

How long would the Sloans let Annie cry before they ran out of patience and hurt her or even killed her? Not long, Charity knew. If she wanted to save her daughter, she had only one choice—to give her captors what they wanted. They could easily hold her down and take her by force. But they seemed to be enjoying this cruel game. Until they grew tired of it, heaven willing, they would let Annie live.

Charity had told herself she would die for her baby. If she could face death, then she could endure this ordeal. But after her time with Black Sun, letting the Sloans touch her would be like killing her own soul. She didn't want to think about who and what she would be by the time they finished with her.

Abner was through eating. With a gassy belch, he tossed his tin plate to the ground and unfolded his skinny frame. Taking his time, he ambled over to Charity and stood grinning down at her. Firelight gleamed on the pistol that hung at his belt. She imagined getting her hands free, wrenching the gun out of the holster and shooting him between the eyes. But she wouldn't do that, Charity knew. The others would still have time to get to Annie.

"Well, pretty girl," he said. "Why don't you show us how much you want that caterwaulin' brat?"

Charity glared up at him like a trapped animal, sickened by the thought of what was to happen next. "I hope you don't expect me to do it with my hands tied," she said in a voice that dripped acid. "That wouldn't be much fun, would it, now?"

Abner's grin broadened. Murmuring an obscene phrase that Charity willed herself not to hear, he pulled his knife out of its sheath and squatted down beside her. The rope had been threaded through the wheel and pulled from behind, lashing her wrists so tightly against the spokes that there was no room to insert the blade. The only way for Abner to cut her free would be to reach around the wheel, beneath the wagon, and ply the knife there.

"Careful." Charity's voice was as spiritless as Mamie's. "You wouldn't want me to bleed on that lovely shirt, would you?"

Abner glanced down at his shirt, which was finely made and obviously stolen. The once-elegant cream linen was streaked with grease and tobacco stains. The cuff of the right sleeve was a grimy black where he'd used it to wipe his nose and mouth. He grinned up at Charity as he reached behind the wheel to cut the rope.

"Funny little bitch," he said. "I like funny lit—"

The words ended in a gurgle as iron fingers

clamped around his wrist and jerked him under the wagon. In the next instant Charity felt the rope drop away from her wrists.

"Stay right where you are, all of you!" Black Sun's voice barked from beneath the wagon. "I've got your friend here. One wrong move and I'll slit his throat!" His voice dropped. "Get your baby, Charity! Then get to the horse and get out of here! Don't stop for anything— not even me!"

Charity was already on her feet. Annie's cries flooded her ears as she plunged toward the wagon where they'd hidden her baby.

She did not see what happened next. She'd reached inside the back of the wagon and had the cradleboard in her arms when a man's voice screamed, "I'll git 'im, Abner!" There was a scuffling sound. A pistol shot rang out in the darkness. The silence that followed was broken only by the sound of Annie's whimpering.

Turning with a liquid, nightmarish slowness, Charity saw one of the Sloan brothers slumped beside the wagon with a smoking gun in his hand. Her heart crawled into her throat as she saw the figure of a man lying facedown beneath the wagon in a pool of blood.

Then she saw the glint of firelight on a dirty

white shirt and the muddy boot sticking out from under the wagon. It wasn't Black Sun she was looking at. It was Abner Sloan.

Roused from her glassy-eyed stupor, one of the women screamed. "Oh, Lord, you shot your own brother, Jess! You shot Abner!"

Mamie rose, trembling, from her place next to the fire. "Well, don't just stand there!" she hissed. "Git that bastard under the wagon!"

Realizing, suddenly, that Black Sun had lost his hostage, the two surviving brothers edged around the wagon with their guns drawn. At first Charity couldn't see Black Sun. Then she glimpsed a shadowy form beneath the wagon box and realized he was still there. Why hadn't he gotten out? Had the bullet that killed Abner hit him, as well?

His pain-roughened voice, rasping out from the shadows, answered her question. "Run, Charity! Get to the horse…ride out of here… and don't look back!"

The brothers danced closer, waiting for a clear shot. Charity knew she should run, but her feet seemed rooted to the ground. She could not leave Black Sun to die. There had to be something she could do.

Then she remembered the tiny pistol—Rueben Potter's pistol—that she'd tucked beneath the padding in Annie's cradleboard.

Her fumbling hand closed around the small, cold weapon. The gun had no bullets, but none of the Sloans would know that.

Mamie's attention was focused on the wagon. Slinging the cradleboard over one shoulder, Charity lunged for the woman, hooked one arm around her throat and jammed the pistol against her temple.

"Throw your guns down!" she shouted at the brothers. "Do it now, or your mother's a dead woman!"

The two men turned toward her, stupefied. The women, sprawled by the fire, stared open-mouthed. Even the hound curled its tail between its legs and slunk out of sight.

"Do what she says," Mamie snapped. "I don't aim to end my days by havin' my head blowed off."

By the time the pistols thudded on the trampled grass, Black Sun had rolled free of the wagon and come around from the far side. Blood was trickling down his ribs and his face looked gray, but his grip on the pistol he'd taken from Abner's body was firm and steady.

"Get their guns, Charity," he said. "We'll

make sure they can't follow us. Then we're getting out of here. It's time to go home."

Charity would remember that night for the rest of her life. After leaving the Sloans with their horses scattered and their shoes flung over the prairie, she and Black Sun had ridden the dun horse back to the foothills where the little pinto waited.

Black Sun's wound had proved not to be serious. The bullet had indeed passed through Abner's body and into his own flesh, but it had not gone deep. Charity had removed it easily and dressed the wound with elder bark. Then they'd ridden until the moon was high, both of them wanting to distance themselves from the horror of the outlaw camp.

At last they'd found a sheltered glade beside a fine silver ribbon of stream. Charity had fed Annie while Black Sun tended to the horses. Then they'd spread the buffalo robes on the ground and fallen into each other's arms.

They hadn't made love that night—both of them were too exhausted for that. But as she'd lain with her head pillowed against his shoulder, listening to the soft rush of his breathing, Charity had known with soul-deep certainty that she'd come home. Wherever Black Sun's life was destined to take him, she and Annie would be there to share it.

Annie would not have an ordinary childhood—and certainly not the sort of upbringing the canyon's wealth would have provided. But she would have a happy childhood, filled with love and laughter and the beauty of the outdoors. She would be raised with a knowledge of both the Arapaho world and the white, so that when the time came she would be free to choose one or the other...or both.

They'd escaped the Sloans more than two weeks ago. Since then, they'd traveled steadily eastward. As he'd done countless times during their trip, Black Sun halted the horses on a low ridge. On the broad plain below, surrounded by a lush sea of waving grass, she could see the clustered lodges of the Arapaho camp. After more than a fortnight of riding, they had finally reached Black Sun's people.

The fluttering sensation in Charity's stomach grew almost unbearable as they rode down the hill. She had asked Black Sun to teach her some Arapaho words and customs as they rode. The lessons had filled their long days on the trail. But now it was as if everything she'd learned had drained away, leaving her mind as empty as a sieve.

She was so anxious for the Arapaho people to like her. What if, in her innocence, she said or did something that offended them?

What if they simply hated her on sight?

As if reading her thoughts, Black Sun reached out and touched her shoulder. "Don't be afraid," he said. "My people will be kind to you. We are not called the Blue Sky people for nothing."

Charity breathed an edgy little sigh. "I know they'll treat me with kindness," she said. "But will they accept me as your woman? Will they accept Annie as your child?"

His hand tightened in a brief squeeze. "In the eyes of Heisonoonin, you are my wife," he said. "They will accept that."

She sensed the underlying tension in his voice. He was doing his best to reassure her, but Charity knew he had his own concerns. His future role with the tribe lay in the hands of his elderly grandfather, Four Winds, as did her own. There was also the question of his young son, Two Feathers. Would the little boy accept a white woman as his mother? Would he join their family or stay with the aunt who'd raised him from babyhood?

By the end of the day, their questions would be answered.

The camp was a large one, between sixty and seventy lodges, Black Sun told her. In the winter, when food was scarce, they separated into small family groups, but now the band had come together for the spring hunt. It was a time of happy abundance, a time for feasting and dancing and the renewal of old friendships.

As she and Black Sun approached the camp, Charity could smell roasting meat and hear the sounds of barking dogs and children's laughter. A group of naked youngsters splashed in a stream. Horses, fat and sleek, grazed in the tall spring grass. Charity kept her gaze lowered as they rode in among the teepees, knowing that it was impolite to stare directly at people. But she could feel a hundred eyes on her back as she and Black Sun dismounted in front of an elaborately painted teepee in the center of the camp. Before he greeted anyone else, Black Sun would speak with Four Winds.

The flap of the teepee was raised, but it was so shadowy inside that it took a moment for Charity's eyes to adjust to the darkness. She could make out the sloping lodge poles that formed the frame of the teepee and the objects that rested against its walls. A painted skin shield and a long-feathered lance caught her gaze, then a long clay pipe and a wondrous assortment of drums, rattles, flutes and baskets. Bundles of drying herbs hung from the poles, perfuming the air with the aromas of sage, pine, yarrow, onion and a melange of other scents she could not begin to name.

The figure sitting cross-legged on a beautiful white buffalo skin looked almost childlike at first. Then, as Charity's eyes adjusted to the low light, she realized she was seeing a man, shriveled with age. His snow-white hair hung like a veil over his shoulders, and he was wearing a fine buckskin shirt decorated with bands of elk teeth. For all his shriveled old body, there was an air of quiet majesty about him.

Black Sun greeted him in Arapaho. The old man looked up at him, revealing a scarred face with a missing eye, which Black Sun had told her had been lost in a long-ago bear attack. His remaining eye appeared clouded, but Charity had been told that he was not entirely blind.

The voice that answered Black Sun was deep and rich, with a ring of authority. His hand—the long, fine fingers free of crippling—motioned for both of them to sit. Charity folded her legs beneath her. Balancing Annie's cradleboard in her arms, she settled herself near the edge of the white buffalo robe. Black Sun sat beside her. The two men spoke briefly in Arapaho before he turned to Charity.

"My grandfather says he cannot see you well. With your permission, he would like to touch you and Annie."

Nodding, Charity leaned toward him. She could hear the pounding of her own heart as the sensitive fingers explored her face and hair and shoulders. Their touch was like gentle rain on her skin.

A smile spread across the old man's face as Annie's small, pink fist closed around his forefinger. How strangely connected the two of them seemed, one so old and one so young, neither of them far removed from their time in the spirit world.

Withdrawing his hands, he smiled again and spoke a few words to Charity. Black Sun translated.

"My grandfather says his fingers have told him you are strong and good of heart. And now if you would care to wait outside, he would like to speak with his grandson alone."

Charity felt a dizzying rush of panic. With Black Sun at her side, she had felt secure. But even the thought of standing alone while people came to stare at her and Annie was enough to make her cringe.

Again, Black Sun seemed to sense what she was feeling. He spoke a few words to his grandfather. "It will be all right," he said, rising and helping Charity to her feet. "Come on, you'll see."

He led her out into the dazzling sunlight. The people in the camp were making an elaborate show of going about their business, pretending to ignore her, but Charity could feel their curious glances whenever she turned away.

"I don't think—" she began, then broke off as she saw a plump, pretty, smiling woman walking straight toward her.

"Charity," Black Sun said, "this is Sweet Grass Woman, the sister of my wife."

Taking Charity's hand, Sweet Grass Woman spoke earnestly in Arapaho.

"She welcomes you," Black Sun translated, "and asks if you would come to her lodge to rest and eat while I visit with my grandfather. She has a baby, too, a little girl. She says that maybe, when they're older, her child and yours will become friends."

Charity swallowed the rising lump in her throat. How could she have been so self-absorbed in her fear that Black Sun's people wouldn't accept her? Sweet Grass Woman had come forward as her first friend. She had opened her arms to the one who'd taken her sister's place in Black Sun's heart.

Blinking back tears, Charity squeezed the woman's plump hand and murmured a thank-you in her halting Arapaho. She had so much to learn from these people, and the first lesson had already been given.

Her eyes caught a subtle movement behind Sweet Grass Woman's skirt. Slowly, like a flower unfolding, a small boy stepped into view. Clad in nothing but a string and a tiny patch of leather, he was as graceful as a wild fawn, lean and golden with melting dark eyes. Those eyes regarded her shyly as his hand emerged from behind his back clutching a bouquet of spring violets.

Charity murmured her thanks in Arapaho as she accepted the gift. Crushed by small, warm fingers, the violets were limp-stemmed and wilted. But to her they were more precious than gold.

When Black Sun spoke, his voice was rich with emotion. "This is Two Feathers," he said softly. "This is our son."

Four Winds listened to the story of his grandson's quest. Black Sun left out no details. If he were to do so, the old man would know.

"And so, did you receive your vision?" he asked when Black Sun had finished. "Was your quest successful?"

Black Sun closed his eyes for a moment, feeling as if he'd just relived all that had happened to him in the past moon—his finding of Charity, their time in the sacred canyon, his dreams and their perilous flight home.

"Not in the way I expected," he answered. "I was seeking one thing. What I received was not what I asked for."

"And what did you ask for?" The old man reached for the clay pipe and balanced it between his spidery hands. The pipe was sacred. Almost everything in the lodge was sacred.

"I wanted to be like you," Black Sun said. "I wanted to be worthy to take your place, as you wished me to. I asked for the wisdom to serve our people, as you have."

"And did you receive that wisdom?"

"No." Black Sun sighed. "My grandfather, I am no more fit to take your place than a sparrow is fit to take the place of an eagle."

A smile played around the old man's mouth. "Perhaps you were never meant to take my place. Perhaps you were meant to be a different kind of eagle. You didn't receive what you asked for. Tell me, what *did* you receive?"

"You met her. And you've seen that I love her. But I never thought I would return from my quest with a *Nih'oo'oo* woman."

"A *Nih'oo'oo* woman, yes. But I can't help believing you were meant to find her, my grandson."

Four Winds lowered his gaze to the sacred pipe in his hands. For a long moment he was silent. Black Sun sat quietly, knowing better than to disturb his grandfather when he was gathering wisdom.

When the old man looked up again, his face shone with understanding. "It all comes clear to me now," he said. "My own visions have shown me a future with the *Nih'oo'oo* spreading over the land like a flood. To keep our people from drowning in that flood, we will need a voice—someone who understands the *Nih'oo'oo* and can reason with them in their own language. When the white man took you and your mother away from us, your feet were set on the path to becoming that voice. When you found the white woman and she healed the hate in your heart, the path was made clear. The two of you will become a bridge between our world and the world of the *Nih'oo'oo*."

"But what about the dreams?" Black Sun dared to ask. "I was given two of them."

"Yes," the old man murmured, lost in thought once more. "Two dreams of the canyon. One dream of the past and one of the future." He reached out and placed his hand on Black Sun's wrist. The grip of his fingers was surprisingly strong.

"You must understand that the canyon is a living thing. It senses what is to come, and it is afraid. Like a child in the night, it has called to you in your dreams. The canyon needs you, my grandson. It is asking you to become its guardian and the keeper of its sacred medicine."

Black Sun struggled to grasp the clarity of his grandfather's wisdom. There were so many questions, so many fears for Charity and their family.

"There's no need for you to return at once," Four Winds said. "As long as the *Siksika* roam the land, the canyon will be safe. But in time they will be driven back by the *Nih'oo'oo*. When that happens, the canyon will call you again and you will answer."

"But what about the future?" Black Sun whispered. "What about the second dream?"

"You have seen the future," Four Winds answered sadly. "The canyon will die. When it happens, you will feel it in your heart, and you will be free to leave. But while the canyon is vulnerable, it will need your protection. It will need your love." The old man released Black Sun's wrist and smiled. "Now I am tired. Go and find your woman and tell her all that I have said. Tomorrow you can bring her to visit me again, with her little baby."

Black Sun walked out into the camp, his heart bursting. It was as if all the painful and tragic events of his life had fallen into place and taken on meaning. He would never be fully Arapaho and, even as Charity's husband, he would never be white. But he had his own place, his own gifts to offer, the love of a beautiful woman and the hope of a happy future together.

For the first time in his life, he felt peace.

Lengthening his stride, he raced through the golden sunlight to find Charity and their children.

Epilogue

April, 1842

They arrived as the sun was setting above the peaks, flooding the cliffs with tones of mauve, amber and rose that melted into purple pools of shadow.

Charity sat beside Black Sun on the wagon bench, filling her eyes with the beauty of the canyon, amazed that it had not changed. Her hand groped for his fingers and found them, squeezing hard. After five long years, they had come home.

"Are we here, Mama?" Annie clambered

onto the bench between them. "Is this where we're going to build our new house?"

"It is," Black Sun said. "Tomorrow morning you can help me choose the spot."

"Over there—no, over there!" Annie bounced up and down, her amulet swinging wildly. One small, sharp elbow jabbed against her mother's rounded belly.

"Careful, now." Charity eased her daughter gently back onto the seat. She had suffered a miscarriage three years earlier, but this baby seemed to be thriving. Black Sun had been willing to wait a few months before moving to the land they planned to settle at the mouth of the canyon, but Charity had wanted her baby to be born here.

She was hoping for a boy. Two Feathers was eleven years old now, and busy learning the life path of an Arapaho warrior. They had left him behind with Sweet Grass Woman to continue his training, but he would be spending the winter months with them. He was a fine, intelligent boy, already showing the promise of his great-grandfather's gifts. Charity couldn't have loved him more, but she wanted to give her husband another son, one he could raise here.

They planned to build a small ranch with a house and corral, where Black Sun could catch and train wild horses. His own dun buffalo pony and the little pinto, who'd become Annie's special pet, were with them now, trailing alongside the wagon. Soon there would be more horses and, Charity hoped, more children, as well.

The canyon itself was to remain sacred. They would not enter it again, not even to visit the secret cave where they had first made love. They would keep it safe for as long as they could until the future foretold in Black Sun's dream came to pass.

Clouds were rolling in above the peaks, blown by a moist wind that carried the promise of rain. Charity loosened the pins from her hair, letting it fly loose as she helped Black Sun secure their first night's camp.

Tonight, when she lay in her husband's arms, they would hear the sound of thunder.

* * * * *

YES! Please send me **The Montana Mavericks Collection** in Larger Print. This collection begins with 3 FREE books and 2 FREE gifts (gifts valued at approx. $20.00 retail) in the first shipment, along with the other first 4 books from the collection! If I do not cancel, I will receive 8 monthly shipments until I have the entire 51-book Montana Mavericks collection. I will receive 2 or 3 FREE books in each shipment and I will pay just $4.99 US/ $5.89 CDN for each of the other four books in each shipment, plus $2.99 for shipping and handling per shipment.*If I decide to keep the entire collection, I'll have paid for only 32 books, because 19 books are FREE! I understand that accepting the 3 free books and gifts places me under no obligation to buy anything. I can always return a shipment and cancel at any time. My free books and gifts are mine to keep no matter what I decide.

263 HCN 2404   463 HCN 2404

Name	(PLEASE PRINT)	
Address		Apt. #
City	State/Prov.	Zip/Postal Code

Signature (if under 18, a parent or guardian must sign)

Mail to the **Reader Service:**

IN U.S.A.: P.O. Box 1867, Buffalo, NY 14240-1867
IN CANADA: P.O. Box 609, Fort Erie, Ontario L2A 5X3

* Terms and prices subject to change without notice. Prices do not include applicable taxes. Sales tax applicable in N.Y. Canadian residents will be charged applicable taxes. This offer is limited to one order per household. All orders subject to approval. Credit or debit balances in a customer's account(s) may be offset by any other outstanding balance owed by or to the customer. Please allow 4 to 6 weeks for delivery. Offer available while quantities last. Offer not available to Quebec residents.

Your Privacy—The Reader Service is committed to protecting your privacy. Our Privacy Policy is available online at www.ReaderService.com or upon request from the Reader Service.

We make a portion of our mailing list available to reputable third parties that offer products we believe may interest you. If you prefer that we not exchange your name with third parties, or if you wish to clarify or modify your communication preferences, please visit us at www.ReaderService.com/consumerschoice or write to us at Reader Service Preference Service, P.O. Box 9062, Buffalo, NY 14269. Include your complete name and address.

MMLPBPA15

REQUEST YOUR FREE BOOKS!
2 FREE NOVELS PLUS 2 FREE GIFTS!

◆ HARLEQUIN®

American Romance®

LOVE, HOME & HAPPINESS

YES! Please send me 2 FREE Harlequin® American Romance® novels and my 2 FREE gifts (gifts are worth about $10). After receiving them, if I don't wish to receive any more books, I can return the shipping statement marked "cancel." If I don't cancel, I will receive 4 brand-new novels every month and be billed just $4.74 per book in the U.S. or $5.49 per book in Canada. That's a savings of at least 12% off the cover price! It's quite a bargain! Shipping and handling is just 50¢ per book in the U.S. and 75¢ per book in Canada.* I understand that accepting the 2 free books and gifts places me under no obligation to buy anything. I can always return a shipment and cancel at any time. Even if I never buy another book, the two free books and gifts are mine to keep forever.

154/354 HDN GHZZ

Name _____ (PLEASE PRINT) _____

Address _____ Apt. #

City _____ State/Prov. _____ Zip/Postal Code

Signature (if under 18, a parent or guardian must sign)

Mail to the **Reader Service:**
IN U.S.A.: P.O. Box 1867, Buffalo, NY 14240-1867
IN CANADA: P.O. Box 609, Fort Erie, Ontario L2A 5X3

Want to try two free books from another line?
Call 1-800-873-8635 or visit www.ReaderService.com.

* Terms and prices subject to change without notice. Prices do not include applicable taxes. Sales tax applicable in N.Y. Canadian residents will be charged applicable taxes. Offer not valid in Quebec. This offer is limited to one order per household. Not valid for current subscribers to Harlequin American Romance books. All orders subject to credit approval. Credit or debit balances in a customer's account(s) may be offset by any other outstanding balance owed by or to the customer. Please allow 4 to 6 weeks for delivery. Offer available while quantities last.

Your Privacy—The Reader Service is committed to protecting your privacy. Our Privacy Policy is available online at www.ReaderService.com or upon request from the Reader Service.

We make a portion of our mailing list available to reputable third parties that offer products we believe may interest you. If you prefer that we not exchange your name with third parties, or if you wish to clarify or modify your communication preferences, please visit us at www.ReaderService.com/consumerchoice or write to us at Reader Service Preference Service, P.O. Box 9062, Buffalo, NY 14240-9062. Include your complete name and address.

HAR15

REQUEST YOUR FREE BOOKS!

2 FREE NOVELS PLUS 2 FREE GIFTS!

H HARLEQUIN®

SPECIAL EDITION

Life, Love & Family

YES! Please send me 2 FREE Harlequin® Special Edition novels and my 2 FREE gifts (gifts are worth about $10). After receiving them, if I don't wish to receive any more books, I can return the shipping statement marked "cancel." If I don't cancel, I will receive 6 brand-new novels every month and be billed just $4.74 per book in the U.S. or $5.49 per book in Canada. That's a savings of at least 12% off the cover price! It's quite a bargain! Shipping and handling is just 50¢ per book in the U.S. and 75¢ per book in Canada.* I understand that accepting the 2 free books and gifts places me under no obligation to buy anything. I can always return a shipment and cancel at any time. Even if I never buy another book, the two free books and gifts are mine to keep forever.

235/335 HDN GH3Z

Name _____ (PLEASE PRINT)

Address _____ Apt. #

City _____ State/Prov. _____ Zip/Postal Code

Signature (if under 18, a parent or guardian must sign)

Mail to the **Reader Service:**
IN U.S.A.: P.O. Box 1867, Buffalo, NY 14240-1867
IN CANADA: P.O. Box 609, Fort Erie, Ontario L2A 5X3

Want to try two free books from another line?
Call 1-800-873-8635 or visit www.ReaderService.com.

* Terms and prices subject to change without notice. Prices do not include applicable taxes. Sales tax applicable in N.Y. Canadian residents will be charged applicable taxes. Offer not valid in Quebec. This offer is limited to one order per household. Not valid for current subscribers to Harlequin Special Edition books. All orders subject to credit approval. Credit or debit balances in a customer's account(s) may be offset by any other outstanding balance owed by or to the customer. Please allow 4 to 6 weeks for delivery. Offer available while quantities last.

Your Privacy—The Reader Service is committed to protecting your privacy. Our Privacy Policy is available online at www.ReaderService.com or upon request from the Reader Service.

We make a portion of our mailing list available to reputable third parties that offer products we believe may interest you. If you prefer that we not exchange your name with third parties, or if you wish to clarify or modify your communication preferences, please visit us at www.ReaderService.com/consumerschoice or write to us at Reader Service Preference Service, P.O. Box 9062, Buffalo, NY 14240-9062. Include your complete name and address.